WRESTLING WITH DEMONS

WRESTLING WITH DEMONS

MAGGIE FEELEY

This book is a work of fiction. The names, characters, places, businesses, organisations and incidents portrayed in it are either the product of the author's imagination or are used fictitiously. Any resemblance to actual persons, living or dead, events or locales is entirely coincidental.

Published 2023 by Crimson
an imprint of Poolbeg Press Ltd.
123 Grange Hill, Baldoyle,
Dublin 13, Ireland
Email: poolbeg@poolbeg.com

© Maggie Feeley 2023

The moral right of the author has been asserted.

© Poolbeg Press Ltd. 2023, copyright for editing, typesetting, layout, design, ebook and cover image.

A catalogue record for this book is available from the British Library.

ISBN 978178199-505-1

All rights reserved. No part of this publication may be reproduced or transmitted in any form or by any means, electronic or mechanical, including photography, recording, or any information storage or retrieval system, without permission in writing from the publisher. The book is sold subject to the condition that it shall not, by way of trade or otherwise, be lent, resold or otherwise circulated without the publisher's prior consent in any form of binding or cover other than that in which it is published and without a similar condition, including this condition, being imposed on the subsequent purchaser.

www.poolbeg.com

About the Author

Maggie has worked as a social researcher and educator in Ireland and is an activist on issues of gender, sexuality and equality. She was born in Roscommon, Ireland, and spent much of her life in Belfast. She now lives in Catalonia with her wife, Ann.

The first Alice Fox mystery, *Murder in the Academy*, was published by Poolbeg in 2021 and *Just Killings*, the second book in the series, in 2022.

Our hopes for a safer, feminist future for everyone: Bojana, Chloë, Jerome, Jessica, Leah, Nessa, Spence and Vicente

Holy Tuesday, 15 April 2014

CHAPTER 1

She'd had a really pleasant day until then. The two boys got off to school and crèche without any protests. Sharon and Jack from next door had called for Riley and the two boys had stood at the front door chatting excitedly about what chocolate eggs they'd get in just a few short days when the Easter Bummy (as Riley called it) finally arrived. He had assumed that the rabbit laid the chocolate eggs, hence it was all about the 'bummy'. She marvelled at where kids could get to in their minds and found herself smiling in a way that hadn't happened for a while now. Then they had skipped off down the road to school as happy as sandboys.

She had wrestled Timmy into the buggy and headed off to the crèche. The sun was shining and everything felt surprisingly hopeful. After leaving the crèche, she picked up two scones at the bakery on the Shankill and headed up to her mother's for a cuppa and a chat. Bull was there on his way out to work, looking peeved. He had been annoyed with her ever since she had got the Exclusion Order against Sammy. Maybe she had deprived him of his weekend party partner. Maybe he was annoyed because she didn't bring him a scone. Who knew with men? They could get themselves in a strop about the strangest things and she wasn't playing that particular guessing game any more, to figure out what demons they were wrestling with. They'd all have to learn to sort their own issues. She and her ma had a grand chat about this and that and she lingered until it was time to head down the road and collect the little fellow. On her maintenance she could only manage to pay for the few hours in crèche but it was better than nothing.

As she pushed the buggy over the cracked pavements towards home, her phone rang and Sammy's name came up on the screen and her peace was shattered. Here we go, she thought. He just can't leave well enough alone. He has to keep on niggling away. She rejected the call but, even so, he had brought down a familiar cloud over the rest of her day. He wasn't one to take no for an answer and she knew in her bones that there would be more to come.

Spy Wednesday, 16 April 2014

CHAPTER 2

On the Wednesday morning early flight from Dublin to Barcelona, Alice Fox stretched her long legs under the seat in front of her and almost purred with contentment. The weather had been clear all the way and she had experienced a Zen-like calm tracking the aerial views of the miles of pine forests and golden beaches that fringed the French Atlantic coast. Unusually for Alice, she had allowed herself to do nothing – no reading or notemaking, no lists or mind maps of possible journal articles. She had simply allowed herself to be in the moment and watch the world below go by. This would be her first ever trip to mainland Europe and she felt lucky to be having this unexpected bonus to her year's research leave in Ireland from CUNY – City University New York.

As they crossed over the Pyrenees, DI Caroline Paton woke beside Alice and took a few sleepy moments to realise where she was. Alice smiled at her partner's confusion and was pleased to see that she had left her sharp, senior-detective persona behind in Belfast. They both really needed this break. They were heading for ten days in the mild Easter weather of Catalonia and were both happy at the prospect of their first break together.

The women's relationship was almost three months old now and had been more eventful than would be the case for most women in their mid-forties. Alice, an ex-detective from Lowell, Massachusetts, was now a visiting post-doctoral scholar in Belfast City College. Caroline headed up the Belfast Murder Squad. A gruesome killing in early January, in DePRec – the college Department of Peace and Reconciliation – where Alice was based, had brought them together. Despite her intensive work in restorative justice in EXIT, a West Belfast youth project, Alice had proved to be integral in solving that case. In the past month, a subsequent double murder had produced victims in both Belfast and Wicklow and, in her role as vulnerable witness support, Alice had once again shown her capacity to catch the scent of killers, to track them and bring them to book. It had surely been a busy start to 2014.

Alice was feeling fortunate. From her detached aerial viewpoint, she slipped into thinking about the way that our brute luck at birth, the place and circumstances into which we are born, determines so much of our life chances. The vast terrain spread out below showed only a minute fraction of the possibilities. The world was large and diverse and the place, the hemisphere where one landed in life, was the result of one giant lottery. In this global game, there were some winners and considerably more losers and in her work with young people in the projects in the US and now in Northern Ireland, Alice witnessed this State social sabotage on a daily basis.

In her restorative justice work Alice supported face-to-face meetings between young offenders and those against whom they were seen to have transgressed. She saw much of her work as preparing young people to participate equally in those conversations and she worked hard to facilitate critical learning about the way the world was organised and encourage lawful, non-violent ways of fighting for change in unjust structures. At the same time she was clear that the biggest offender was the system that left some hungry, angry and hopeless while others flourished. Within that wider inequality, the justice system too was becoming increasingly problematic for Alice and she realised that she and Caroline had some serious talking to do to reconcile their diverse viewpoints. Caroline implemented the law without question whereas Alice saw the legal system as part of the problem. She could see there might be trouble ahead when this conversation took place but for now they were leaving all ideas of crime, death and detection behind and heading to the Catalan village of Begur for a much-needed rest. Begur was on the Costa Brava, about a two-hour drive north of Barcelona. They had rented a car and would drive there.

Wide-awake now, Caroline leaned in closer to Alice who was in the window seat and exclaimed, "Just look at that view, Alice!"

They were flying over an extensive range of snow-covered mountains set against an azure sky. It was a breathtakingly lovely sight and they could hear others around them echo their appreciation of this aerial view of the high Pyrenees.

They remained happily pressed against each other as the snow below gradually thinned and their flight moved down over the foothills of the mountains. Soon these too gave way to an arid, dusty-looking landscape of ploughed fields and small clusters of houses in Catalan villages. Then the deep-blue water of the Mediterranean rose up to meet them as the wing of the Aer Lingus jet banked and headed south along the coast. In only moments, the massive expanse of the city of Barcelona spread out to their right and, as they turned smoothly over the great metropolis and made their gradual descent, they were able to see the fine detail of some small rural holdings that bordered the airport.

As the plane touched down, Caroline kissed her lover softly on the cheek. "Welcome to Spain, Alice Fox. I hope you'll love this area as much as I do."

"I'm surely open to that idea." Alice smiled her sideways smile and kissed her lover back. "What's not to like?" she said as a small voice deep within whispered the warning ... "be careful what you wish for".

CHAPTER 3

Back in Murder Squad headquarters in Belfast's Grosvenor Road Station, DS Bill Burrows was acting head in DI Caroline Paton's absence. With DC Ian McVeigh and IT specialist Constable Zara Pradić, he was methodically clearing a backlog of paperwork. This included responding to requests for information from legal people preparing for a number of court proceedings in relation to recently solved murders. Paton ran a tight ship and locating responses for legal discovery was meticulous work but not usually a problem. Pradić's magical touch with all things IT was already making this drudge-work a lot easier.

The Good Friday Agreement negotiated by the political parties in the North, and the British and Irish government, was signed on the tenth of April 1998. Post-agreement times in Northern Ireland meant that death did not occupy as much of the local media headlines as it had done during the thirty years of the Troubles. Nevertheless the

Murder Squad dealt with around twenty homocides annually and Detective Superintendent Graham McCluskey preciously guarded their impeccable record. He left the squad pretty much to their own devices but liked to be kept informed of developments and maintained his public role as spokesperson at press gatherings and other media events. He had called Burrows that morning to check that they were managing in DI Paton's absence and to remind him that he wanted to know immediately of any new developments. Burrows thought that life would be much easier if there were no new cases for the time being but, if there was a fresh murder, he knew they were well able to deal with it. He and McVeigh had a solid record of working together and Zara Pradić, who was new to the squad during the last case, had IT wizardry that made her worth several colleagues. Pradić, a young woman in her mid-thirties, was notable for her gleaming jade-green hair and her dislike of small talk. Co-workers joked that they were not really sure if she slept or not as they frequently left her in the squad HQ only to find her there the next morning when they returned. She was a bit of a mystery in that regard.

The three colleagues were just about to head to the canteen for an early lunch when the phone rang. Burrows knew in his bones this wasn't a routine call. It was as if he could hear the urgency in the ring tone, even though it was just the same as it ever was.

"Murder Squad – DS Burrows here," he answered smartly.

He made hand-signals to McVeigh and Pradić to hold off on the canteen trip. They stopped in their tracks and listened to his side of the conversation.

"And the address of the incident?" He paused and hurriedly wrote something on the message pad on his desk. "That's the new development off the Lower Shankill, isn't it?" He rolled his eyes at his colleagues who had returned to their desks to hear what was coming down the tracks towards them. "We'll be there directly."

He finished the call and reached for his coat.

"Multiple murder off the Shankill. Sounds like a domestic. Woman and two small boys dead … the alert was raised by a friend who was worried about her neighbour not responding to calls. The local guys broke down the door and then called us directly." He paused and considered his next steps carefully. "Pradić, you stay put and we'll call you for digital support. I'll alert the DS from the car. McVeigh, you're the chauffeur." He handed him the slip of paper.

Pradić read it over Ian's shoulder and was already searching the address on Google Maps before they left the room.

"OK!" said Burrows resolutely. "Let's show them what we can do."

CHAPTER 4

Settled in their rental car, Alice and Caroline took the AP7 north from Barcelona, in the direction of Girona and France. As the capital of Catalonia, Barcelona was immensely popular with tourists, but the women had decided to avoid it this time. The city was notoriously crowded all year round and they were determined to have a peaceful, relaxing time. Back at home, Caroline had embarked on tackling unresolved childhood trauma and bustling, aggressive city streets were not on the agenda this trip. The senior detective had been coming to the same small hotel in Begur for at least ten years and had never been disappointed by her time there. She had enthusiastically assured Alice that the quiet village was her favourite place in the world, which was high praise indeed from someone who didn't often do superlatives. Because it was the weekend retreat and holiday resort of wealthy people from Barcelona, its traditional character had been well protected from over-development and the worst expressions of Costa

Brava excess. At the same time, unlike many resorts, Begur had a resident population of several thousand all year round and the village's vibrant culture reflected an authentic representation of Catalan life.

Caroline told Alice that the first time she had been to Begur was for a mid-September break after a very difficult case. She had landed accidentally into the celebrations for the feast of Santa Reparada, the village patron saint. The entire population, from small children to senior citizens, was gathered in the plaça and she had spent hours, over several very large gin and tonics, watching them dance to the gentle music of a local band. It was like being on a film set from the fifties, she said. A group of older women in their summer finery had been sitting on the stone bench that ran the length of the side of the church wall of soft local stone that formed the backdrop to the village square. Another two sides were taken up with brightly lit, small bars that had tables outside where onlookers gathered to eat, sip their drinks and enjoy the spectacle of local life. Four narrow streets filtered people in and out of the scene.

In the post-retirement group of dancers, there appeared to be only one available male partner who worked his way around the older women and made sure each had a chance to dance. The local Lothario had a very appropriate thin moustache and seemed extremely pleased with his role. Caroline had watched one woman in particular who was determined to get more than her fair number of turns and was amused by her strategy. "She managed her point anyway," she laughed when she related the experience to Alice. Young families and teenagers all danced alongside their elders, learning the steps and happily greeting friends as they danced around the square. Caroline had been captivated by the charm and innocence of it all and lost her heart to Begur village, once and for all. It had become her happy place for all subsequent breaks from her daily life hunting down Northern Ireland's murderers. Now she was obviously delighted to be sharing it with Alice who secretly hoped that this odyssey would not disappoint either of them.

The motorway was not too busy and, as Caroline drove, Alice watched a mix of commercial and rural settings flash by. Surprising sunshine-yellow fields of rapeseed caught Alice's eye and raised a slight longing in her for home. Olive oil was clearly another local product and at one point she spotted that particular soft sage-green of an olive plantation that stretched for several miles. In the open countryside there were occasional low, red-roofed country houses that had arched covered spaces for eating outside in hot weather. When they got within sight of the deep-blue Mediterranean there were larger housing complexes built into the slopes and in the distance along the coast some high-rise apartments blocked the view of the sea. Clearly some of the area had lost the battle to maintain its local charm and given way to the developers.

Evidence of the Catalan independence movement was visible all along the road. The striped red-and-yellow flags, some with the white star in a blue triangle, were everywhere – flying from buildings, on cars and lorry-stickers and painted on gable walls and farm outhouses.

"What do you know about the politics of the area, Caro?" Alice inquired. "The flags are surely very popular. Shades of Belfast except that here they seem to be agreed on the colours!"

Caroline moved into the outside lane and deftly manoeuvred her way past a number of big lorries that looked a bit unstable. "It's a big topic here and one that raises the hackles of those on both sides of the argument." She moved safely back to the inside lane and smiled at Alice. "There's a very long history of a Catalan independence movement that goes back centuries and has French as well as Spanish supporters. Communities on both sides of the Pyrenees that separate France and Spain identify as Catalan. Basically there is a triangle of territory in the north-eastern part of the country, where we are now, that is a recognised autonomous Catalan region. Some go as far as calling it a nation. As well as having a widely spoken language and distinct cultural traditions, the region is very wealthy. A lot of the major banks are Catalan … anyway, the separatists claim they could afford to be a distinct economic area and want to totally sever links with the rest of Spain."

"I see," said Alice. "There are some resonances with Northern Ireland then but with different complications, eh?"

"Well, Catalan people are very much divided on whether they think independence is desirable or not, so I suppose political and cultural conflict would be a common theme. After the Spanish civil war in the thirties, under Franco there was massive repression of the Catalan language and other cultural expressions. Now, you'll often see people dancing in the street … a dance called the sardana that looks a bit like a simplified version of Irish set dancing, I suppose, although that's not an area I've ever taken a lot of interest in." Caroline came from a Protestant background and in Northern Ireland their cultural touchstone was often Scotland rather than the twenty-six counties that made up the Irish Republic. "The music too was repressed for decades here but you hear it now anywhere there is a fiesta or to accompany the sardana. The instruments sound almost medieval … they sound a bit squeaky and high-pitched but are also very haunting. Catalan is widely spoken."

"So I won't get to practise my Spanish then?" Alice feigned disappointment.

"Everybody is bilingual. They speak Castilian too – Spanish, that is – but use Catalan in preference. They are friendly people and if you make an effort to speak Spanish they'll answer you. I've picked up a few words and phrases down the years but often I resort to English and most people understand that and speak what they can with tourists. You'll see that there won't be a problem being understood."

They had left the motorway now and were driving along a major coastal road with frequent exits to the coastal resorts. As the kilometre count to the French border on the road signage got smaller, Alice realised she was excited to be so near to France. They planned to take a day and visit the French coastal town of Collioure, just over the border. Alice had read up on the region and knew Collioure to be a fishing village that, because of its special light quality, was famed as a location of choice for painters like Matisse, Picasso and Dalí. Apparently locals in Collioure fished sardines and anchovies in long, narrow, brightly painted sailing boats and, as she became aware of her own hunger, Alice looked forward to that visit more urgently.

The clunking of the indicator signalled that they were turning off and Begur was now signposted as just a few kilometres away.

"We'll be there in no time," Caroline said happily.

They drove through well-kept vineyards, fading mimosa trees and then steadily uphill through a wooded area. Straight ahead now the village rose up before them in a spiral of narrow streets topped by an ancient circular stone castle where a large Catalan flag fluttered gently in the breeze. A tasteful sign at the edge of the village announced, *Begur es autèntic* and the intrepid travellers felt the relief of having finally arrived.

As if to welcome them, the village church bell confidently struck twelve o'clock.

CHAPTER 5

On Belfast's notorious Shankill Road the tattered Union flags danced sadly in an April wind. On the gable wall at the end of Goliath Row loomed a stark image of balaclava-wearing figures brandishing rifles and incongruously professing allegiance to the Queen. McVeigh silently wondered if this glorification of cultural violence made the kind that took place in families, behind closed doors, more likely or easier to perpetrate. The murder scene they were heading towards struck a deep chord with him. He and his wife Sally had a little boy who was just nine months old and the idea that he would ever be angry enough to harm him or his mum was anathema to him.

Burrows broke into his young partner's reflections. "I think this is going to be a bit of a horror scene, Ian." The older man was often looking out for teaching moments for his young colleague. "I always find that focusing meticulously on the evidential detail makes it a little less horrendous – and also helps the investigation."

Burrows was such a kind mentor, Ian thought. He had really got very lucky to have him as a guide, and increasingly as a friend. They worked so closely together in the most gruesome of circumstances that it was almost inevitable that their relationship would become companionable.

"Thanks, Bill. I was just thinking this is going to be a messy one and wondering how to cushion the impact. Thanks for the advice. It makes sense."

"I'm not sure that there's any way of lessening the horror of what we see … but I do think we can go in with the idea of concentrating on the facts and delay the emotional response until we're in the comfort of our own safe homes."

In this frame of mind they both braced themselves for what awaited them inside the newly constructed row of small town houses.

Blue-and-white tape indicated the outer cordon of the crime scene and separated their destination from the adjoining houses. A woman was furtively watching the activity in the street from behind the net curtains of the house next door. Burrows decided they would talk to her as soon as they were finished at the scene. She must have heard something of what had gone on. These small houses had thin walls and sound carried.

They suited up in the forensic gazebo already in place in the small garden outside the house. There was a one-way system so those entering did not pick up contamination from those leaving.

They presented their ID and the uniformed officer at the door of the house gave them a summary of what was known so far. He was very young and looked cowed under the weight of this, maybe his first, major incident.

"We got a call through from emergency services just after ten this morning. It was from the woman next door. Apparently her wee lad usually walked to school with the oldest fella here in this house. The younger one has been attending a local crèche." He lost his way for a moment in his account and then pulled himself back. "The neighbour was worried when the young fella didn't appear for school and she couldn't get any answer at the door or on the mobile. She said that she had heard shouting and door-banging the previous evening but that wasn't unusual. The woman in this house, Donna Nelson, was separated from her husband and when he came around apparently there was often argy-bargy. It was only when there was no sign of them this morning – even though the lights were on downstairs – that she thought something might have happened and made the call."

The forensic pathologist Cynthia Boylan, with whom they had all too frequent opportunities for collaboration, and her assistant George arrived as Burrows and McVeigh were talking with the uniformed officer.

"See you inside, Dr Boylan," Burrows said by way of greeting.

"Right you are, Senior Investigating Officer." She saluted and winked at Burrows. "DI Paton picked a good time for her holiday in the sun! We'll have to make sure we don't give her anything to complain about when she gets back." And she put her briefcase down and lifted a set of PPE – Personal Protective Equipment – from the pile inside the tent.

Burrows and McVeigh signed into the Crime Scene Log that was being managed by the uniformed PSNI in the small hallway. They paused to survey the lay of the land. Aside from those who had carried out a first scan of the scene, they were looking at fresh evidence of the Belfast Murder Squad's latest case.

"The dead woman is in the kitchen," the officer announced, "and the two kids are in the small bedroom upstairs on the right. No-one has been in since we put the tape in place, sir."

The two detectives moved cautiously forward, noting the mirror that was askew on the wall and avoiding the stains on the wooden floor that were probably made from blood on the killer's trainers.

"Make sure nothing is disturbed till forensics get here," Burrows said sharply to the policeman as he edged the living-room door open with his elbow.

It was clear that this was a home where there were small boys. A plastic basket of action toys sat under the front window and someone had made an elaborate Lego construction that was perched precariously on one end of a coffee table. Some magazines and a small schoolbag had been pushed out of the way to make room for the coloured bricks. There was a large television screen mounted on the wall opposite a cream fabric sofa where a few small items of children's clothes and an empty snack paper lay. A number of birthday cards with the number 2 had been hung over the top edge of the TV. Both men recognised the normal debris of the bedtime struggle. The boys had probably been put to bed before the trouble had started and this end of the room seemed untouched by the subsequent violence.

A framed photo of the mother and two boys sat on top of a small china cabinet that might have been an old family piece or been bought in a charity shop. The blonde woman in the picture had an arm around each child and was smiling eagerly. Burrows gauged that the children must be about five and two years old. He wondered if the father had taken the picture in happier days.

The kitchen/diner space was around to the right in the L-shaped room. It was in shadow as the blinds were down on the two small windows. The mound of the woman's body was face down on the floor by the kitchen sink and a sizeable pool of blood had escaped to the left of the remains. It had congealed and darkened now, giving some clues as to the span of time since the assault had happened. She was wearing tight denim jeans and a lemon T-shirt that was drawn upwards, revealing a section of pale skin on her back. There were smudges of blood on the woman's body as if her killer's hands had touched her after she had fallen. One of her purple house slippers had fallen off and lay at an awkward angle to her bare foot. There were dark crimson splatters on the front of the cupboards under the sink. Some dishes had been washed and remained on the draining board to the left. The back door was to the extreme right of the rear wall and appeared to be bolted. A mobile phone with a shattered screen was lying face-upwards by the door as if it had been thrown forcefully against a hard surface. Alongside the opposite wall there was a small wooden table that held a ketchup bottle and a glass saltcellar, both of which had been knocked over. A wooden chair with a red seat lay on its side.

"Under the table, Sarge," murmured McVeigh and pointed to a large bloodied knife against the skirting board where it had been thrown during a struggle.

"OK! It's a tragic mess all right but the plot is probably not too complicated, I think. The same sad story of a thwarted partner repeats itself. We've seen this too many times, haven't we, Ian?"

Cynthia Boylan and George had come in behind Burrows and McVeigh. She was nodding in agreement. Burrows and McVeigh moved to the side to allow them access. George rapidly took a series of photos of the scene and then stood back. Burrows remarked to himself how well they all knew their steps in this macabre dance routine. They advanced and retired around each other with a sensitivity that might well have been choreographed. A faint smell of whatever had been made for the children's dinner hung in the air, evoking memories of his own kids when they were small. They had all made it successfully to adulthood now, he thought with gratitude.

The pathologist knelt carefully by the right side of the dead woman and gently leaned across and eased the body towards her onto its back. The dead woman's blonde hair fell back from her face and it became clear that she had been brutally assaulted. Her face and body, which had relaxed in death, showed the blueish discoloration associated with livor mortis. The pathologist pointed to the bruised appearance on the woman's body and the swollen and bruised left eye and thick smears of dried blood in the area around her nose and mouth.

"This staining of the body is caused by the pooling of blood in the areas closest to the ground. You can see that it differs from these injuries that were caused prior to death."

The woman's arms now lay stiffly by her sides and both hands were open as if to accept something being offered to her. Her lemon T-shirt had three distinct gouge-marks in the chest area where she had been stabbed with force.

Boylan made a cursory examination of the woman's nails and spoke quietly. "She clearly put up a fight. Our perp may well show signs of having been in a scrap."

"The cause of death is fairly clear here," said Cynthia. "We have full rigor mortis so she has been dead for between eight to twenty-four hours. You'll have other factors to add into that equation, DS Burrows, that should give you a possible time of death. If we have a look at the children now, I'll take them all back to base and we'll prepare for the full examination from there. Probably tomorrow morning, Bill. I'll confirm an exact time later."

She wasn't her usual chipper self, Burrows noted. The killing of children took the wind out of most sails, even those of the experienced pathologist.

Burrows led the way up the narrow staircase, noting a few blood smears on the carpet, walls and banister. So, he killed the mother first and then the children. An image of his own kids tucked up in bed of an evening flashed through his head. He wondered what the crazed thought process of this killer might have been. Maybe he couldn't stand the idea that the kids would know he'd killed their mother. His sons' approval was still important to him. Burrows stopped there and refocussed his mind in the here and now. It was never good to speculate to the extent that you missed the detail of the moment. He was conscious that directing this investigation was down to him now and he needed to be as sharp as he could be and not leave himself open to criticism from DS McCluskey or anyone else.

The bathroom was straight ahead and the children's room was to the right above the kitchen. The mother's room was located at the front of the house, facing out to the street. There was a bloodied towel on the floor of the bathroom, suggesting that the killer had tried to wash his hands either before or after being in the children's room. Either was feasible and forensics would be able to clear that up.

Very gently, Burrows edged open the door with the glossy superman poster and two coloured wooden initials: an R and a T. The curtains were drawn and the light was off in the small room but enough weak sun shone through to show the horror that was arranged in the room. Two small bodies lay close together in the bottom bunk. Burrows switched on the light carefully with his gloved hand. The bedclothes had been pulled back from the boys and their small bodies lay rigid, side by side, in matching dinosaur pyjamas. Their limbs lay tangled in the aftermath of their final struggle against their father's deadly actions. Both boys were deathly pale. On the floor beside the beds lay a pillow with bloodied handprints that suggested the man had asphyxiated his sons and made no attempt to conceal the evidence.

DC McVeigh and Dr Boylan stood behind Burrows, absorbing the tragedy before them. Here was the result of an anger that had been devoid of reason or hope … a fury without any interruption or softening even in the face of those dinosaur pyjamas and the affection shown by his firstborn son who at some stage had left his own upper bunk to lie beside his little brother, perhaps to comfort him as their parents argued noisily in the kitchen below. This man, this husband, this father had been thwarted in some part of his identity to the extent that a red mist had clouded his mind to all that he had once loved and controlled, so that he had felt compelled to obliterate it. For those who had never felt threatened in this way it was incomprehensible but, for those present, confronted repeatedly with such actions of angry men, there was a familiarity, if not anything as deep as an understanding.

"Do your best with the photos, George," Burrows said sombrely. "We'll wait for forensics and then Ian and I will talk to the neighbour who made the call. Then we'll get the local lads organised with the house-to-house calls."

McVeigh was reading a message on his phone.

"Zara has tracked down the address the husband had moved to, through Social Security records. There was a recent Exclusion Order against him and he's back with his parents, apparently."

"Of course he is," said Burrows knowingly. "We'll get someone out there from the local station and have him brought into the Grosvenor Road Station. Make sure they bring his trainers and his clothes too and send them through to forensics. He can wait for us there until we get back. Ring through, Ian, and get him put on suicide watch. I don't want him taking the easy way out. These bully boys, for all their bravado, can often be loath to face the music."

They went downstairs and met the forensics team coming through the front door.

"We'll leave you to it, guys." Burrows spoke from the bottom stair as the two men made their way into the narrow hall. "The murder weapon's under the kitchen table. Human remains in the kitchen and upstairs. Bloody prints in both the bathroom and the children's room. Hopefully we'll have our perp before the day's out so let's get a robust evidence trail in place ASAP."

CHAPTER 6

Caroline parked on a double yellow line outside an ornate three-storey building at the corner of two narrow streets in the village of Begur.

"It's OK to park here for a few moments while we check in," she said, to explain her contravention of parking procedures.

Alice smiled at her lover's fastidious attention to the rules. "We are on our holidays, Caro. Let yourself off the hook."

Stepping out of the car, at the same moment she saw two orange trees laden with fruit overhanging a nearby car park and smelt the aroma of vanilla and coffee coming from a local café. Under a clear cobalt sky, Begur and its effortless good looks was getting off to a very good start. The village rose up a hill towards the medieval castle at its peak. It spread upwards rather than outwards and the soft honeyed-stone buildings were easy on the eye.

Of course Alice had checked the hotel out online but the reality was often quite different. In this instance, Hotel Aiguaclara was even more charming than the online images suggested. She had read that the building was one of a series of Indiana Mansions in the village, built by returning emigrants who had gone to Cuba when times were tough in Spain. The plaque outside the hotel explained that Bonaventura Caner Bataller, born in Begur, had gone to Cuba in 1845 and returned in 1866 to construct this 'colonial palace'. In this case, it stated that he had made a fortune using his knowledge of the cork plantations that were plentiful at the time on the Costa Brava. There was evidence now that some of these pioneers had traded in slaves as well as other more acceptable merchandise and Alice wondered how noble the endeavours of Bataller had been.

The current owners, Joan and Clara, had restored it to make a ten-bedroom, boutique hotel created in the ethos of '*fet amb love*' – a combination of Catalan and English meaning 'made with love'. Joan was Catalan for John and was often confused with the English woman's name of the same spelling. Those expecting the owners to be two women were surprised when Joan turned out to be a tall, dark and handsome ex-rugby-player. Through the glass panel of the inside door, they could see a large heart made out of sparkling lights that made the house motto clear to all newcomers.

A dark-haired, smiling man in his mid-forties opened the door. He was wearing jeans and a brightly coloured shirt, his wrist festooned with beaded and leather bracelets.

He enveloped Caroline in a bear hug saying, "Welcome back, Caroline!" with what seemed like genuine delight. Then, much to Alice's surprise, he turned to her and kissed her noisily on both cheeks. "You are very welcome to Aiguaclara, Alice. We hope that you will have a peaceful stay with us." As Alice recovered her composure he continued. "Caroline has told me that you like to run long distances in the morning and so I have prepared a map for you of some suitable routes." He smiled broadly. "I am an enthusiastic cyclist so I understand the need to be outdoors."

And he waved them from the spacious, tiled foyer of the old house into the colonial-style office and indicated two seats facing the desk.

The inside doors of the office opened onto an area covered in glass that was set out as a restaurant with an outdoor bar and terrace. In the outside area, a series of low couches constructed from wooden pallets were upholstered in soft green leather. Old enamelled advertising placards and two rusting bicycles hung amidst the green creepers that covered the external walls.

Joan deftly opened a bottle of cava with a joyful pop and poured three glasses. "We will drink to your arrival in Aiguaclara while we complete the necessary documentation. Clara is at a market. She said she will see you later."

Caroline had explained that Clara was an avid collector and restorer of old items that she found in local markets and the décor of Aiguaclara was testament to this. With great style and flawless taste, Clara made the case against endless consumerism very articulately. Alice detested formulaic hotel environments and felt very at home in this hotel that defied that approach to life. She was already feeling an unexpected affinity to this couple and this place.

As they handed over passports and Joan completed the administration demanded by the Spanish authorities, Alice sipped the cava and reviewed her surroundings. They had done a good job. The essence of the colonial house was still safely in place, unspoiled by the approach of adding recycled pieces of furniture and lights, old luggage and judiciously chosen modern art. The original polished wood, colourful tiling and wrought-iron work were still in place, and twinkling lights and enlarged sepia photos of the area in bygone days added to the charm.

Coupled with the early start, the sparkling wine made Alice instantly drowsy and she was relieved when Joan lifted their two bags and led the way to their room. It was on the first floor. Climbing the stairs, they passed windows looking out onto the village, with sills stacked with books for borrowing. In one corner an old wooden clothes stand held a long-legged man's vintage knitted swimming costume. Clara had a sense of humour too, Alice mused. The first-floor landing was lined on one side with large laundry cupboards which lay open, piled with freshly washed bed linen. Housekeeping was clearly in progress. The other side had a long sideboard piled high with an array of old suitcases of all shapes and sizes. The long windows at the far end were open onto the street and the richly planted balcony of the house opposite. Alice, who enjoyed plain, old-style comforts, found the whole environment captivating.

Joan deposited their bags inside Room 3 and left them, saying, "We knew you'd be hungry, so there is a snack here to get you through till you've had a siesta. See you later."

Alice had the impression of staying with friends rather than in a hotel and thought these proprietors were very good indeed at what they did.

The bedroom was as charming as the rest of the hotel. A small sitting room and spacious bedroom both opened onto a balcony with reclining chairs that looked up at the castle. The bathroom had an old freestanding bathtub and shower and all three rooms had exquisitely patterned floor tiles.

"I love that this is only a two-star hotel," Caroline enthused. "Because they don't tick all the boxes required by those who allocate star ratings, they don't get recognition in that way but they are repeatedly Number One in hotels of the Costa Brava. Don't you love it, Alice?"

"I do, Caro. I can see why it's your happy place and I am looking forward to exploring but please tell me I can get into that delightful bed right now. I am ready to fall over. Let's have a proper Spanish siesta before we do anything else."

* * *

Several hours later, as Caroline continued to sleep peacefully, Alice donned her running gear and slipped silently from their room. She didn't plan to go far but a circuit of the village would help clear her head and allow her to get her bearings. She would wait until the following morning to start on the coastal track that Joan had marked out for her.

The odour of warm pine trees and fresh bread filled her nose as she headed back along the route by which they had arrived and found herself on the road that seemed to go around the edge of the village. She ran more slowly than usual so that she could take in the surroundings. On her left, in the near distance, she saw the deep blue Mediterranean and a line of small islands further north towards France. The coastline in the distance looked fairly built up but the immediate area was verdant and not overly developed. What building there was along the coast seemed to be mostly large individual houses nestled into the sheer slopes leading towards the sea. Some were traditional white buildings with typical tiled roofs. The more recent models were variously shaped white boxes with glass walls that maximised the stunning views for the lucky owners. This was clearly the land of the wealthy holidaymaker who could afford a second home that was bigger than the average community centre in the projects where Alice worked with young offenders in Massachusetts. The Fox family had a modest wooden holiday home in Wellfleet on Cape Cod and Alice recognised their privilege and also her father's hard work and foresight that had allowed them to own such a place. She wondered about some of these massive second properties that obviously brought wealth to an area and also created a new service industry where the poor became the servants and cleaners of the well-off. It was good that there was a lot of work in the area but complicated in that it was as a consequence of massive social inequality.

Alice ran with ease and breathed the soft Spanish evening air with satisfaction. On her right she could make out a network of narrow village streets where the front doors of houses opened onto the street. She imagined this must be where local families had lived for generations. Those who worked in the tourist industries – the cleaners and bar staff and restaurant workers and their families – were more likely to live in the nearest big town where there would be social housing and cheaper rental options. In these small streets there would be expats too and those from nearby cities who bought small local houses and gentrified them so that prices rose and excluded young native residents from settling in their homeplace. The pattern was familiar across the continents, Alice ruminated, and yet she could see the lure of spending weekends and holidays in this lovely place. The problem was that everybody didn't have those choices.

She passed by a patch of well-tended allotments where an abundance of vegetables was growing and turned into a small road that led upwards through a pine forest. Her route was making a wide circle around the village and the castle remained a central landmark guiding her along. The steep gradient slowed her pace and she could see how the village of Begur had been cautiously developed with modest holiday houses and apartments, none of which exceeded two or three storeys in height. A tight rein was evidently kept on building regulations within the village itself. The wider landscape too reflected this restraint with no high-rise constructions and plentiful amounts of forestation softening the impact of any new building. Its privileged holiday clientele protected Begur, kept it exclusive and ensured that overcrowding did not pollute the nature of the area. She had been uncertain about the meaning of the sign on the outskirts of the village but now she could see that 'autèntic' meant unspoiled and protected by the money and taste of those who wanted to keep it like that.

The forest gave way to a small collection of older houses with vegetable gardens and fruit trees side by side with more recent small apartment blocks painted terra cotta and somehow managing to look like part of the landscape. There was a small supermarket and a series of estate-agent offices on the far edge of the village and a steep hill led back down to the main road, past the cemetery and the end of the circuit of the village. It had taken only thirty minutes, despite there being several very challenging slopes.

Back in the hotel, Alice found a note from Caroline to say she was in the square with Clara and that she should join them. She hopped in the shower and found she was quite eager to meet the second part of the Aiguaclara enterprise.

CHAPTER 7

In Number 8 Goliath Row on Belfast's Shankill Road, Burrows and McVeigh were sitting on a red-leather sofa opposite a thirty-something woman. Sharon Dunwoody looked not unlike her deceased neighbour. Alike in age, colouring and lone-parent status, she explained to the detectives that the women and their five-year-old sons had become friends since moving into this new development six months previously. McVeigh had made strong tea for them all and found a few biscuits in a tin which he had put on a plate on the coffee table. Even the arrangement of the room mirrored that of her friend next door, he thought.

"I can't believe what you're telling me," Sharon said, cradling the warm cup in her hands for comfort. At the same time she looked pleadingly at Burrows as if to suggest he had made a mistake and the reel could be rewound and the bleak reality rewritten.

Burrows nodded with genuine sympathy. He had confirmed her worst suspicion that there were three fatalities next door. There was no point in holding off, he reckoned. It would be announced shortly on the radio hourly news bulletin and the woman had already formed her own view from what she had seen and overheard.

"I'm afraid that it's true, Sharon. I am so sorry for your loss of your neighbour and friend. Take your time ... and when you're ready we would be very grateful for anything that you can tell us that would help us find her killer and bring them to justice." He paused and waited as the woman slowly registered his request.

She looked at Burrows directly and her eyes filled with tears that spilled over and rolled down her cheeks. McVeigh passed a small packet of tissues from his pocket across to her.

"I have a new little boy," he said by way of explanation. "There's always something to mop up ..." and he smiled awkwardly. Somehow mentioning his healthy, living child seemed crass in this circumstance but the woman recognised a familiar story and returned the smile.

"Some men are so stupid," she began, hesitated and then continued. "It was Sammy, of course, Donna's ex-husband who did it. Sammy Marshall's his name. He's been living in his parents' house further up the Shankill since Donna got the Exclusion Order against him and changed her name back to her maiden name – Nelson. That really annoyed him something shocking."

"Would that be in Alameda Crescent, do you know?" Burrows enquired.

"Aye. That's right. His da works in the City Council as a binman, I think."

McVeigh and Burrows exchanged a glance that affirmed the same address as the one provided earlier by Pradić. Hopefully some uniformed officers were already there, gathering his belongings and bringing Mr Marshall in for questioning.

"Let's take this slowly, Sharon. No need to rush. You were saying that some men are stupid ... why do you say that?"

The woman looked at Burrows as if to say that the answer was obvious but, when he remained silent, she continued. "Well, first they tell us they love us and everything is hunky-dory. Everyone is dancing in step. They set up home with us, have children with us and then they don't like having to share our attention with the kids and it all goes downhill from there. I go to the Shankill Women's Centre and the number of women in the same boat is amazing. There actually is a pattern, you know, that a lot of women discover the hard way." She looked around her room as if reliving how her version of the story had played out. "And who ends up with all the responsibility for the kids? They swan around at the weekend and take them for a treat, throw a bit of money at the problem and then drop them back, full of sugar and upset not to have their lovely da living with them. Then we become the ones responsible for their misery."

"What was the story next door then?" asked McVeigh who was hoping that he would never in any way fit into the model of masculinity that Sharon described.

She was less distressed now, maybe distracted by the conversation. "Well, Sammy was one of the ones who took to throwing his weight around. He was a violent bastard. Mind you, they're always careful enough to vent their anger on people weaker than them. You never hear of them taking a swing at their boss, for example. My fella just wanted to pretend he was still a teenager who could go drinking and picking up women whenever he felt like it – which was often." She shook her head in exasperation and exhaled through her nose and mouth as if to expel the memory of it all. "At least he wasn't violent, I suppose. Just useless as a partner you could count on." Again she became absorbed in her recollections.

Burrows nudged her gently back to the present. "Sharon, can you tell us a bit about Donna and what you know about what happened last night?"

"Well, I was talking to her yesterday evening because the wee lads, my Jack and her Riley, were playing together in her house and I came in to get my one at teatime – around six o'clock, I suppose. I think the news was on the telly. They had been building a Lego thing and I had to wait for them to finish so me and Donna were having a chat while she fed the smallest one – Timmy. He was just two a few weeks ago." She covered her mouth with her hand, widened and closed her eyes at the horror of what picture her mind had conjured. "She told me that Sammy was on the warpath. He had phoned her several times that day to say he was coming round and 'fuck the Exclusion Order'. He said that neither she nor the courts had the right to stop him seeing his boys and she had better not think that she could. I told her she should phone your lot and let them know but she said there was no point until he'd actually breached the exclusion order. The cops would do nothing."

Burrows and McVeigh exchanged a look that suggested that the woman might well have had a point but neither spoke. How so-called 'domestics' were dealt with was always a difficult one.

"I said I'd be next door if she needed me and took my lad home. After he was in bed, I sat down to watch *EastEnders* and registered that all was quiet at Number Six."

"OK, Sharon, that's all very helpful. Did you see Sammy arriving next door later that evening?" Burrows asked gently.

"Look," she said earnestly. "The thing is that he's a very crafty bugger. He was frequently violent with her when he was living there but he'd turn up the music or the TV loud so that you couldn't really be sure what was what. It was only when Donna told me what he was like that I began to see the way he operated." She looked defeated by the knowledge that she was unable to know with certainty what her friend had to contend with. "I didn't see him arrive so I suppose I couldn't swear it was him."

Everyone these days watched a lot of crime programmes on the TV and was conscious of what counted as evidence in legal cases. This wasn't always useful, thought Burrows, but he dismissed this distraction from the moment.

"I understand that you didn't see anything but what exactly did you hear, Sharon?" he calmly asked.

"Well, I did hear a door bang after nine some time and I thought: I hope that's not Sammy. But everything was quiet for a while and so I thought I was mistaken. The hall and the stairs are between Donna's living room and mine so that stops the sound carrying."

"I see," said Burrows, hoping that there might be something more concrete coming.

"Then, not long afterwards, when I was in the kitchen where there's a shared wall between us, I clearly heard the shouting. I heard his voice and Donna's although I couldn't make out the words. He was shouting and swearing and her voice was less loud and not so angry. I assumed she was reasoning with him because of the boys up above."

Both detectives were nodding encouragingly.

"Then the shouting stopped and there was a thud like something was knocked over. It got quiet and I thought that maybe he had calmed down as there was nothing after that, and maybe twenty minutes or so later the front door banged and I saw him leave and walk off towards the Shankill."

"And during that twenty minutes, Sharon, what did you hear?" Burrows asked.

The woman thought about the question and shook her head as if to try and release a memory that was eluding her.

"I don't remember hearing anything. I may just have been sitting here in a daze. Sometimes I am so tired at the end of the day that I don't remember how I've put the evening in. It just all becomes a blur." She looked at them to see if this was a familiar experience for them too.

Burrows changed tack. "When you saw Marshall leaving, did you see him clearly? Did you see his face?"

Sharon looked at him despondently and shook her head.

"Did Donna have other callers? Were there other men that visited her?" Burrows knew the question was loaded but did not try to soften it.

Sharon was clearly reaching the end of her stamina. She looked at Burrows and again shook her head. "There was just her brother. He called sometimes and he and Sammy went out drinking a lot for a while and then that eased off when she got the Exclusion Order. Donna told me that she asked him to support her and stop going about with Sammy. I haven't seen him around here very much lately."

"Did you try to contact Donna after you saw Sammy leaving?" McVeigh asked quietly. "Did you check if she was OK?"

Sharon looked distraught. "I had the phone in my hand to text her when my Jack came down the stairs in a state. Said he'd had a nightmare and could he have a glass of milk and a biscuit. It was probably the noise next door that spooked him." She looked at the men as if appealing for their understanding. "You know how it is. It took ages to get him settled and by then all was calm next door and I went to bed myself. It was only when Donna didn't answer the door when we called for Riley to walk to school with us next morning that I started to worry, but I went to the school with my fella first, so he wouldn't be late like. I did some messages on the road and then it was when I got back and still couldn't get any response from Donna that I phoned the police."

Burrows turned his pen over and back in his hand and thought about how this poor woman must feel. "Don't torture yourself, Sharon. The truth is you probably couldn't have made a difference. This is not your fault in any way. I'm sure you were a good neighbour and friend to Donna … and, as I said earlier, I am sorry for your loss."

"Do you have someone you can call to stay with you for a while?" McVeigh considered the practicalities of the rest of the woman's day. "There will be a lot of activity next door and eventually the press will be looking for someone to interview. You might like to avoid that." He wondered what the hopes were of escaping the press gang when they had the scent of a story but Sharon was smart enough to read the situation, he thought.

"I planned on going to the Shankill Women's Centre this afternoon so I will just go ahead and do that. I've already phoned them. Someone there will have picked up Jack from school and the company will help me get through the rest of the day."

"We can arrange for someone from Police Welfare to call if that would be useful." Burrows raised his bushy eyebrows to accompany his suggestion.

"I'm comfortable in the Women's Centre – thanks anyway. They've experience of all the shit thrown at women around there and Jack will be taken care of in the crèche. He knows the other kids there too." She was shaking her head slowly from side to side. "I tried to get Donna to come to the Centre with me but she wasn't ready for that.

It's a shame ... but maybe there was no avoiding this. These men can literally get away with blue murder."

As they left, Burrows and McVeigh checked their messages. There were several from Pradić asking them to get in touch as soon as possible and a voicemail from DS McCluskey asking for an immediate update.

At that moment both their phones rang in tandem.

"OK, Ian," said Burrows. "Let's see what's making us so bloody popular all of a sudden."

CHAPTER 8

In the soft evening light, the village square in Begur lived up to Caroline's description. Alice had the sense of walking onto a film set where the other actors had already taken their places. She stopped on the edge of the plaça and observed. The high, pale stone wall of the church formed one side of the square and a stone bench that ran the length of the wall formed a natural stopping place for those who wanted to pause for a while. A couple of older men chatted animatedly while young parents watched their children play safely in the central open space. Alice noted a constant trickle of people who walked across the square, up one of the tributary side roads and then appeared out of another. There was obviously a circuit of the village that could be done by families and couples before settling down into their evening activities.

"Alice!"

Her reverie was interrupted by Caroline's voice as she waved to her to signal where she was.

Bar de Plaça faced the church wall and Caroline was sitting with a beautiful, dark-haired woman. She had a soft tanned complexion and was smiling widely in Alice's direction.

"This is Clara," announced Caroline as if she had found a prized trophy.

The woman stood up and opened her arms to Alice.

"Welcome to Begur, Alice Fox," she said as she embraced Alice warmly. "Come and have a cava and something to eat."

They sat and she made a sign to one of the waiters who promptly produced another glass.

"How was your run around the village?" she enquired. "Joan is excited to have another person who likes to be in the outdoors. He really loves this."

Her English was fluent and pronounced with a rhythm and intonation that made the mundane sound more attractive than usual.

As they chatted, Alice admired Clara's excellent communication skills: direct eye contact, attentive listening and a tendency to emphasise points with a touch of the hand that was pointed but not invasive. It was clear why this winning couple were so successful in their business. They had hit upon a model of welcoming people to their hotel that emphasised all things affective and it seemed as if it was a genuine and lived philosophy. She was enthralled.

"Clara was just telling me the local gossip."

Caroline was as relaxed and contented as Alice had ever seen her – except perhaps when they got a day off at a weekend in Belfast and they went walking in the Mourne Mountains.

Here, the gentle April heat and the presence of a cast of others all intent on the pursuit of contentment, enhanced that joyful feeling of escape. The cava was cool and refreshing and Alice decided to restrain her characteristic pondering on social issues for the moment. She promptly gave up thinking and sipped her cava with more abandon.

* * *

Before she left on this short break Alice had spent some time discussing the future with Hugo, the youth leader in the EXIT youth project where she worked several days a week. They had become close through their mutual interest in the eight young people with whom they worked intensely. Now, in hindsight, Alice could see that from the beginning there had been a spark between them that might have led to a different kind of relationship. Although not entirely immune to Hugo's charms, Alice had been focused on her more pressing inclination towards DI Caroline Paton. Of course, she and Hugo were more on an ideological wavelength than she and Caroline, and they had quickly become close because of the intensity of their work and the issues it raised. She spent half of her working week with Hugo and frequently that timeframe could expand when a young person was troubled and needed additional investment of time. Recently that had been the case when a member of the group, Jed, had been grappling with some shocking revelations about his father. Jed's mother, Brenda, and Alice had become friends and the woman's struggle to get justice for those abused as children in the care of the State had won her respect and admiration. For the second time in her eight months in Ireland, and much to her surprise, Alice had found herself embroiled in a murder enquiry where her sharp research skills had been central to resolving the mystery.

Before she left for her break in Begur, Hugo had been telling her about an interesting men's project in Catalonia. They had been discussing ways in which they could encourage the young men in their group to express their masculinity in non-violent and alternative ways to what was generally modelled in their community. Hugo had connections with a number of European groups through funded projects he had taken part in. The Catalonian branch of the Spanish Men's Gender Equality Association was getting noticed for its work with young men in schools and youth groups that challenged traditional expressions and limitations of masculinity. If the opportunity presented itself, Alice hoped to follow up on the group and maybe even visit them. She had reasonably good Spanish and would be able to understand enough to make a visit worthwhile and, of course, most people nowadays had some English which would ease the communication. For now, she would wait and see what shape the coming days took and not introduce work into the mix too soon.

* * *

The table in Bar de Plaça was now filled with small plates of tapas and Alice was enjoying sharing these with the other two women and drinking her second glass of cava. Clara was explaining something to Caroline about an Easter event, which was due to take place that evening, in a nearby village. It involved the re-enactment of a procession that dated from medieval times when local people remembered the loss of life that resulted from a series of plagues and pandemics. A Christian element had been added on to the original event but Clara explained it was possible to omit the religious bits and just attend the dance spectacle that night.

"In Catalan it is called La Danza de la Muerte."

"I've heard of it but I've never been," said Caroline.

"This is the only place that the Dance of the Dead takes place now in all of Europe. It is really impressive. The streets are lit only by candles and torches and two adults and two children dressed as skeletons dance to the beat of a solitary drum. They remind us that life is short and we must not forget this."

Clara spoke with enthusiasm about this local event and Alice thought it sounded fascinating.

"It sounds like the perfect night out for the head of the Belfast Murder Squad." She winked at Caroline.

"It takes place in a very small area of the town of Verges and it is hard to get tickets but if you would like to go I'm sure we could manage something. Joan and I are going after dinner in the hotel. We can all go together if you like."

And so the entertainment for the first night of the holiday was decided and they arranged to meet in the hotel foyer at ten o'clock.

CHAPTER 9

As evening began to draw in, back in the car on the Shankill Road Burrows phoned through to Zara Pradić to get an update on what was going on back at HQ. He preferred to have as much detail as possible before getting in touch with the Superintendent. He knew McCluskey didn't like any ambiguity in the information he received and for the moment Burrows didn't feel he had the full grasp of the situation. It would be better if he could report the good news story that the suspected perpetrator was safely in custody. That would make a more fulsome press statement than something woolly about 'pursuing a definite line of inquiry'.

"Hello, Zara, what can you tell me about the progress on bringing Sammy Marshall in for questioning?" Burrows put his phone on loudspeaker and McVeigh listened attentively as he negotiated the right turn onto the Westlink that would get them back to the Murder Squad offices in Grosvenor Road Station in as short a time as possible.

"Things have got a little more complicated." Pradić did not waste time on small talk. Her accent was a blend of Belfast and something more melodic that was easy on the ear. "When the uniformed officers called to his parents' home this afternoon they found only the mother, who was very upset. She told them that her son had come home in the wee small hours of the morning and they hadn't seen him then. They assumed he had been drinking somewhere and that he had gone straight to sleep. After lunchtime, when the father was already back at work, two men called to the house and they had dragged Sammy out of bed and taken him away with them. The mother was trying to decide what to do when the uniforms called to bring Sammy in for questioning. It seems the two men were from an organisation active in the area. Mrs Marshall said that Sammy had got on the wrong side of some people and she was afraid to call the police in case they got angry and hurt her son."

"Well, we can be sure that if the local lads were annoyed with Sammy before, they'll be even more angry when they hear what he's done to his wife and children." Something that had seemed very straightforward was turning into a much more convoluted situation. "Get an alert out for Sammy Marshall and see what the local PSNIs can give us on the thugs that are operating in their area."

Burrows felt his blood pressure rise at the thought of what lay ahead but he knew that DI Paton would deal with it step by step and not allow herself or the Squad to be hassled out of their rhythm in the investigation. He inhaled deeply and continued calmly.

"We'll be there in ten, Zara, and I'll get the Super off your back between this and then. In the meantime you keep doing what you do best and see what you can find out online about the Marshalls and Donna's family. They are also from the Shankill area and the surname is Nelson."

Pradić ended the call without any further chat and both Burrows and McVeigh knew that at her workstation of multiple screens she would uncover what she could in the shortest time possible.

Without any further prevarication, Burrows phoned through to Police Headquarters and asked to be put through to Detective Superintendent McCluskey.

When he announced himself to the secretary, she said, "Ah, DS Burrows. Your call is expected."

"I am eager to hear your update, DS Burrows." McCluskey's tone was curt and inhospitable.

There was no room for any extraneous detail. Burrows gave an account of the three victims and the evidence of the neighbour that pointed to the ex-husband. At this stage, McCluskey was making satisfied noises until Burrows added the complication that the suspect was now missing, possibly being held by a local paramilitary group with whom he had some unfinished business.

"I don't like the sound of that one bit."

The senior officer made Burrows feel that it was somehow his fault that Marshall had evaded being brought in for questioning.

"I understand the gravity of the situation, sir." Burrows mustered his most confident voice. "I am on my way back to Grosvenor Road Station now and will send you a draft press release immediately. Then we will get on with trying to determine the whereabouts of Sammy Marshall."

Listening carefully, McVeigh thought that Burrows had made their task seem a lot easier than it might turn out to be but he could see that the sergeant had made no promises and that was a good way to buy time and delay the pressure from on high.

It was already getting dark as they drove through the security barriers back at base. Both men felt the weight of the task facing them and the absence of DI Paton who usually shielded them from this all-important layer of responsibility. There was no doubt that everyone was wishing Paton could be instantly beamed home from Begur to deal with all this mess but Burrows was equally determined to prove his capability. He knew he had what it took to get this job done and he would have Sammy Marshall in the interview room just as soon as he could manage it.

* * *

In a grim lock-up behind a row of bricked-up houses, Sammy Marshall was experiencing a great degree of discomfort. He was numb with both cold and fear and hoping earnestly that the boys just wanted to frighten him and did not have any plan to rough him up. He had heard about the treatment of others who owed them money or who had transgressed the code of behaviour enforced locally by members of this gang. There were irreparable injuries done to knees and elbows and psychological consequences that meant the fear of leaving the house became too much to bear. Many moved away from their family and homeplace, never to return.

The men who had collected him earlier had been far from gentle. They were built like tanks and didn't need to enforce their orders. He had seen them before, hanging around the gym, and knew better than to struggle with them. In their line of business it was enough that they said something, and obedience followed. In the first place they hadn't even given him the time to get dressed and so he was in the same T-shirt and boxers that he had been wearing when he was in Donna's. He had gone from there to an unofficial drinking den run by a local supporters' club and had drunk a lot of straight vodka. He had kept his jacket on to conceal Donna's mess on his sweatshirt and when he got home, in his drunken state, he'd dumped his jeans and sweatshirt straight into the washing machine. His ma would put a wash on as usual without looking at what was in there and that would be the evidence out of the way. He had scrubbed his hands and nails as best he could although the toilets in the club had no soap and it was too dark to see clearly. He had told himself that he wouldn't be a suspect because of the Exclusion Order, not realising that he was finding cause for comfort now in the very reason for his anger. Sammy Marshall didn't really do irony.

Until then, he had not allowed himself to contemplate what he had done to his ex-wife and his boys aside from the odd flash of his sons' bewildered faces as he had lowered the pillow and held it firmly in place over both of them. After his initial flight from Goliath Row he had felt only relief at getting away and then the release from awareness produced by the successive shots of vodka. When he finally staggered home early next morning he had slept a troubled, drunken sleep and woken dry-mouthed to see two brutish figures looming over his bed. At first he had thought he was still asleep and in the grip of a nightmare. Any semblance of dreaming had rapidly become replaced by stark reality as the gruff-voiced commands had been issued and rough arms had pulled him from the bed. His first thought was that it was the cops but then he figured out that it was some local heft sent by a totally different, potentially more dreadful authority. In the bedroom doorway his mother had been standing, her hand on her chest and her lips moving as if in prayer or maybe some muttered entreaty to these men to leave her boy alone. One of them had turned sharply to her and pointed a finger in her face.

"No calls to the fucking cops now, missus, or you'll make matters much worse for him than they are already. *Do you hear me?*"

She had nodded only very slightly but she would obey them without question. Everyone knew the penalty of defiance.

Sammy knew his mother would try to contact his father at work but it would be hours before he knocked off and be able to get home. He didn't know anyway if the oul fella would be able to exercise any influence over his captors or those that had dispatched them. His father was a wimp of a man. He had steered clear of involvement in local politics and the subsequent groups that had been formed Post-Agreement to manage petty crime, drugs and moneylending in the area. His parents were church-going people who didn't drink or socialise in local clubs and bars. They were keen grandparents and found it hard when he and Donna had split up and he didn't want them to maintain contact with Donna and the boys. In fact, he had made it clear that he wanted them to take his side and leave it to him to sort things out in his own way. After that they had stepped back even though they loved the boys, and Donna too if the truth were told. That plan for sorting things out hadn't gone too well now, he thought. What a bloody mess!

CHAPTER 10

In the car that evening, Joan was explaining the local phenomenon of the tramontana – a wind that comes from the Pyrenees and is loved by some and drives others into deep depression. An elderly uncle of his who had lived in the area all his life told the story of how when the tramontana blew, his mother would put newspaper under his clothes, front and back, so that he wouldn't be cold going and coming from school. The same uncle related how when the wind was strong on their way to school, he and his friend would unzip their jerkins and extend their arms to the side so that the wind filled their coats like wings. He maintained that on occasions they could be lifted off the ground and had the real sensation of flight. Joan, who had been raised in Barcelona and come to Begur for the summer each year, had never had this childhood experience and was dubious about these stories. He explained that they were part of local lore and there were several versions told by older people from Begur about the role of the wind in their lives. Alice had noted that the wind symbol appeared frequently on the weekly weather forecast for the area and was interested to see if they would actually get to experience the tramontana. She smiled to herself at the mental images she conjured up of Oz-type adventures in the wind.

After a short drive from Begur, there was an air of quiet expectation as Alice and Caroline, Joan and Clara drove from the darkness towards the warm glow of the Verges village lights. In the headlights they could see that red-and-gold Catalan flags lined the access road and flapped like sails in the evening breeze. Joan parked on the outskirts on some rough ground that had been cleared for the purpose and was being efficiently managed by a group of young people. They were all wearing black T-shirts bearing an image of the Grim Reaper and black bandanas that gave them a look of swashbuckling pirates. The four merged into the group of fellow pilgrims and were carried forward by the crowd towards their common end. Flaming torches attached to the walls of buildings generated macabre moving shadows from the constant stream of visitors that edged along the narrow streets of sandstone houses. The air was filled with the muffled voices of those gathering for the event that would culminate at around midnight with the celebrated Danza de la Muerte.

As they were absorbed into the human snake moving towards the village centre, it became clear that the crowd was following its appointed path and there was little room for freethinking. In the distance, the sound of music competed with the animated chatter of those gathering for the fiesta. Alice was sure that her own reflections about life's journey were being shared by many around her and realised that she was already captivated by the experience of this ancient ritual.

As they neared the more concentrated lights of the *plaça major*, Joan turned left up a small alley and they found themselves in a candlelit café. An odd air of jollity and camaraderie filled the sombre space. The man behind the bar was wearing the same outfit as those managing the car park and he shouted a greeting to them in Catalan. Joan responded in the strangely soft-sounding language and they were soon seated at a small table with glasses of cava and a plate of assorted tapas.

"So!" began Joan. "Here we are, doing what our ancestors have done for centuries." He raised his glass and as they followed suit the bubbles caught the light of the candle flame. "Let's drink to life and not wasting any of our moments."

"*To life – la vida!*" declared Clara with infectious fervour.

And they clinked their glasses together to life, remembering all at once its joys and its inevitable ending.

"*Just this!*" said Clara, managing to hold them captive in the optimism of the instant.

Alice became aware of Caroline's attention being drawn from the immediate activity and chat at the table. She had assumed a familiar work expression and was staring fixedly at a couple seated at a table in the darkest corner of the room. A thirty-something man, tanned and with shoulder-length brown curly hair was talking seriously with a slightly older, stocky fellow whose back was towards their table. Alice touched her partner's hand gently and raised her eyebrows to inquire what was going on.

Joan and Clara were speaking in Spanish about a message that had arrived on Joan's phone. Inquiries about the hotel were constant.

"It's OK, Alice. Nothing too worrying, I'm sure."

Alice could read clearly that Caroline's expression belied her assurances. She looked perplexed and preoccupied.

"Appropriately enough, I think I've just seen a ghost." Caroline shook her head to make it clear that any further elaboration would keep until they were alone later.

When they rejoined the procession the sense of excitement had heightened and there was the haunting sound of reedy Catalan music filling the warm air. They took their places on the rows of wooden seats that were set out around the village square. The arrangement left a wide passageway for the performers that led across from one narrow, dark side street towards the open doors of the church. Set off to the side a small raised platform held a group of musicians – men and women of diverse ages all dressed in black and playing their strange wind instruments with a mix of pride and composure.

Alice's first exposure to Catalan culture had got her thinking. Even at this late hour, family groups included all the generations. Small children, teenagers, parents rocking babies in their arms and grandparents sat side-by-side listening respectfully to the music and waving to friends that they spotted around the audience. There was a sense of shared identity, a deep connection to the place and an underlying, open kindness that Alice had observed since her arrival. She was still trying to figure it out but for now her impression of the Catalan ethos was entirely positive. It reminded her a little of the sense of solidarity she had experienced on a visit with Hugo to the republican Felons Club in West Belfast where political prisoners and their supporters gathered to socialise and participate in shared activities. Here in Verges, with the wider generational element she saw a similar cultural camaraderie without the emphasis on alcohol or solidarity in adversity.

As the village clock edged towards twelve, the musicians finished their performance to enthusiastic applause and then for a few moments the crowd was still. The clock rang out midnight clearly into the silence and then the sound of a woman singing slowly in Latin filled the air. The small programme on her seat told Alice that this was Rufus Wainwright's arrangement of the 'Agnus Dei'. It was haunting and uncompromising and entirely congruous with the ancient ceremony originally performed to ward off the destructive impact of plagues and pandemics. The contemporary Christian message of the ritual was clear although for many, like herself, Alice assumed it would be interpreted in its more pagan form.

The deep sound of a drum came from a distance, somewhere along the narrow street, signalling that the dance had already begun. It approached gradually and built, raising the level of anticipation in the crowd until the steady heartbeat resounded through the square, playing out a slow, measured, rhythmical beat. Children moved in closer to their parents and couples held each other's hands more firmly. Before the participants were actually physically present, their long, eerie shadows danced across the stone facades moving in time to the age-old throb of wood on tightly stretched skin.

First to come into view was a figure that looked for all the world like a human skeleton. It was a tall man dressed in black with an intricate, luminous, white skeletal pattern on the front. As the black merged with the darkness, his fleshless arms, legs and body came to life as he danced and turned at one with the staccato stroke of the drum. The man was wearing a grotesque, skull-shaped helmet and carrying a scythe whose shadow swung back and forward above the heads of the crowd. Along the blade of the scythe was written '*Nemini Parco*'. "No one is spared," whispered Joan.

As the first figure hopped and turned, moving forward very slowly, two children followed also dressed as skeletons and wearing the ghostly skull headgear. As they danced to the haunting drumbeat, one held aloft a clock with no hands and the other a bowl of ashes, which the bearer held out and displayed to the crowd. Then came the fourth figure playing the drum and a fifth holding a flag with something written on it. Again Joan provided the translation. "Time is short," he whispered and reached for Clara's hand and held it tightly.

Behind these figures and apparently serving the purpose of providing additional light for the performance, there emerged five more figures wearing purple robes and holding flaming torches. While the skeletons danced to the drumbeat, the figures behind walked slowly and held their torches aloft.

The light-bearers wore pointed hoods that looked, for Alice, too much like the regalia of the Ku Klux Klan. She glanced in distaste at Joan for some explanation. "They are members of the local brotherhood," he said. "These are traditional robes and have nothing to do with your KKK. They were traditionally worn by penitents in Holy Week processions." Alice accepted his account but was left with a residual sense of displeasure that came, she accepted, from her own shameful, national cultural baggage.

The ghostly procession danced its way through the crowd in the direction of the open, now brightly illuminated church doors. Here they stopped and, bending forward at the waist, bowed slowly towards a statue of the crucifixion in the church porch. They held this position in silence for several moments and then stood erect, turned and bowed slowly towards the audience. This abrupt ending was met first with respectful applause that was then accompanied by joyful whooping and built towards a cacophony that seemed to proclaim the joy of life and, at least for the moment, the collective escape from life's ending.

Alice had been watching the children in the crowd near her and wondering what they made of all this grim entertainment. Their expressions didn't suggest they were horrified in any way and she assumed that their parents gave them adequate guidance before the event to ensure that they understood the message. Certainly there would be many for whom the religious theme would be central but for others perhaps this was a healthy way of reminding us of the need to make the most of life while we can before death comes looking for us. It was an impressive performance and she couldn't help but wonder how Caroline, whose daily business was concerned with untimely visits from the Grim Reaper, had received it.

* * *

The impact of La Danza de la Muerte and the lateness of the hour had meant that the journey home in the car was a quiet affair and the couples had said goodbye at the door of the hotel.

"Are you going to tell me about your ghost, Caro?" Alice asked as soon as they had locked the door of their room.

Caroline nodded and sat down in the armchair in the small sitting room at the entrance to their suite and kicked off her shoes. Alice lay on the day bed facing her, full of attention.

"OK," Caroline began. "Back in the late nineties when I was first working in the Murder Squad there was a particularly awful killing of an eighty-four-year-old woman. Her name was Maudie Prior. She was raped and her throat was cut in her own home and all apparently for the paltry sum of twenty-three pounds. The killer wasn't very bright and made no attempt to conceal evidence. Forensics had prints and sperm and any amount of other hooks to hang him on. In fact, many people would have been happy to see him hang, while others argued that he himself was a victim of the system." She paused as if replaying the media debate that had raged at the time. "Anyway, there was CCTV nearby that clearly identified a local youth and he confessed straight away, as soon as we brought him in."

The story was not unfamiliar to Alice and she just nodded as Caroline continued with her story.

"He was an eighteen-year-old who couldn't read or write and was serially bullied at school. It was clear he was trying to establish his tough-guy identity with his peers and he was held on remand in the Maze Prison while the legal case and various psychological tests were prepared."

She looked exhausted as she related the story and Alice could see that there was a twist coming.

"He was duly tried and convicted and given fourteen years. It probably would have given him time to catch up on his missed education but there was an appeal and he was acquitted on a technicality and awarded a substantial compensatory payment. You can imagine the impact of that on a guy whose ego had continuously taken such a battering. Overnight he became cock of the walk. Last I heard of him, he was leaving Northern Ireland for good and planned to set up a business in Scotland with his newly acquired girlfriend. I heard nothing more until tonight when I saw him in the corner of the bar engrossed in conversation with another guy. His name was Jordan Campbell and I guess now that he must have made a new life for himself around these parts." She met Alice's concerned regard and shook her head from side to side to indicate that there was no need for anxiety about her safety. "I was only a small player in that case and I don't think he recognised me this evening. I have to give him the benefit of the doubt ... he took his second chance with both hands and has made a decent new start here. We are talking about nearly twenty years ago now."

There was a tacit agreement to let sleeping dogs lie and, without much more chat, they went directly to bed. Alice fell into a fitful sleep with the insistent rhythm of the drum from the earlier procession sounding ominously in her head.

CHAPTER 11

The dismal circumstances of Sammy Marshall's detention gave him an expanse of time to consider his situation. The gloom in which he was now detained was mirrored by the growing darkness of his state of mind. Little by little now, eyes and mouth wrapped with some type of thick, plastic sticky tape and handcuffed to the wall like an animal, the actual bloody mess he had made of his family crept into full view in his consciousness. Between his lurid recollections of the carnage he had created, the freezing cold and his brutal hangover, his nerves jangled with the force of a physical tornado.

Last night Donna had been feisty at first and said he had no rights to be there – in his own house. That had really irked him and he had smacked her. He felt his temper flare again. The main reason he was in trouble with these thugs was because he still had to pay the maintenance for the kids he couldn't see and a mortgage for a house he was excluded from. Where were his rights in all that? How come these bitches of women had all the power nowadays? She had been so sure that the cops would take her side if she called them. She bragged that the courts had given her a number to phone if he ever tried to breach the Exclusion Order – if she ever felt that she was at risk. "*I'll show you fucking risk!*" he had shouted in her smug face as he'd grabbed her mobile and flung it against the wall. She would not be talking to anyone about him.

Then she came at him and they struggled and he'd lost his balance and had gone down with a wallop. He must have lost it altogether then and grabbed the big knife from the rack on the work surface and stabbed her until he'd shut her squealing mouth once and for all. He didn't remember actually sticking the knife in but the knife was in his hands and she was dead so there was no arguing with that evidence. He had thrown the knife under the table and rubbed his hands on his sweatshirt. He was surprised how tacky her blood was. It stuck like glue to his hands and he had gone up to the bathroom to try to wash it off.

And then there were the kids. He hadn't hesitated once he'd silenced Donna. He couldn't have the boys left judging him. He just knew instinctively they had to go too. Recently, Riley was already acting strange with him and he knew Donna had been filling his head with stories about him and his tempers. Last time he'd seen them the kid had said, "We liked you better when you weren't angry all the time, Daddy." There was no way a five-year-old had thought that remark up for himself. That was Donna's doing – spreading her poison into the kids – making them uneasy and suspicious of him. But he'd put paid to all of that. What sort of eejit did she think he was that he would stand for it, that he'd keep paying for everything while she sat about in her new house and acted the fucking lady?

He had lost track of time and his world was now permanently pitch dark. His other senses heightened by his now sightless eyes, he could hear agitated scuffling that made him think there were rats in the garage with him. He was terrified of rats and felt his bowels loosening at the thought that they might attack him. He heard himself whimper but knew that there was no one else there to help him. How long did they expect him to stay there trussed up like a lump of meat? It was freezing cold and he was only half dressed. His hangover had expanded to become a full body trauma and he was afraid that any minute he would vomit and choke himself to death. He worked at the tape across his mouth, wriggling his jaw and pushing hard against the tape with his tongue until it hurt. It loosened only slightly but he was finally able to suck in a little of the fetid air and it was a small relief.

When they'd taken him from under the blanket on the back seat of the car he was shoved against a wall as they'd unlocked a rusted overhead garage door. He couldn't recognise the place at all. Then inside, they had taped his mouth and eyes, attached him to a ring on the wall and said something about giving him time to think about 'paying his lawful debts or accepting the fucking consequences'. As the overhead door swung down and was locked outside he was left in unrelenting darkness. He could see nothing at all.

Sammy was struggling to figure out why he had been dragged in over the unpaid debt. It was Bull, Donna's brother, who had sorted the loan for him in the first place. He said he knew that Sammy would be good for the money when he got himself sorted and that he would look out for him. Bull hadn't got involved when Sammy and Donna had split up. Even though he and his sister got on OK together it was Sammy and Bull who were close friends and spent the most time together. Donna was always caught up with the kids and Sammy needed adult company and a few drinks to help him relax. Bull seemed to get that. He was always keen to have Sammy along when he had business to do in local clubs or even a few jaunts out of town to meet up with contacts out in the sticks. Riding round in the flash car and an endless supply of uppers and free shots kept Sammy happy and he had been gutted when Bull had suddenly dropped him. They had been like brothers, he thought. That fucking Exclusion Order had wrecked everything and the tears of misery stung his eyes behind the adhesive tape.

It was clear that when his two jailers returned he would have to have a good argument to put forward about paying what he owed or they might lose patience with him. He couldn't fathom why Bull would lift him now because of the unpaid loan when back in Goliath Row there were much greater reasons for him to be punished. He was sure to know that since earlier in the day and yet it was puzzling that he hadn't done anything about it.

Images of the hurts that Bull and his henchmen could cause him made his stomach churn. His mouth was parched from the drink and he had eaten nothing since the previous teatime when his ma had produced her classic liver and onions. A mouthful of burning bile rose from his throat and he retched the acidic, foul-smelling liquid that escaped the slightly loosened gag and ran down his chin and the front of his T-shirt. As his sense of panic about his options rose, he found himself wondering if he might not be better off being found by the cops and safely locked up in a cell. He heard a car door slam nearby and felt liquid faeces soak the seat of his boxers and hot urine sting his freezing legs, as he lost all control of himself.

* * *

Pradić did not disappoint with her online investigations. When Burrows and McVeigh entered the Murder Squad offices, she immediately swung her chair around and made it clear she was ready to report her findings.

"I have found quite a lot online about Sammy Marshall. I've made notes and sent them to you but the summary is he has form for drink driving and has lost his licence for two years, starting from a few months ago. An Exclusion Order was granted after his wife provided evidence that he was repeatedly violent with her. There were corroborating statements entered in evidence, from their son Riley's primary school teacher and the little one's crèche, that showed the kids were upset and on a number of occasions the mother showed up with only thinly disguised facial bruises."

Burrows was nodding and smiled appreciatively at Pradić. "Good work, Zara. The more we have on him the better, so that when we find him, we can nail him."

"Donna Nelson's supervisor from a part-time job she had in the office at the local Tesco had also entered a statement backing her story of repeated abuse by Marshall. He said she had to stop work in the long run as she had too much to contend with at home."

Burrows and McVeigh were listening attentively. It was clear that Marshall had the profile of an abuser.

"Donna Nelson's family don't feature much in the court proceedings taken by their daughter. She does have a brother, his name is Robert but he is known as Bull, and he has quite a reputation for dealing drugs and extracting money with menaces – but he has avoided conviction so far. He's smart. Rumour has it he is part of a Shankill gang involved in protection and using strong-arm tactics to secure overdue payments. He and Sammy Marshall have history. They were friends on Facebook although there has been little or no activity between them since Donna's Exclusion Order was issued. Prior to that, there were images of them partying in local clubs and seeming to be very close."

How close was close, Burrows wondered. "Interesting," he said. "It sounds as if there had been a falling-out between those two. If Marshall was overdue with paying his debts and Bull had an axe to grind about his treatment of his sister, there might well be a family connection here. Let's get Family Liaison out to both families first thing tomorrow. The local uniforms will have been out to break the news to the Nelsons." He turned to McVeigh. "Ian, can you organise to take Sandra Woods and head out there first thing in the morning? Talk to the grandparents and the brother and see if you can get any lead on where Marshall might be being held. We'll need the brother or the grandparents to come in and ID the bodies. I'll be here to manage that. For now let's check what intel the local PSNIs might have on premises used for gang business in their area. They will keep plugging away this evening at the house-to-house calls and the search for Marshall. We'll also see what the Anti-terrorism people have about gangland activities in the Loyalist west of the city. Who is involved and are there known premises that they work out of. They still have feet on the ground in that regard, I'm sure."

He turned back to Zara. "Any record of Marshall hurting the children?"

"There are reports filed by Social Welfare, in relation to the Exclusion Order, about the oldest boy showing signs of distress at school. He was normally a quiet young boy but became uncharacteristically aggressive in the playground. There was a home visit where Donna, the mother, said he was upset by his father's behaviour, and was bedwetting and having persistent nightmares. No report of physical harm to the children."

Pradić had spoken unemotionally but her expression had hardened as she listed the child's symptoms and Burrows wondered momentarily about her own history.

"OK. Let's find Marshall as soon as we can and bring him in. If the Bull fella gets to him first we may be looking at an additional fatality and a much harder job of ever pinning it on anybody. Ian, you focus on the families. Zara, track down the business on Bull Nelson and associates through whatever channels you can. Also see what there is by way of CCTV around the murder scene, his drinking hole and Marshall's route home. I'll look after the Super, the local door-to-door enquiries and the various autopsies and forensics."

His manner was calm and competent and his colleagues responded with fresh energy.

"Let's see where we can get to in the few hours before this evening's review meeting," he said, launching a final motivational push, and settled down at his desk.

DI Paton's office door was closed and despite the fact that he was taking the lead in her absence he would not have dreamed of moving into her space. He drafted an initial press statement and emailed it to DS McCluskey. Then he contacted his colleagues in-house to flag the possibility of needing some extra support in the coming days. His phone rang and at the same time Pradić was signalling that she had found something interesting. This was all moving in the right direction, he thought, as he reached for his desk phone.

* * *

Sammy Marshall's teeth were chattering with cold and terror as the metal up-and-over door was flung open with excessive force. A switch was pulled and he recognised the sound of fluorescent lights stuttering into action. Behind the blindfold, he sensed that the space around him was flooded with light and the waft of fresh air filled his nostrils with his own stench. He struggled to interpret the signs of what was happening now. He had heard a car arrive and two doors banging shut. There would be two of them – and maybe another one still in the driving seat. He heard two distinct voices grunting and goading each other as they wrestled with the stubborn roller-shutter door. Then there was the sound of sharp exhalation and muttered expletives as his jailers surveyed their quarry.

"For fuck's sake! He's shit himself!" And then there was derisive laughter as they mocked him for his complete loss of bottle. "Oh Sammy! You haven't stood up to this wee bit of pressure too well, have you? You are really stinking, man. I wonder how this will look on social media."

He heard their phones clicking and their guffaws as they reviewed their handiwork. He could only snivel and hope that they wouldn't hurt him any more than he hurt already. They ripped the tape from his mouth and roughly poured in some water. He swallowed and strained his head forward for some more.

"Lucky for you that the boss is busy with some family stuff. We just called by to let you know that he wants you to hang on here for a bit …"

He heard them snigger at their unintentional witticism.

"He'll be around to talk to you tomorrow himself … man to man, like."

Snorting with laughter they moved away, the lights were extinguished and the metal gate was closed down and locked from the outside. Almost immediately the two car doors slammed shut and the engine fired noisily as they drove away.

Sammy sagged forward as a wave of uncontrollable panic overwhelmed him. He was on his own here for the night and the prospect was totally nerve-shattering.

Maundy Thursday, 17 April 2014

CHAPTER 12

The joyful chattering of swallows and swifts woke the women the following morning. Alice counted the church clock ringing three-quarters of an hour as she opened the shutters and the window and slid back into bed. Caroline was slow to waken in the mornings and Alice lay quietly beside her as the senior detective gradually accepted the intrusion of the new day. Alice wondered how they would spend this first full day of their break. They had agreed not to look at news from home and, whatever effort this required of Caroline, it was no great penance for Alice.

The hotel breakfast was from nine to eleven and so there was no pressure to get moving any more quickly than suited Caroline's holiday tempo. Alice headed to the shower and left Caroline to her own pace of seizing the day. She hadn't been too long under the very pleasant rain-head shower when she heard her lover's mobile phone announce an incoming call. Her parents maybe, Alice mused, and reconcentrated her attentions on the pleasure of the hot shower and the very satisfying aroma of the musky shower products. Even the small things were well looked after in this establishment.

Once out of the shower, Alice was surprised to see Caroline out of bed and looking more alert than she would have expected.

"That was DS McCluskey," Caroline said. "Seems like our ghost has risen, well and truly."

Alice swathed herself more securely in her towel and sat on the edge of the bed. "What do you mean? What's happened?"

"It seems as if the Grim Reaper called in a soul in Verges earlier this morning, maybe even while we were still watching the performance. A local man who was caught earlier on security cameras in the company of a native of Northern Ireland was found dead this morning with his throat cut. One Jordi Campbell, as he is now known, is being sought for questioning and McCluskey has, very apologetically, asked if I can become involved. The local Policia will be here at eleven."

"Can't he send Burrows or McVeigh to handle it?" Alice felt aggrieved that the holiday was already stymied on their first full day.

Caroline twisted her mouth and shook her head. "Seems they're busy enough with a triple murder and an abduction so that's a definite 'no'."

And that's the end of the news embargo too, Alice thought to herself.

"He did say that I can add on the days at the end so that is something."

Alice wondered if her own allocation of leave was also assumed to be elastic but didn't think it was the time to be raising her own interests.

"Well, I do have something Hugo asked me to follow up on, so I'll get on with that while you're busy with the Spanish Policia."

Alice sounded more fractious than she actually was and, as they headed down for breakfast, there was a certain chill in the air that Joan and Clara's enthusiastic good mornings did nothing to allay.

* * *

Alice took some time to read stuff that Hugo had sent her about the group whose work he thought might be interesting for them. She didn't really want to work today but with Caro downstairs meeting the local police she didn't have a lot of options. She sat on the terrace of their suite in the hotel and searched on the Internet for what she could find about the group. All that Hugo had given her was the group's name – Associació Homes Igualitaris, meaning the 'Association of Egalitarian Men'. It was affiliated to the Spanish national group 'Asociación Hombres por la Igualdad de Género' – 'Men's Association for Gender Equality' or AHIGE.

The Catalan group had been set up in 2009 and was actively working to engage men in gender-equality activities. There were programmes of awareness-raising in schools and communities and a network of events for boys, fathers and even those who had been convicted of gender-based violent crimes against women and gay men. AHIGE argued that sexism and machismo are common enemies of both men and women and that men stood to gain, rather than lose, from greater gender equality. The group's online materials engaged Alice's attention immediately. They resonated deeply with her own observations of the young men she worked with who were so easily dragged into acting out their masculinity in violent ways that damaged themselves as well as others.

Her annoyance with Caroline and the whole business of their break being interrupted had already disappeared and she was regretting the sulk she had got into over breakfast. Sitting here in the April sunshine, she felt relaxed and privileged and was sorry that she had sent Caroline off to cope with things alone.

At breakfast, after a few frosty minutes Caroline had laid her hand gently over Alice's. "I was wondering if your Spanish is up to acting as interpreter in my discussion with the local police?" she launched tentatively. "I'd be very grateful …" She had tried a usually winning seductive tone but Alice wasn't convinced.

"See how you manage on your own first," she responded, "and you can let me know later if you really need me. I'm sure these guys speak English well enough." She had regretted her stubbornness almost immediately but hadn't backed down.

She was reading a convincing argument about how sexism impacted men's health in a negative way when her phone buzzed and a text from Caroline came through. **I am in the basement sitting room with the local detectives and could really use your help with the language. Neither man has great English and things are moving very slowly.** An emoji kiss softened the demand.

On my way, replied Alice and as she saved her readings onto the desktop and headed for the door, she felt her mood lift and her interest in this new investigation take hold. I'm really such a pushover, she thought, and laughed to herself.

CHAPTER 13

First thing on Holy Thursday morning, McVeigh and Family Liaison Officer, Sandra Woods, knocked on the door of the Nelson household. McVeigh noted that the front door was reinforced and that the Nelsons had invested heavily in their protection from unwanted intruders. There was a flashy black Merc parked at the door that seriously outclassed all the other vehicles parked at neighbouring houses, including the patrol car that Burrows had asked to be there in case there was some gangland feud at the bottom of all this. McVeigh was hopeful that the car meant Bull was on the premises.

As they waited at the door, the young detective tried to empathise with a family that had just lost a sister, a daughter, two small grandsons and nephews. The shock and anger would be sizeable, he thought, as he heard footsteps inside and a seriously body-built man in his late thirties opened the door. Bull. He and Woods held their ID out and Bull snorted disdainfully and stood aside to allow them to come in.

The house was a fifties semi and smelt of cigarettes and fried food overlaid with a sickly room freshener. Bull walked ahead of them into an open-plan living room and kitchen that had been extended and furnished with highend L-shaped leather sofas. There was a well-stocked corner bar at the front end of the room. The dining and kitchen area at the back was also like an image from a style magazine with an oval smoked-glass dining table and marble-topped kitchen surfaces.

A middle-aged couple were sitting on one sofa with mugs of cold tea and a plate of tired-looking biscuits in front of them.

"Your lot have already been here several times yesterday," the younger member of the Nelson family grunted. "I hope you're coming to say you've got the bastard who did this." He pointed in an off-hand manner towards two places on the sofa where McVeigh and Woods should sit.

Something in Bull's tone suggested to McVeigh that he might be bluffing but he decided to play along and see where things went. If it was Bull who had arranged for Sammy Marshall to be lifted, he wouldn't have had time yet to confront him with his sister's killing.

"We are here to say that we are sorry for your loss." He addressed his remarks to the older couple. "And that we are making every effort to apprehend the person or persons who killed your daughter and grandchildren, as quickly as possible."

The couple looked shell-shocked and the woman might well have taken a tranquiliser, judging by the glaze over her eyes and the size of her pupils.

"Anything at all that you can tell us that might help us find Donna and the boys' killer would be very useful."

Bull Nelson grimaced and shook his head as if to dislodge something that was annoying him. "Let's not play games here. We all know that Sammy Marshall did this. He's been working up to it for a while now. He can't pay his debts and he can't control his fucking temper."

The standards by which Bull Nelson judged Marshall were interesting, McVeigh reflected.

"I told our Donna that a fucking Exclusion Order wasn't worth the paper it was written on. The dogs on the street know that. Your lot don't want to get involved in domestics."

His face paled then and McVeigh could see that there was something working on him. McVeigh left the silence hanging between them.

"Donna phoned me on Tuesday evening, earlier on," Bull went on, "and said Marshall was threatening to come around. I told her not to open the door and to ring me if he came." A nerve pulsed in his cheek and he shook his head again in exasperation.

"Can you say what time that was?" McVeigh asked gently, wondering if what he was looking at was predominantly grief or guilt.

"*Of course I bloody can!*" He spat the words as if he would not countenance being taken for a fool. He held up his phone. "Last call from Donna was at 5.57pm. She was making the boys' tea while she was talking to me. I think the woman next door was with her."

"That is very useful, Mr Nelson," Sandra Woods interjected. "Can you say if your sister made any further calls to you on Tuesday evening, even if they were missed calls."

"There were no missed calls. If there had been I would have been round there like a shot." He looked at his parents as if to get assurance that he would in no way be held accountable for what had happened.

His father gave him the nod he was looking for and muttered under his breath, "Of course you would have, son."

"When our officers called to Sammy Marshall's parents' house yesterday between 12.30 and 1.00 they were told that Sammy had already been taken away by two men. These men had warned his mother against contacting the police or there would be further trouble for her son." McVeigh paused to see the impact of this information on Bull Nelson.

The man was studiously examining the backs of his hands, working at some scratches across his knuckles as if trying to remember what had caused them. There were a number of nicks on his cheek too that might have been explained by a slip shaving – or might not.

"If you have any idea who is holding Marshall or where he might be," McVeigh continued, "I would ask you to share that information and let us bring him in right now for questioning."

Bull exhaled sharply again and fixed McVeigh with a stony look.

A chill ran up the young detective's back and he concentrated on not showing any response. "We urgently want to bring your sister's and nephews' killer to justice, Mr Nelson."

"Well, your urgent is too late now, officer," he said coldly. "And we need to acknowledge that our ideas of what justice might be in this case may be very different."

McVeigh could see that Bull was not just about brute physical strength but also had a sharp mind that he was able to put to work when he wanted to. Well, he could play the strategic game too, McVeigh thought as he observed his opponent sitting opposite him. They couldn't be sure if Marshall was being held at the instigation of his ex-brother-in-law or whether it was another gang altogether that Marshall had fallen out with. It might take a while longer to find out what was going on there but McVeigh was almost certain that Bull was having Sammy Marshall held somewhere until he could decide what to do with him. The pressing question was why Nelson would want Sammy kept offside at this moment in time. If Bull had arranged for Sammy to be taken and held, because of his unpaid debts and harassment of his sister, then Donna's death had rendered that move obsolete. He was more than likely letting Marshall sweat for the moment but he needed to find a way out of impeding a murder inquiry without losing face or attracting attention to his own unlawful activities. McVeigh could also imagine that by now Marshall was hoping that the police found him first.

"I'm sure that we'll speak further about these matters, Mr Nelson," McVeigh said quietly. "For now, I'm afraid I'll have to ask if you will go to Grosvenor Road Station and meet Detective Sergeant Burrows there. He's expecting you and will need you to identify the remains of your sister and nephews."

Bull Nelson blanched and for the first time allowed his distress to become visible. He looked hopefully at his parents but realised immediately that this was his task, not theirs, to complete.

"DS Burrows will accompany you to the mortuary," McVeigh added.

Bull remained seated and showed no signs of complying with McVeigh's request.

"Constable Woods is from our family liaison section and will stay here with Mr and Mrs Marshall for as long as necessary." McVeigh raised his eyebrows at Sandra Woods and she immediately rose and took charge of the situation.

"Let's start by getting the kettle on for a fresh cuppa, will we?" And she moved towards the kitchen area.

Bull Marshall stood up reluctantly and put on a leather jacket that was on the back of a chair in the dining area. Then he moved grudgingly towards the door. His mother sobbed as he began to leave, as if picturing the difficult task that faced him.

"I'll be back as soon as I can, Ma," he said as he left the room.

McVeigh also took his leave and headed for the Marshall house where the second Liaison Officer would already be waiting with another family whose child's future hung in the balance. None of the current options for Sammy Marshall were even slightly optimistic.

CHAPTER 14

At the sound of Alice coming down the spiral metal staircase leading to the basement space of Hotel Aiguaclara, Caroline and the two men sitting with her turned and watched her descend.

The men were youngish, dressed in casual clothes. Both were dark-haired and had a tanned complexion. They wore open-necked shirts and jeans and one wore a leather jacket. The younger man had a small, neatly trimmed beard. Alice judged that the other was the superior officer.

The two men stood.

Caroline smiled broadly and said slowly, "This is Doctor Alice Fox who has kindly agreed to interpret for us. Hopefully now we will be able to make some progress."

Alice shook hands with the men and sat opposite them, beside Caroline.

"I'll finish the introductions and bring you up to date first, Alice, and then we can continue."

The men nodded their agreement.

"This is Detective José Mantego." Caroline gestured towards the older man, "and this is Detective Carlos Tapia Rodriguez. They are from the Girona Mossos d'Esquadra, Criminal Investigation Division."

The men resumed their seats.

Caroline continued. "The Mossos are the autonomous Catalan Police Force who are taking charge of a murder that happened in Verges early this morning. I've explained that we attended the event last night and that I recognised Campbell from several decades ago when he was involved in a Belfast Murder Squad case. Some people returning to their car after a late meal found the man that Campbell was with in the café. He was in a field on the outskirts of Verges with his throat cut. The victim's name is Xavier Duxo. That's about as far as we've got."

She gestured to the men that it was OK to continue.

The detectives spoke rapidly to each other in what Alice assumed was Catalan and then spoke in an accented Castilian that Alice tuned into without any difficulty. Both as a detective and a youth worker she had worked in Hispanic communities in Lowell. Nearly twenty per cent of the population in that area of Massachusetts were Latin American and, for as long as she could remember, Alice had both friends and colleagues who were Spanish-speaking. She had learned Spanish at high school and then taken evening classes to become more proficient.

It appeared that José Mantego was the senior of the two detectives and he did most of the talking. Rodriguez was the note-taker although his approach to the task was definitely minimalist. He was holding a pen and a notebook on which there was very little written.

Mantego outlined the context of the case and then paused so that Alice could translate for Caroline.

"I'm not translating absolutely literally, Caroline, but I'll give you as accurate a general idea as possible. It seems that after the Danza de le Muerte in Verges there is always a fair amount of fiesta. People who are not in a hurry home stay around and have a few drinks and eat at some of the local restaurants. It is a good night for local businesses and they try to capitalise on the crowds. Detective Mantego explained that Verges is a small place and limited in its tourist opportunities. The numbers that come into the village on this night exceed those of any other date in their tourist calendar."

Caroline signalled a little impatiently that she got the message and Mantego continued.

Alice listened attentively and then relayed the information to Caroline. The interpreter role was not new to her as she had often been an impromptu translator in Lowell PD.

"The body of the murdered man was lying at the edge of a field, partially concealed by thickly planted bamboo. A young couple who had gone to collect their car down in the field, which was used as a car park for the night, saw the body illuminated in their headlights and reported it to the police. They attended the scene immediately and the victim, Xavier Duxo, was known to them. The Irishman he was with on the CCTV cameras and in the café was also known to them for crimes here in Catalonia and also in Ireland." Alice could see that Mantego's failure to accurately identify Northern Ireland irritated Caroline but she focussed on interpreting what he said as accurately as she could. "Duxo, the victim, was a controversial character who belonged to a newish right-wing political party."

Caroline asked for some background on the party and Mantego obliged.

Alice relayed the detail of the exchange smoothly, conscious yet again of the parallels between Northern Ireland and Catalonia: "Vox have raised spectres of the Spanish Civil War which have never been fully laid to rest. In Spain, the Civil War is not openly discussed. It divided families and communities at the time back in the thirties and has continued to do so ever since."

Mantego waited for Caroline to respond but she remained silent. Alice guessed that she wasn't interested in this protracted history lesson and wanted to get to the point but the detective had his own agenda, it seemed. She continued to interpret his words for Caroline who did not display much engagement with what she heard.

"There are mass graves all over the country where the fascist falangists buried republicans that they had killed and many families are still hoping to find their loved ones and give them a decent burial. Vox, it seems, has reprised Franco's war cry of 'Viva España' and used it to demonise migrants, feminists and the Catalan independence movement. They have annoyed a lot of people."

"I don't follow," said Caroline to Alice, furrowing her brow. "I can't see what would position those three particular groups against the extreme nationalist position."

Alice relayed the comment and Mantego's subsequent reply.

"Each in their own way is seen as a threat to the fabric of traditional Spanish values. Catalan independents want to divide the nation by separating a valuable and productive part of Spain from the rest of the country. Feminists fundamentally threaten the patriarchal structure to which nationalists are devoted and migrants, especially Muslim people, are linked to the invading Moors that occupied Spain way back many centuries ago. Vox are reinventing history to suit their own ends."

Alice waited to see what Caroline had to say to all this but she just looked bemused and Mantego continued.

"Vox do not have much support in Catalonia. At least not open support anyway. But the Mossos know that those who propose extreme right-wing measures are growing in popularity throughout Europe. He says the American Tea Party is another example of these views."

At this point the detective addressed his comments directly to Alice. "I am sure, Dr Fox, that you are familiar with the expression of this ideological position in your own country."

Alice nodded her agreement that this was the case but chose not to digress from her role as interpreter. Mantego's attempts to get a political discussion under way was proving unsuccessful, Alice noted. There was probably quite a lot that could be said about the competing political identities in many countries but now was not the moment.

"What I'm really struggling to see is how a guy from Northern Ireland could be tangled up in such matters." Caroline sounded genuinely bewildered.

Alice relayed her comment and Mantego seemed loath to be too specific. Alice translated.

"He says that at this point they are trying to find Campbell and ask for his explanation as to why he was in the company of Xavier Duxo around the time that Duxo was murdered. They have asked the Irish police to help with that information-gathering and Detective McCluskey has suggested that you can help them with that."

Alice could see that Caroline was amused by Mantego's reduction of her superior's rank and status.

Mantego continued and Alice passed on his comments.

"Detective Mantego says that when they find Jordi Campbell they think that you will be of much help in our questioning of him. He says that both of us will help them." Alice tried to maintain a blank expression although she could see that Caroline was unimpressed by

Mantego's assumptions. His final remark had been made as a slightly arrogant statement of fact. Alice translated it as such and she could see that the next few days could become more crowded with policework than tourist activities. She was resigned to go with the flow and waited for Caroline's response.

"Detective Superintendent Graham McCluskey of the Police Service of *Northern* Ireland," Caroline stressed the word '*northern*', "has asked us to cooperate with you and of course we will comply with his wishes. We will gather what information we can on Campbell's historic and more recent activities and forward those to you. We expect that you will reciprocate. When we are all up to date with the relevant documents, then we can discuss what additional collaboration you require of us."

After Alice had translated, Caroline didn't wait for any further discussion but stood up, shook hands with the men and left the room.

Alice said her own goodbyes and followed Caroline upstairs to their room.

CHAPTER 15

Back in the car, DC Ian McVeigh called directly into Murder Squad HQ and got through immediately to Zara Pradić. After asking for a trace to be put on Bull Nelson's phone, he stayed on the line to talk to Burrows. Pradić would get the phone under surveillance lickety-quick.

"Bull Nelson is on his way in to you, sarge," he said. "His sister had phoned him before six o'clock Tuesday evening to say she was frightened and that Sammy Marshall was threatening to breach the Exclusion Order. He told her not to let him in and to call if she needed him. She clearly wasn't able to make that call before Marshall stopped her."

"OK, Ian. How are you reading it?"

"At first I wasn't sure if he was mired in grief or guilt but I'd say it was most likely guilt. I'd say he feels he should have been more responsive to Donna's call but his previous friendship with Sammy may have stopped him interfering. There must have been some legacy of loyalty there that made him reluctant to get involved between them." He paused momentarily and then decided to go with his gut. "I may be wrong but I actually think that independently, without knowing about the murder, he had Marshall lifted to put the frighteners on him. It might have been about Marshall's debt or his repeated violence towards Donna or both. In any case he got his timing very badly wrong."

Burrows got the message immediately. "Now, if that's the case, he's faced with a real dilemma. If initially he only wanted to give Sammy Marshall a fright now he's going to have to decide whether to execute him, hand him over to us or at least let him go so we can pick him up. We need to make that the most appealing option for him." He paused for thought. "If that is the way of things, it won't do much to appease him when he sees the remains of his sister and nephews." At the back of his mind was a niggle that Bull might have an altogether different motive for causing a distraction with the disappearance of Sammy but the thought slipped away before he could get hold of it.

There was a silence between the colleagues as they contemplated the complexity of what had begun as a straightforward domestic. If such a thing actually ever existed, McVeigh found himself thinking.

"I'm nearly at the Marshall house now. I'll see if I can find out anything useful here that will help convince Bull to let his ex-brother-in-law go into police custody. If he was sure we had the evidence to convict Marshall that might help. Bull won't want to be up on a murder charge either although I'd say he'd be hands-off from that kind of dirty stuff. He's clearly the man who issues the orders. DC Woods has stayed with the Nelsons so she'll maybe find out something that will prove useful. I'll check in with her later."

Both men understood that Bull's ego was under severe pressure in this situation. He was angry and frustrated by the turn of events. Then there was his position in the eyes of the men who worked for him and a sense of duty to his parents, his sister and the boys. There would also have been love somewhere in the mix even if that was something that Bull might not easily admit to. McVeigh wondered what kind of uncle he had been to the boys. The young detective hadn't failed to notice that for all his tough exterior Bull needed his parents' approval and was careful to let his mother know when he would be back home. Not really the behaviours associated with a hard man. He wondered if Bull was in a relationship with someone who could exercise influence over him. He'd see what the Marshalls knew about all that.

At the house, a man in his late fifties, wearing a high-vis jacket bearing the City Council Cleansing Department logo, opened the door. From the narrow hallway, McVeigh could see the uniformed family liaison officer sitting at the kitchen table with Mrs Marshall and he nodded to her and beckoned Mr Marshall into the small front room to speak to him in private.

* * *

Burrows was ready for Bull Nelson when the desk sergeant in Grosvenor Road Station phoned through to say the man was asking for him in reception. Burrows waited a while to give the guy some quiet time to consider his situation. He had found that often these bully boys didn't allow themselves to think and the shock to them of discovering what was in their own heads was sometimes quite useful.

Burrows had a lot of sympathy for young men these days. He had a grown-up son and daughter and had watched his own son battle with the pressures of becoming a man in a place that had all the usual peer pressures and social-media stuff aimed at boys. As well as all that,

Belfast had a particular history of violent masculinity that was painted on the walls for all to see. It was hard for young men to stay true to themselves and remain in touch with their humanity. Education helped and he was glad his fella had stayed in school and developed an academic interest in history and politics. He lived in Scotland now and, like most of his peers, showed no inclination to return to the North. It was a kind of Plantation of Ulster in reverse, he thought to himself.

Burrows was a believer in getting kids to stay connected. Often parents let them slip away in the mistaken belief they were giving them some freedom and privacy. His son laughed now about how his father had used occasions when he had him trapped in the car to make him talk about how he was. He said that in hindsight he had secretly loved those chats even though he might have tried to avoid them. So many families nowadays didn't even sit down to eat together, Burrows thought wistfully. Everyone ate separately in front of the TV or in their bedrooms. How did parents expect to know what was happening in their kids' lives when they never had a conversation with them?

He stood up and told Pradić he was taking someone downstairs to the morgue to ID the remains from the morning's case. "I'll be in the interview room downstairs after that if anyone needs me. Can you keep chasing the possible whereabouts of places these guys use to entertain their clients?"

She met his gaze with her characteristic stony expression and nodded, understanding the time pressures only too clearly.

Burrows made his way out to the entrance area of the station and the desk sergeant pointed towards a hefty guy sitting in the waiting area, intently examining his hands.

"Mr Nelson?" Burrows inquired and the man looked up.

"Aye," he said. "That's me alright."

"I'm Detective Sergeant Bill Burrows." He extended his hand. "I am very sorry for your loss. I am the chief investigating officer in the murder of your sister and nephews." He held eye contact with the younger man as they shook, observing the pain and confusion he saw there and the dread about the task that awaited him. Identifying the remains of a family member was traumatic, even for the seemingly most hardened men. "I know that this is a most difficult thing to do, Mr Nelson. Unfortunately, it is absolutely necessary and we assumed you would want to spare your parents the ordeal."

Bull Nelson nodded unenthusiastically and stood up, flexing his knees and plunging his hands deep into the pockets of his designer jeans.

"If you come with me now we'll head down to the morgue. The pathologist has prepared the remains so you'll be spared seeing the worst of the damage caused by the murderer." Burrows was carefully choosing his words so that Bull Nelson might be inclined to talk to him when the ID was finished. He knew Bull was in for an emotional roller coaster. "I will stay with you throughout, Mr Nelson, but if you wish to have time alone with your family members I will be happy to wait outside whenever you say."

Burrows led the way downstairs and along to the end of the corridor where the pathology department lay behind a set of double doors.

"Good afternoon, DS Burrows," Cynthia Boylan called chirpily from her office. "Everything is ready for you."

Low lighting softened the impact of the mortuary room where three gurneys were arranged side-by-side with a space of few feet in between. The slight size of the smallest boy's body meant that there was barely any rise and fall to the sheet covering him. In the geography of death this was the lowlands, Burrows thought. It was as if the covering sheet was merely a little wrinkled rather than concealing the small frame of a child. His older brother made only a slightly bigger impression in terms of his body volume. Donna Nelson's remains bore witness to a longer life with a substantial number of years in which to cement relations with her brother.

Bull Nelson paused inside the door of the room as if to consider if backing out was an option.

Burrows waited at the head of the sister's remains. "Let me know when you are ready, Mr Nelson, and I'll turn back the covers."

* * *

DC Sandra Woods had easily settled into her role as FLO with Mr and Mrs Nelson. After putting on the kettle she had removed her uniform jacket and put on a coloured cardigan she had brought to undo the impact of her police uniform. She had found over the years that this gesture helped family members relax and open up to her and so she always made sure to have such a garment in her bag. She asked Mrs Nelson to direct her to the teabags and the woman rose from her daze and became involved with the other woman in the familiar kitchen activity.

"I always find a cup of tea helps most situations feel a little bit better," said Sandra.

"Our Donna loved her cup of tea," said the woman. "She was up here with me only on Tuesday morning when the kids were at school and crèche and we had a grand old chat. Her da was down at the men's shed." She nodded at her husband as if to explain that it was his absence that had made the chat with her daughter possible.

"How did Donna and her brother get along, Mrs Nelson? Were they close?"

Mrs Nelson furrowed her brow and looked as if she was struggling to produce an answer to Sandra's straightforward question. "Well …" she began hesitantly, "Bull can be sensitive, you know, and he can take things too seriously. They got on most of the time but our Donna ribbed him sometimes and she didn't know when to stop. Like, she used to joke with him that he and Sammy were more of a couple than she and Sammy were. It niggled him something shocking."

"Did Donna come up to visit often?" Sandra asked as she opened the fridge to get some milk. She had lined up three mugs and now pointed the milk bottle at the other woman. "Do you and Mr Nelson like your milk before or after?"

"Just do your own, officer, and I'll do his and mine. It's quicker than explaining."

"Call me Sandra, won't you? It's less formal."

"Alright." Mrs Nelson was relaxing into the conversation.

"And did you see your grandsons much?" Sandra continued conversationally.

"We've actually seen them more since Donna and Sammy split up. Their daddy sometimes takes them on Saturdays but not regularly and his parents don't spend time with them like they used to. More time for us, I suppose." She smiled at this remark and then almost simultaneously realised that these good times were over and her face dissolved in tears of abject grief.

Sandra allowed the woman to cry and handed her fresh tissues from a supply in her cardigan pocket.

"There are no words to say how much I sympathise with your sadness, Mrs Nelson. I have little ones of my own and I understand how precious they are."

When the cups of tea had been distributed, Constable Woods

gently probed Mrs Marshall to continue her story. "You were saying that Sammy's mum and dad didn't see so much of the children. Why was that, do you think?"

"Oh, Sammy was cross about the whole break-up and didn't know how to accept it." Mrs Nelson looked to her husband for help explaining.

He looked a little baffled at first but pulled himself back to the moment. He spoke quietly and deliberately as if he had thought these things through over some time. "Sammy was a man who liked things done his way. He wasn't what you'd call cooperative." He checked with his wife to see if she agreed with his statement and she nodded sadly, fully alert again now and engaged in the conversation. Her husband continued. "If it wasn't his plan then he could dig his heels in and get quite awkward." Mr Nelson paused and took a deep breath and continued. "Our Donna wasn't great at just doing what she was told without questioning and that made him angry a lot of the time. They never managed to find an easy way of getting along together – and you need that in a marriage." He smiled weakly at his wife as if to confirm that they had learned this lesson together over the years. She returned his look sadly.

"Did your son Bull get on well with his brother-in-law – with Sammy?" Sandra knew the areas that she needed to explore and forged ahead while the mood was in her favour.

Mrs Nelson's mouth turned slightly upwards and Sandra could see how charismatic the happier version of the woman might be.

"You know, Sandra, they were the best of mates for a long time. Maybe even as much as six or seven years. Certainly since before Sharon had the boys. Our Bull wasn't big into having girlfriends. He didn't seem that bothered but he would have gone out with Donna and Sammy and then when Donna had Riley, he and Sammy would have gone out drinking when Donna couldn't be bothered. She always seemed happy for them to be friends. I supposed it meant she knew Sammy was in her brother's company. That he was safe, like."

Sandra understood that everyone was happier for Sammy to be with a family member than out on his own and open to distraction but she could hear there was something unsaid in Mrs Nelson's reply. She nodded to show she was following and Mrs Nelson continued.

"I'm not quite sure what broke the boys up …" Again she consulted her husband but this time he just shook his head. "Our Bull began to get quite well off. He helps out a lot of local businesses and they are generous with him in return."

Sandra thought that Mrs Nelson's presentation of running a protection racket made it sound almost charitable.

"He drives an expensive car and likes nice clothes. He has a business interest in a local gym where men go to do bodybuilding and boxing and Sammy spent a lot of time there. I think it might have been jealousy that came between them at first. Sammy was a casual labourer and got work when he could. He didn't have the cash at his disposal that Bull would have. It was Bull that helped them get the house and Sammy never was able to pay him back."

Here Mr Nelson interjected. "Yes, love. But what did for it once and for all was when Bull discovered Sammy was hitting our Donna. For all that he's a big tough guy, he wouldn't hold with beating a woman. Especially not his sister. I'd say that finished him. When our Donna had to get the Exclusion Order because she was afraid for herself and the boys, he had nothing more to do with Sammy. I was a bit surprised he didn't get involved like and try to warn Sammy off but I guess because they had been close …" He stopped there as if he couldn't seem to make sense himself of what he was saying. "Our Bull acts tougher than he is," he said thoughtfully. "I think he just didn't want to get involved between Donna and Sammy. He has a strong loyal streak. Now I'd say he's regretting he didn't do more … I can see he's blaming himself for not doing something."

His eyes welled with tears and Constable Sandra Woods inwardly marvelled at the nature of family relationships and just how complicated they could become.

She excused herself for a few moments and texted DS Burrows to confirm just how close Sammy and Bull had been. He might be able to use that as a lever to locate Marshall.

CHAPTER 16

In Room 3 of the Hotel Aiguaclara, Alice and Caroline found themselves on the cusp of a difficult moment. They could ignore the frosty moments from earlier and allow them to fester slowly or they could have that awkward conversation and allow their already sturdy relationship to have a solid future.

Caroline looked at Alice with a rather sulky pout and raised her eyebrows. A loaded silence hung between them.

OK, thought Alice ... I suppose I was the one being cranky. She took a deep breath. "I'm sorry for being awkward earlier. Truth is that I woke up feeling in full holiday mode, accompanied by sunshine and joyful migrant birds. I went to take a shower with good times on my mind and by the time I came back you were already back at work. I guess I felt cheated." She shrugged. "But I'm all grown up and I got over it and here we are now embarked on another adventure." She smiled her winning smile and the tension was dispelled.

"Well, I'm not totally innocent either," Caroline volunteered. "I could have told McCluskey that I needed to consult you." She laughed at the unlikely prospect of stalling her superior in that way. "I could have at least given some semblance of considering the impact of all of this on you and your time off. I'm sorry too."

"OK. We're good then," said Alice cheerfully. "So what's on the agenda now?"

"I thought maybe we could rewind and start the day differently." Caroline looked suddenly shy about her bold suggestion.

Alice turned on her heel, went into the bathroom and slammed the door. As Caroline wondered if she had said something inappropriate, Alice reappeared naked, wrapped in her towel and smiling lasciviously.

"OK, Caro. Let's start here. I really think you got up too quickly this morning and a small nap is called for before we start work …"

And Alice let her towel slip to the floor and began to slowly unbutton her partner's shirt.

Caroline replied hoarsely. "*Mmmm*, well … I suppose a thirty-minute lunch break is allowed for a working detective … and possibly a little longer when she's actually on holiday."

* * *

Before lunch, while DI Paton contacted Constable Pradić to enlist her support in accessing Jordan Campbell's case records, Alice did some of her own searches. She read in a newspaper report that back in the nineties, at the time of his arrest, Campbell was part of a cross-community literacy programme being held in a local college. The course was for young people on the Youth Training Programme (YTP), which was compulsory for those who left school without qualifications or any possibility of work. In order to receive a minimal welfare allowance, and to be conveniently removed from unemployment statistics, enrolment on a training course was required. These might have a vocational basis or, as in the case of Campbell's course, allowed the opportunity to revisit missed basic educational opportunities. The Learn As You Earn (LAYE) course, the article explained, only worked with those who voluntarily opted to try to improve their literacy skills. Alice could see that making learning literacy compulsory would not work at all. She knew young people both in the United States and Belfast who had unmet literacy needs and she knew that forcing them to learn would be a total non-starter. It said something significant about Jordan Campbell, Alice thought, that he had signed up voluntarilly to improve his basic skills. She valued these small signs of redemption when she could find them. All too often they were overlooked and a young person was damned outright. Judging by his actions to date, most would say that Campbell had not earned the right to any good faith at all but she would keep an open mind for the moment and hope for some real signs of redemption.

Alice could hear Caroline in the background talking to Burrows.

"Sounds as if you are doing all the right things, Bill. Just be careful not to jump to any conclusions until the evidence is there to support them. Careful steps. The secret is to keep McCluskey well up to date and then he'll leave you in peace … No way, Bill. I'm not getting involved at all. I'll do what I can in terms of the case here and then I'll get back to my holiday."

In her head, Alice was calculating where Hugo might have been when Jordan Campbell was first arrested. She knew he had worked in youth programmes for decades now and it wasn't beyond the bounds of possibility that he was familiar with the Campbell case. She sent him a voice message saying that she had done some research about men's training group and planned to meet up with them when she could arrange a suitable time. She also asked him if he knew anything about the LAYE course and the tragic affair of Jordan Campbell.

Caroline broke into her thinking when she exclaimed, "Technology can be quite the tormentor with its speedy results! I have two files already: one from Pradić that contains all the case evidence and the court proceedings on Campbell's original trial and appeal, and the second from José Mantego about Campbell's brush with the law here in Catalonia. Looks as if Mantego has put the entire file through Google translate. The language is very convoluted."

"He's obviously trying to be helpful," Alice replied. "I can have a look at the original if it's in Castilian. Ask him to send that too and we'll go through them together later." She laughed mischievously. "Is this what's known as a busman's holiday, DI Paton?" She ducked to avoid the low-flying glasses case that was hurled in her direction.

* * *

While the two women had a very pleasant lunch in Bar de Plaça, Alice received a text response from Hugo. **Wondering what you're up to in Spain and with whom! Leave it with me for a few hours. I need to phone someone I worked with back then. I'll call you later this evening. All good here in EXIT although of course you are missed.** This was accompanied by a winking emoji that made Alice smile. She needed to think seriously about Hugo's suggestion that she stay on and take up a paid post in EXIT after her visiting scholarship was done. There was her family back in Lowell to consider, her potential academic book contract and of course her relationship with Caroline. This relaxing break was all of a sudden getting very pressured and Alice laughed out loud at the fascinating turns her life could take without any effort whatsoever on her part.

CHAPTER 17

Bull Nelson's henchmen sat in the office above the Smart Guy's Gym, drinking Diet Coke and playing games on their iPhones. A local radio chat show was playing in the background and occasionally one or other of them would grunt in response to something that was said. They were waiting for a new order to come through from Bull about what to do with Sammy Marshall. He was in pretty poor shape the last time they saw him and should probably be given some more water if he wasn't to dehydrate altogether after losing so much body fluid.

They knew better than to take the initiative and suggest any course of action to Bull. They had begun working for him since just after they had left school and now, some fifteen years later, their loyalty was deeply ingrained. They did not question his instructions and in return he generously looked after them and their families, meaning they had access to material wealth way beyond that of their peers.

It was clear that both men were growing in terms of agitation. Bull's business activities skated very close to the edge of criminality but he was shrewd about leaving no paper trail and up until now they had steered clear of PSNI attention. He had a few of the local police working in his interests and that kept him, and them, out of trouble. Now, this business with Sammy Marshall was turning into a right shit-show, in more ways than one. Word had been out on the street since yesterday morning that Donna and the kids were dead and whatever security Bull had arranged locally would not protect him from the close scrutiny of the Belfast Murder Squad who must clearly want to talk to Sammy. Both of the men holed up in the gym wanted this episode with Sammy Marshall over and done with before any of that heat extended to them.

* * *

While Pradić waited for the trace on Bull Nelson's phone to become active, she pursued other sources of intelligence on criminal gangs in the Greater Shankill area. Local police had said there were too many possibilities to be specific but that they would follow up on what they had and get back to her. She wouldn't be holding her breath on that one.

In Holywood Barracks, those charged with gathering and using intelligence to protect British interests and ensure the stability of the peace process were slow to respond. Pradić knew that their allegiance to their sources might well trump the need to locate a perp who was as good as, if not actually, already dead. It was hard to believe that Bull Nelson was the captor of Marshall. Earlier she had found an image posted on social media of Marshall and Bull Nelson in the weights room of a Gym on the Shankill. The strapline, "**Sammy and Bull – Best of Buds?**", had seemed a little sardonic and she had forwarded it to Burrows. She wondered if there was an underlying implication about the exact nature of their relationship.

She filed the question for later just as an electronic tone in her earphones alerted her that Bull Nelson's phone data was now accessible. She flicked open a file of metadata and prepared to study it closely.

*　*　*

Sammy Marshall's father was still wearing his Council work clothes and he gave off a strong odour of sweat and refuse. He and McVeigh sat in the cramped front room of the fifties social housing and the detective watched as the older man wrung his hands in despair. Marshall must be nearing retirement age, McVeigh thought, but he was familiar with people's need to work until the last possible minute so that they could move directly onto the state pension. Unlike the Nelson home, this was not a wealthy household. The furnishings were worn and ancient and as far as he could see there had been no decorating done for decades. There were some framed religious tracts on the walls and Marshall Senior bore all the signs of a church-going man who found his son's lifestyle completely bewildering.

"I just can't fathom the mess our Sammy has got himself into. He had a lovely wife and two beautiful boys that loved him but instead of being at home where he belonged, he was out running with Bull Nelson at all hours of the night doing god knows what. When I said to him that he was asking for trouble, he just laughed at me." The man was distraught, trying to explain his relationship with his son. "What would I know, he would say over and over to me, but at least I can sleep easily knowing I've done my best for my family. I can't believe what he has done to Donna and those little angels."

He seemed to be finding it hard to breathe and McVeigh was worried he was working himself up to a cardiac arrest.

"Have you any idea where the men who came here this morning might have taken your son?"

The man shook his head and puffed air in small spurts through his lips. "Sorry, son. I haven't a clue … but if I did I'd go there now and get him myself so that he could be made to face up to the consequences of his actions. He will find no refuge here in this house. I'm done with him." And he put his head in his hands and gave himself up to wracking sobs that seemed to come from deep inside his body.

McVeigh stood and beckoned to the Family Liaison Officer who had come out into the hall as the sound of Mr Marshall's grief grew in volume. He signalled to her that a cup of tea might be in order and left to return to the station where he might be of more use.

Pradić called him in the car. She told him that Burrows was interviewing Bull Nelson and that she had just found some disturbing images of Sammy Marshall posted on social media. "He was wearing only his underwear and looking as if he had wet himself – and possibly worse. No hope of tracking them as they'd been posted from a burner phone and the background was too indistinct to identify." She explained that she thought he looked as if he was in great distress.

McVeigh found he felt little sympathy for Marshall's plight but nonetheless hurried back so that he could add his weight to the search.

CHAPTER 18

Hugo was true to his word and by evening he had sent Alice a long email summarising what he had discovered from past colleagues about Jordan Campbell. He said that he thought it was easier to put it all in writing than to trust himself to remember the detail when speaking to her. If she needed to call him to clarify anything, he would be home all evening.

She read the email with interest.

Hi Alice!

Your instincts were, as ever, sharp and I was working in the youth sector back then when the case concerning Jordan Campbell occurred. I remember how shocking it was from a lot of perspectives … that a quiet young man had committed such heinous acts against an elderly woman who was completely unknown to him, that he had not received any social, psychological or educational supports from

the system throughout his life up to that point, that he was convicted and sentenced and then that the conviction was found to be flawed and he was rapidly released and compensated with no opportunity of a retrial even though he had admitted the offence. It was memorable for a whole range of reasons that I know you will totally understand without my labouring the point.

Anyway, Jordan Campbell was from a YTP scheme on the Shankill so I didn't have any direct contact with him although we did work across communities even in those days. The programme was specially for young people with mild learning difficulties and I spoke today with one of the workers from that time that I know from the Young Offenders Centre. I also managed to track down the woman who ran the LAYE course back then who has now transferred her affections to Higher Education. Anyway, here's the gist of what I've learned.

Jordan somehow managed to make his way through the school system without learning any literacy or numeracy. It's not possible that his learning challenges weren't noticed, as he couldn't have participated in any classes with his total absence of basic skills. I suppose it is possible that teachers just gave up on him and allowed him to sit in class and didn't ask him to participate beyond that. I can only assume that, because of the widespread systemic disruption caused by the Troubles back then, referrals to Special Schools or classes where his needs should have been addressed must not have happened. He was a quiet lad, apparently, and wouldn't have attracted any attention to himself. That in itself is another reason maybe why he was just left alone. He didn't demand attention so he didn't get any.

Anyway, in the YTP scheme, which was all male, he was badly bullied and the guy who worked there told me that he was probably encouraged to volunteer for the literacy programme to escape the relentless aggressions from the other lads. The other guys called him 'Florrie' apparently although the guy said he could never discover why. Campbell would be visibly angry when this happened but he never retaliated either verbally or physically. The guy said that sometimes he looked ready to explode but it never happened. I guess he vented all that rage on the poor woman he attacked – maybe to show them all just how macho he could be. Sure enough, when he was arrested for the rape, robbery and murder of an octagenarian, he gained a certain degree of notoriety in his peer group. I won't bother to repeat the comments that his behaviour generated, none of which were sympathetic to the victim. 'Florrie' was well and truly laid to rest and replaced by some macho alternative.

The woman who created the LAYE scheme prided herself on taking each young person and giving them a new start as learners. Her hymn sheet would have been similar to ours. They could leave past failures behind and got very intensive supports to help get their literacy up to at least a functional level. The programme was full time, and holistic in that they did general life skills, social awareness, creative activities and anything that contributed to facilitating the development of a rounded individual.

She remembered Jordan very clearly. She said that not only were his literacy and other basic skills almost non-existent but that she had quickly deduced that the reason for his silence was that his language and cognitive development was also very delayed. She said she thought that he missed the meaning of a lot of what went on around him. He of course knew instinctively when he was being mocked and taunted but maybe not the reasons why that was so. Not only was he unable to tell the time but he also had no concept of the passage of time and other things that we take for granted when speaking to a teenager. Another example she gave me was that he didn't understand the concept of rhyme, of words sounding the same as one another, and so he was challenging for even the crackshot literacy tutors that she employed to work with these young men and women. They were beginning to make some progress when he was arrested for rape, robbery and murder of an elderly women and his learning was abruptly suspended.

Another detail she remembered was that the young Jordan was very painfully thin and looked malnourished. He always ate voraciously if there was food provided as part of a group activity and so she deduced that maybe he wasn't too well fed at home. She discovered one day that he wore two pairs of jeans to make his body appear more developed than was the case.

The woman told me how horrified they were when he was arrested and they read the reports of his case. She was called as witness by the defence who tried to make the case that he was not able to distinguish between right and wrong and therefore couldn't be held responsible for his actions. She wasn't happy about being complicit in attempts to excuse his violent treatment of a vulnerable older woman and yet she could see that he was a victim too in many ways. She remembered the day he came into the project after he was released and compensated. He had his new girlfriend in tow and the lads in the group displayed a new respect for him that she found nauseating but she didn't feel she could make it part of a critical discussion with them after he left.

His plan then, twenty years ago, was to go to Scotland with the young woman and set her up in a hairdressing business with some of his compo money. Neither of my two informants heard anything more about him after that but I guess you'll be able to fill in some blanks at your end.

I did try to find out about his personal life, his family, his childhood etc but no one had any light to shed on any of that. Reports in the papers said that he lived alone with his father who was reportedly quite mentally ill but I have no information relating to any of that. Perhaps the legal case files will have some of that detail.

Anyway, Alice! Another sad story of a young life gone awry and the wholesale damage that can bring with it. I hope you find that his subsequent life experience was a bit better.

Call if you need further elucidation.

Best,

Hugo

Alice spent a long time considering the content of Hugo's email. She had known many versions of Jordan Campbell, both as a police officer when they broke the law and as a youth worker who tried to stop them getting into trouble in the first place. It was hard to get a young person to understand social responsibility when nothing in their life experience had modelled that principle in action. No one had taken account of their poverty, poor housing, marginalised parents, inadequate schooling, all of which inevitably led to them feeling pushed to the criminal margins of their community. In her restorative justice work where she helped prepare young offenders to meet up with those they had aggrieved, she was constantly coming up against examples of those double standards. For her they all boiled down to inequalities of one kind or another and needed to be tackled at the root before anything would change. If, as some people perceived it, the wealthy had everything and they had little or nothing, then violence and theft were almost inevitable. In a way she thought they were an articulation of their refusal to passively accept their unfair lot but she couldn't say that out loud to many people.

Alice's father had been killed outright in a motor collision with a young joyrider who was high on a cocktail of drugs. He was a working police officer at the time and for most of his family and colleagues the case was cut and dried. The guy deserved to be locked up for as long as possible to pay for his actions. Alice, her sister Sam and her mother had participated in a restorative justice programme where they met with the convicted young man and discussed what had happened and the consequences for all concerned. It had been painful and ultimately life-changing for her. Her sister too had changed her views as a result of the process but her mother had been too hurt to hear the young man's experience clearly. Her brother, Red, who was a firefighter in Lowell, Massachusetts, had refused to engage with the process and thought that participation alone was a form of betrayal of their father. There were subjects that the Fox family did not deal with any longer out of a certainty that there would be no satisfactory outcome.

Caroline pulled Alice out of her reflections by kissing the back of her neck and adopting an exaggeratedly pleading voice. "Any chance that we might go and get some dinner? I'm going cross-eyed reading about Campbell and his exploits."

Alice knew that now was not the moment to begin the discussion of how harmed Jordan Campbell may have been but she knew in her bones that time was coming soon. She really hoped that they could find some common ground because she wasn't sure their relationship would survive a fundamental disagreement about something so central to both their lives. For now, food and some excellent local wine sounded like a welcome delaying tactic.

CHAPTER 19

On the shared drive for the Murder Squad inquiry, the forensic science people had uploaded visual and documentary analysis of their findings in Donna Nelson's home. The evidence gathered from the trainers and clothes gathered by local uniformed officers from Marshall's home that morning would make a damning case against Sammy Marshall. His mother had been too distraught when he was taken away to do her daily wash and so his jeans and sweatshirt had remained untouched since he had dumped them in the washing machine the previous evening. He was clearly still wearing his underwear which would tell its own story if it ever turned up. The autopsies scheduled for first thing the following day would have little to add that was of evidential significance but would provide damning detail of Marshall's actions that would help in his conviction and sentencing. His prints were on the murder weapon and he had left bloody footprints in several places around the house. When he was finally apprehended, Burrows was sure he would still have damning traces of Donna's blood under his nails and on his body. DS Bill Burrow's nagging worry was that Sammy Marshall might be found dead before he could be made accountable for his rampage of killing. He was determined to avoid that if at all possible but he needed a break in locating Marshall and bringing him in. Every member of the force in the Shankill area knew this was a priority and Burrows was banking on his luck changing sooner rather than later.

Earlier in the Grosvenor Road Barrack's morgue, Bull Nelson and Burrows had shared some moments of quiet intimacy. Nelson had been understandably shaken about the identification of the remains of his sister and nephews and Burrows hoped that his vulnerability might generate a situation in which Bull would lower his guard and help them to discover Marshall's whereabouts. Afterwards in the interview room, Burrows had poured tea for them both and sat back across the table from Bull. The younger man had not broken down while identifying his sister and her boys but he had tensed his body so tightly that in both his cheeks a nerve pulsed continuously and his eyes blinked involuntarily as if in a minor epileptic event. It was surprising the lengths that a man would go to not to cry, Burrows thought, even when considering the remains of three members of his family.

"I know that was hard for you," Burrows began. "There is nothing that can prepare you for seeing members of your family that have suffered violent death." He considered Bull's tough exterior and wondered how he had come by his nickname. It suggested he had earned the reputation of displaying no weakness and meeting conflict head on. Burrows wasn't sure there were any weapons in his interviewing arsenal against that kind of deep resolve. He plumped for honesty rather than game-playing.

"Our job now is to bring the perpetrator of these killings in and to have the evidence gathered to ensure he is convicted in the courts. Don't you think that people need to face the public and account for their actions? Otherwise there is no point in having laws." He paused again to gauge the impression his words were having.

Bull Nelson remained mulishly silent.

Burrows forged ahead with his message. "I can tell you that the forensic evidence against Sammy Marshall will be robust. I want to get him in here to answer for himself as soon as possible. If you can help us achieve that goal, Bull, I urge you to help us pick him up right now. There are officers waiting to act as soon as we have a location." He looked at the man sitting unresponsive and seemingly disconnected from the conversation. "I am asking you to help us here. We want to get justice done for Donna and the boys. If Sammy Marshall is let off the hook, Donna and the boys will be denied justice. I know you don't want that to happen."

Bull looked at Burrows with an expression that articulately expressed his reservations about what the justice system had to offer his sister and her sons, but he still said nothing.

So many people in this place think they have a monopoly on defining justice, thought Burrows. How can we ever get past all this mistrust?

Before he could think of any response to his own question there was a knock on the door and a uniformed police officer stepped inside.

"You're needed immediately upstairs, DS Burrows."

Bull Nelson didn't look too happy about being left waiting but Burrows thought it would do him no harm to be given some time to review his options. The uniformed officer took his place inside the interview-room door and nodded almost imperceptibly to Bull.

"Thank you, Officer Caldwell," Burrows said as he left the room.

* * *

For decades now, some women from the Falls Women's Centre and their counterparts from the Shankill Road Women's Centre had been meeting to collaborate about common issues. Especially in the early years, these meetings had taken place cautiously and in secret. There was every chance that they might have been viewed as a potential risk or even as a betrayal by those men who had taken on responsibility for security in localities where the police were unwelcome. Even women who were sympathetic to a particular local political stance could see that some women's issues were best approached collaboratively and suspended their other differences for that purpose.

Women on both sides of the divided North, urban and rural, experienced poverty, sexual and domestic violence, reproductive injustice, discrimination in work and a host of other gender-based harms. Their covert gatherings allowed common ground and understanding to grow and, as confidence and friendship solidified, some novel things happened. Women from the Shankill and the Village, both areas with a perceived Loyalist identity might be seen walking behind a funeral on the Falls Road. Women from Republican areas like Ardoyne and Andersonstown were observed showing personal solidarity with women whose politics differed from theirs but who had gender-related discriminations in common. Women found ways of going where their men would not go and built bridges that had been unimaginable in earlier times of great division.

Today, in post-Agreement Belfast, as they had done innumerable times, two of these women travelled together to share their sympathies for a woman and her children murdered by an angry man. It was a well-worn path irrespective of the area of the city, the colour of the paving stones or of the flags flying from the lampposts.

The women, Paula and Grace, sat in the front of the car crossing from the Falls Road through the open security gates on Northumberland Street that led across to the Shankill Road. They would meet their counterparts at the Shankill Women's Centre and walk to Goliath Row from there.

"I can't believe we're heading to another vigil for another murdered woman … and this time two small boys as well." Paula unwrapped two liquorice toffees and handed one to Grace who was driving. "There've been pictures of the perp on the internet since this morning … I think the suggestion of a big Reclaim the Night March for the weekend is good. Saturday would be best when the town is full of people out for the night. It would get attention, especially so closely linked to the killings earlier in the week."

Suddenly the car pulled to a halt.

Paula looked at Grace in alarm. "What are you doing, Grace? Why are you stopping?"

"Look at that crazy guy there wandering across the waste ground, Paula. The one in the dirty boxers. Is that not the face you've been looking at all morning on social media? I think we've found us a real live perp!"

She swung the car alongside the waste ground towards the man and screeched to a halt.

"Help me to try and get him in the back, Paula. Don't worry, I have a plan. Let's get back to the Falls before those peelers spot us."

* * *

In the end, the command to let Sammy Marshall go had come not from Bull himself but from one of his loyal PSNI officers. It was in the form of a one-word, prearranged code that let Marshall's two custodians know that extreme urgency was required. They didn't waste a second and the message was acted upon without delay. By the time the internal PSNI request to go to a lock-up behind the leisure centre was issued, Marshall was already staggering across some waste ground on the lower Shankill Road, looking very much the worse for wear.

Suddenly released from captivity, still with the sticky tape on his eyes and mouth, Sammy had felt the fresh wind on his face and had fallen to his knees, expecting the final shot to come at any moment. He was sure he was destined to finish his life in a ditch. When it became clear that there would be no shot and that he was in fact alone on some rough ground, he had torn the sticky tape off and lost some clumps of his thin blonde hair in the process. His face was marked with adhesive, tears, snot and the remains of his earlier bilious retching.

Confronted by Sammy, some young fellows smoking on the way back from school had run home to their mothers. They were spooked not just by the revolting smell but by his wild expression which was a mixture of relief at being free and the madness that comes from having been so close to his own violent death. He desperately wanted to be home in his own bed but his expectations were tempered by the memory of his captors' threats and his own knowledge of what he'd done to his family. Surely there must very soon be a reckoning coming his way?

The strident sound of police sirens came almost as a comfort and yet, before the PSNIs had time to reach the spot where he was standing, a car screeched to a halt beside him and he was bundled into the back seat and covered with a blanket. The car took off at speed and the sound of sirens faded along with his fleeting hope of escape. He wrapped both his arms around his head and tried to withdraw from this reality that he knew was all of his own making. He considered the possibility that perhaps he had actually died and this continuous sequence of captures and confinements was to be his hell for all eternity. A woman's voice interrupted his deranged thought process and left him terrorised for another whole host of reasons. It was clear to Sammy that she was a Fenian.

CHAPTER 20

The restaurant where they went for dinner was no more than five minutes' walk from Hotel Aiguaclara. Much of Begur's charm, Alice reckoned, was that a large range of the facilities that make a holiday pleasant were available in a very small and accessible amount of space. Bars, restaurants, tasteful clothes and jewellery shops, stylish household furnishings for second homes, locally grown vegetables, a number of good quality fish, meat, wine and deli shops were all condensed into two or three small streets running from the plaça that made up the village centre. However, this was not just a holiday location but somewhere that people lived all year round and Alice was sure that the majority of the village shops were aimed at weekend and holiday clients. Locals must go to the nearby big towns to satisfy their shopping needs in outlets that recognised the existence of those on a limited budget. The obvious privilege of Begur was challenging in that it didn't allow you to forget that your advantage was at the cost of others.

As they settled at their candlelit table on a covered terrace overlooking a beautifully planted small square, inevitably the conversation turned to their preoccupation with Jordi Campbell. That afternoon, Caroline had read a good deal of the material about the initial murder investigation that complemented the background detail provided by Hugo.

"I haven't looked at the Catalan files yet. I think it's better if we do that together because of the language stuff. Maybe tomorrow morning."

Alice nodded agreement and poured them chilled local white wine.

"I remember how shocking this case was at the time," Caroline reflected as she swirled her finger through the condensation on her cool glass. "It was something to do with the small amount of money taken alongside the gravity of the attack. Rape and murder sat incongruously beside petty theft. There was jewellery and other small valuables that he didn't seem to notice. It never really made sense at the time. If what you wanted was money why would you go beyond that with such colossal consequences for the woman first of all, but also for yourself as the perpetrator? If your interest was in committing a violent attack, why bother with such a small amount of money and leave the other stuff untouched? The pieces never seemed to fit."

"Was it ever construed as a gendered assault?" Alice asked tentatively. "It was after all sexual and violent, as well as murderous, of course, and the perpetrator was a young man attacking a less powerful, older woman." She raised her eyebrows at Caroline to stress her point.

Caroline shook her head in response. "Well, it was classified as murder back in the day as that was seen as the predominant crime. The robbery was entirely secondary and barely worth a mention except in its association to the murder. The rape, because it was of such an elderly woman by a teenager, baffled people at the time. I think that it mostly served to contribute additional weight to the utterly dysfunctional character of Campbell. He was totally demonised in the press. Actually, they had a field day with the whole case from sensational start to very messy finish, as far as the final outcome was concerned."

"My reading of it from what Hugo wrote in his email was that Campbell was a very harmed individual. It sounds more like an act of desperation than a carefully planned assault. He seems to have been a very disturbed, unhappy young man and he lost all control in this poor woman's house. I wonder why he went there in the first place? What emerged about that in the case notes? Did she live near him? Were they related?" Alice wondered how much effort went into understanding the young man at a time when the Troubles were the major preoccupation in policing and less was known about the consequences of social harm. Of course, the woman was the primary victim but Campbell seemed like a needy kid who wasn't getting much remedial support.

"At the time it was viewed as a premeditated crime in that he brought the weapon with him from his own home," Caroline said. "His father identified the knife as one from their kitchen and he showed no understanding as to why his son would behave in that way. He said he and his son never really talked about things. The family didn't know the woman, who lived a short bus ride from them, and Campbell himself offered no explanation for why he behaved as he did." She shrugged her shoulders. "I wasn't involved in the actual questioning but I remember he said things like, 'I just did it', and 'I wanted to see what it was like'. There was a psychiatric report and one from the person responsible for his training programme. They said he had learning difficulties and limited comprehension of what was going on around him but the fact that he went there with a weapon and behaved as he did seemed to show he knew enough to be held responsible."

Caroline looked at Alice, sensing the ideological chasm that was opening between them. She sighed and ate an olive from the dish in front of her. "Alice, don't let's do this now. I know we come at these issues from different places but that doesn't mean we have to argue or fall out about it."

Her voice had taken on a note of entreaty that Alice didn't like much. "I'm not arguing, Caro. I just find it interesting that gender wasn't perceived to be an issue in this clearly gendered crime. It isn't surprising that gender inequality is so persistent when it's often not even named as part of the problem."

"I know where this is heading," said Caroline, sounding exhausted by the prospect. "Can't we just let it sit for the moment until we have time to discuss it properly?"

Alice paused to choose her words carefully. She had no desire for them to argue but neither did she want to be silenced about views that she had worked hard to figure out. "I don't want something to come between us that might be sorted out very easily by having a conversation or two." She purposely made the issue sound less devisive than she feared it might be. "Of course I'm prepared for us to differ about things but I'd like to know what they are and what's at the root of our difference."

Their main course arrived and the server had some tricky action to do to take their fish off the bone. It was a conversation-stopper and carried out in a tense silence.

When the task was complete and the waiter had left, they began to eat.

"I know what it means to be a police officer, Caro. The job is about catching people responsible for committing crimes and getting them convicted. There isn't much room for nuance in our interpretation of the law … especially in your work, which is all about murder."

"Well, that's true enough, Alice. Dead is dead and there isn't any arguing with that." Caroline sounded irritated.

She ate her fish half-heartedly and Alice regretted that this conversation was happening now when they should have been mindlessly enjoying the good food and wine. Still … she had begun so she continued doggedly.

"I suppose if I didn't care about you it wouldn't matter so much. I find myself getting tetchy with you around work stuff and I think it's better to get to the bottom of that. In other respects we rub along together very well …"

Caroline laughed. "That's one way of putting it."

Alice joined in the joke and sipped at her wine. She felt her mood lighten as she contemplated the pleasure they gave each other most of the time.

"OK. We have a lot going for us, I think, Caro. I admire your fighting spirit and the way your mind works when you're solving a case. I love your indomitable courage that tenaciously follows the scent until you get your killer." She smiled as she noted that her lover's appetite was picking up and she was now eating with relish. She forged ahead with her attempt to explain herself. "The fact that you let me know the other Caroline … the one who was hurt and harmed and has hard work to do to sort all that childhood stuff out … well, it's a gift to me. Our intimacy is precious. You fill me up with your tenderness and I don't want that to end …" She hesitated about where to go next with all this.

Caroline's eyes had hardened as the inevitable 'but' hung in the atmosphere and Alice could see she was becoming defensive. Maybe she was bullishly pushing an issue that would resolve itself in time without this effort or maybe it was altogether the wrong moment … but she had to trust her gut that kept bringing their different belief systems into question and needing to resolve that. She changed tack from making pronouncements to asking a question.

"I know by now that my views jar with you sometimes when I'm droning on about social justice and all that, isn't that so?"

Caroline looked directly at her and smiled in a distant kind of way. She wasn't easily going to fall for Alice's questioning strategy.

"Most of the time, Alice, I'm intent on doing my job – which is to act in accordance with the law as it stands at the moment. I don't always think that the law is perfect but that's a different issue. While I'm head of the Murder Squad my task is to find killers, not to understand why they've done what they did. When you were a detective I'm sure you were the same, eh?"

"I guess so." Alice tried to remember what preoccupied her younger self.

"I think that your work now, Alice, is about thinking and theorising whereas I'm still doing the practical chase-and-apprehend routine. I don't mean that I don't also think about the cases and of course the motives involved … but arguing legal points and questioning the mitigating factors for an individual perp is not my concern." She looked directly at Alice and made her final point with admirable clarity and simplicity. "Nor do I think that I would be a better detective if I took on critiquing the law and applying some kind of judgement about whether or not a murderer had been harmed by the State or systemic inequality before I slapped the cuffs on him – or her. And

I'm not saying that I won't have those conversations with you. I will happily do that but it will be between us and not part of what I'm paid to do which is to bring a murderer to book."

She signalled to the waiter and pointed to the wine bottle that was now empty. "*Uno mas*," she said and smiled mischievously at Alice. "You're driving me to drink, Alice Fox."

The sky was a deep indigo and a new crescent moon hung high over the village and cast a delicate light on the square below.

Alice felt her uncertainty dissipate as her admiration and respect for Caroline was fully reinstated by her explanation. "I'm such a mutt, Caro!" She laughed at herself. "Forgive me?"

"No apologies needed. I think we make a good team. You can do the contextual reflection and I'll stick to the evidence base and together we'll throw a wider net around our suspect. Now help me with this wine or I'll need to be carried home."

They raised their glasses that caught the sparkling lights around the terrace roof.

"Sounds like a plan to me," said Alice who recovered her appetite and found that cold grilled fish could be very tasty indeed.

CHAPTER 21

While he waited for Burrows to return to the interview room, the need to send a message to release Sammy Marshall had bypassed Bull altogether. It had been taken care of, in his interests, by an officer whose love of fancy holidays, smart clothes and electronic goods exceeded his loyalty to his PSNI oath. He sold his services to the highest bidder and in this case Bull Nelson had bought his complete fidelity. He and Bull had spoken earlier when news of Donna's death had reached him and he was made aware of Bull's awkward timing issue. Bull already had Sammy Marshall locked up when the PSNIs called to the house to relay the news of Donna and the boys' murder. He explained that he wasn't able to think straight now. The friendly PSNI understood immediately that it was one thing putting the frighteners on a prick like Marshall but getting embroiled in a murder inquiry was an altogether different matter. He noted that Bull had wisely opted for leaving it to others to operate on his behalf. The officer knew that it wasn't that Bull would shy away from ordering an execution. It was probably more that this was too personal and he found himself unusually indecisive. He had liked Sammy a lot and been reluctant to break his ties with him but in the end Donna's upset was too great and he needed to teach Sammy a lesson. Now he was clearly wracked with guilt and frustration that he had left it all too late. It was much better to back away from the whole mess. Someone else would have to deal with Sammy Marshall. As soon as Bull's loyal policeman got wind that the Murder Squad moves to locate Marshall were reaching a climax, he had acted immediately and in the certainty that his reward would be generous. While Bull was helping with inquiries in Grosvenor Road, he wouldn't be under suspicion for what was happening somewhere else. Any connection between Marshall's detention and Bull needed to be eliminated and now was the moment for action. Whatever way you looked at it, he thought, Marshall's goose was cooked so there was no question of any moral dilemma for this trusted member of the PSNI.

* * *

In the heel of the hunt, Bull Nelson's cooperation became unnecessary as events took on a momentum all of their own. The message of Marshall's location on the Shankill reached the Murder Squad before Burrows had time to fully exercise his persuasive powers over Bull. One of Pradić's inquiries had paid off and an all-person alert had gone out to local officers with the location of the lock-up and the order that Marshall was to be released from his holding place, arrested immediately and taken to Murder Squad HQ.

Burrows had left Bull in the interview room and returned to the office only to hear that the uniformed officers that had gone to collect Marshall had missed him. The lock-up was empty, leaving potent evidence that Marshall had lost an array of bodily fluids during his time there. Burrows got forensics onto gathering what data they could without any delay and issued an urgent order for Marshall to be arrested on sight.

McVeigh arrived just in time to witness Burrows' disappointment that Marshall had escaped arrest and had disappeared almost immediately. Uniformed officers reported that some local young lads had seen someone that might have been Marshall but couldn't say what had become of him. Burrows now had to consider the possibility that Marshall had, somewhat farcically, been abducted for the second time in as many days.

"Let's try to figure out who would have an interest in having Marshall escape arrest. What about his family? How likely is that as an option, Ian?"

"Very doubtful." McVeigh shook his head resolutely from side to side. "For one thing the father doesn't have a car and anyway the Family Liaison is still there. I'll check but she'd have let us know if he'd gone out."

Burrows' brow furrowed more deeply as he searched for a potential explanation for Marshall's disappearance. "Bull is still here waiting for the rest of his interview so he isn't directly implicated. If the two heavies were his and they've been given a tip-off to let Marshall go then they're unlikely to have recaptured him. They'll have got off-side sharpish. We're back to square one here." He looked distraught but pulled it together. "Ian, it might be worth having another chat with Sharon, Donna's neighbour. Ask her if Donna had any new partner on the go that might want to have a man-to-man chat with Marshall.

I'll finish my interview with Bull. I doubt he'll want Marshall to get away from us either so we may be able to enlist him as an unlikely ally." He turned to Pradić who was looking intently at her various screens. "Anything you want to add, Zara?"

"I'm checking webcams in the area, DS Burrows, and also any whispers on social media in relation to the images of Marshall in the lock-up. That and other visuals are featuring in a lot of chats from a whole range of quarters. His face must be becoming very well known in some internet circles by this stage." She took a sip of her cold coffee and looked meaningfully at Burrows. "It seems as if whoever was holding him knew we were on to them. They were alerted by someone and let him go just ahead of our guys getting there. They are obviously well-connected to be able to act ahead of us … unless it was just coincidental and they planned to let him go anyway. I suppose there is no point in wasting time now in chasing after leaked messages."

She looked determined to keep on the case and Burrows knew she would not be wasting any time.

"I know that you are doing stuff for DI Paton as well, Zara, but keep at it."

"The community and women's networks are across this too, Sergeant Burrows. The frequency of violent attacks on women and families recently is generating a lot of community anxiety. I've seen notices going around about a vigil this evening outside Donna Nelson's house. It might be useful having some eyes there, just in case. Will I alert the locals?"

Burrows thought that sounded reasonable.

"Good idea, Zara. Before that you might see what Sandra Woods is up to. If the Nelson family wanted to go to the vigil, she might accompany them and that would be useful for us too. I'll go and finish up with Bull Nelson. We'll have a case review first thing in the morning and see where we can go from here. Thanks, Zara."

And he headed back unenthusiastically to continue his talk with Bull Nelson. He'd see if there was anything useful to be salvaged from this interview and then he'd have to contemplate updating McCluskey, which was probably the least attractive item on his list of things to do.

* * *

Outside Donna Nelson's house bunches of flowers had begun to accumulate against the wooden fence, interspersed with children's drawings and tea lights. The house was still sealed off and the white police gazebo and rustling crime-scene tape suggested a morbidly carnival atmosphere. Someone had placed a copy of the family portrait of Donna and the two boys inside a plastic folder and stapled it in place on the wooden fence. As the evening light faded the flickering candles looked desolate in the small cul de sac where the short row of houses faced out onto a brick wall laden with graffittied opinions on life. An intermittent stream of women, some with small children in buggies, stopped by the temporary shrine to leave an offering.

One small boy aged about five carefully placed a warrior figure amongst the flowers and candles. "Riley was in his class at school," the young woman with him said to Sandra Woods who was standing beside Mr and Mrs Nelson. "There but for fortune …" she said solemnly and she took her son by the hand and hurried off, pulling her thin jacket around her. It provided little protection against the evening chill, Sandra Woods observed. As the Nelsons were comforted by some of those in attendance, Woods watched carefully for anything that might be worth reporting to the detectives.

* * *

In Number 8, Sharon Dunwoody's son was in the living room when McVeigh called on her for a second time in as many days. He was sitting on the sofa with a picture book in his lap and wearing earphones. His mum took her place beside him and McVeigh sat opposite her.

"I'm trying to distract him," whispered his mum. "There is no way to explain all this madness to a child." She shook her head in bewilderment. "How do innocent young boys like this grow into the men who do these things?" She looked angry as she looked at her son and considered how impossible it was to protect him from all this harm. "He and Riley were close. They walked to and from school together every day. They were in the same class and they played together in the evenings. There's very little avoiding the news. It's everywhere and there were even counsellors in the school this afternoon telling the kids stories and preparing them for what they're going to hear … and I suppose what they're going to feel."

McVeigh just listened and nodded sympathetically. There was nothing he could add to soften the message.

"I'm sorry I have to come and talk to you again, Sharon. Especially when you have your own grief to contend with as well as taking care of Jack. I'm sure that you might want to go to the vigil as well?" McVeigh framed this as a question as he wasn't sure if Sharon would think taking Jack to the gathering was a good idea.

She just exhaled and waved her hands to suggest uncertainty and hopelessness. McVeigh nodded in understanding.

"I wonder if you know, Sharon, if Donna had another partner on the scene or someone who she was close to that it might be useful for us to talk to?"

"No. Definitely not. She would have talked to me about most things and I know she was just trying to get a bit of peace and quiet for her and the boys. The last thing she would have wanted was another man." She laughed derisively. "No offence to you, but those of us who have had unhappy relationships are not really eager to repeat the experience. I know there are some men who have managed to get past the chest-beating primate stage, but they are few and far between. Mostly we women just want a quiet life and maybe the occasional night out with mates who won't try to complicate our lives."

McVeigh could see that made sense. Of course he and Sally had discussed gender issues and he knew his limitations. Sally had asked him, when they'd last discussed sexism, if he ever challenged other men about remarks they made that objectified women. Of course he'd had to admit that he never did and she had said that meant he was enabling sexist behaviour to continue. "What sort of a man do you want your son to be? What sort of world do you want him to grow up in?" She had posed the question and said she'd leave him to think about that and the subject hadn't arisen since. Here in this woman's living room, he was beginning to understand what his wife had meant.

Jack had reached the end of his story and taken off the headphones and moved over beside his mum. "I hear singing, Ma," he said in a quiet voice. "I think it's outside Riley's house. Can we go and see?"

"Yes, son. We'll go now. Where's the picture you drew of you and Riley. Show it to DC McVeigh while I get our coats. I have some flowers too that we can leave for Donna. I think she'd like that, don't you?"

The child nodded uncertainly and brought his picture to show McVeigh.

"It's me and Riley playing with our Lego. It was our favourite thing to do."

He looked at McVeigh for a response and the detective found himself choked by the child's trust and sincerity. He couldn't help but think of the two small boys next door and the ultimate betrayal of how their own father had ended their young lives.

He remembered his mother's saying when children had been harmed by someone: "Hanging is too good for them," and now he understood where she was coming from. He touched the child's small hand gently and said, "It's the best picture I've ever seen, Jack. I think Riley would really like it."

And the little boy was pleased and turned towards his mother who was holding his warm coat out to him.

"If you think of anything, Sharon, you know where I am."

And they left the house together, letting the door close softly behind them.

CHAPTER 22

After dinner, and the second bottle of wine, Caroline ditched her plan to continue her reading of the casework relating to the man now known as Jordi Campbell. She went straight to bed with a large glass of water and was asleep almost immediately.

It was a calm, warm night and only the very occasional car or group of passing people disturbed the silence as Alice sat in a sun lounger on the terrace and phoned Hugo. It was only nine thirty in Belfast and she knew he would be just home from working with their EXIT group.

He greeted her warmly. "Hey, Alice Fox! It's good to hear from you. How are things in sunny Spain and why the sudden interest in the Campbell case? I hope that you are not getting lured into another murder inquiry?" He chuckled at his own outlandish suggestion. In the relatively short time that he'd known her, Alice Fox had already been an active participant in resolving two murder cases.

"Well, actually, Hugo, you are not too far from the mark." She decided to go for a full reveal. "I'm here for a week's break with Caroline Paton and she has been asked by her superior to get involved in something here in which Campbell may be implicated. That's entirely between us, of course ... both of those items of information." She waited to see how he would take the news of her being with Caroline.

There was a loaded pause, then he replied a little quietly, "Well, that's unexpected news ... on both counts. I had no idea ... you are really quite the dark horse, Alice." He laughed heartily. "I'm not sure, if you decide to make an application for membership to the Felons Club, that it will be accepted but I suppose I could always put in a good word for you, if need be!"

Alice smiled at Hugo's boundless generosity of spirit. The PSNIs had yet to overcome the suspicions about their legacy of biased behaviour in nationalist areas of Northern Ireland. Hugo's father had been interned without trial during the troubles and was a bit of a republican legend in his community and there were many like him who had little reason to trust the police. Alice understood the need for discretion about her personal involvement with a senior police officer. She had to be similarly cautious about her disclosure of her own history in Lowell PD in the US communities where she had worked. She understood why there was mutual mistrust between certain communities and the police and the complicated nature of resolving that relationship. It had been a measure of her trust in Hugo that she had shared her relationship with Caroline. They had talked at great length about many social issues as they prepared to work with the EXIT group. They had a shared respect and a common value system and so she was glad to have removed this area of concealment from between them.

"I knew I could count on you, Hugo," she said meaningfully, knowing he would understand. "My involvement in the inquiry is solely as interpreter between Caroline and the Catalan police – the Mossos d'Esquadra but I am getting interested in Campbell, who seems very like someone we might have worked with, if we had been about then."

"True. I had a similar response when I was trying to find out stuff for you earlier. It's heartening that we have better supports in place now than back then. Good to know there is *some* progress." He stressed 'some' in a way that implied that improvement was lacking in other areas and Alice waited for him to explain. "This triple murder on the Shankill has raised a lot of dust around the area of men's violence against women – and 'domestic violence' as they term it. I have never really been able to get the 'domestic' part of the phrase. I know it's used to refer to the location within the home and family but 'domestic' somehow infers that it's a tamer form of violent aggression. It dilutes the severity of what actually happens."

"I know, Hugo. I guess you need a good alternative that is universally recognised so that women who need help know where to look … naming and renaming things is important. I haven't read the news so I'm not sure exactly what has happened there."

Hugo sighed deeply. "Well, it's a sadly familiar story. On the Shankill Road, a woman and her two small sons, aged two and five, were killed by a man believed to be the children's father and her ex-husband … although none of that is confirmed. She had an Exclusion Order out against him for previous violent episodes but he got into the house last night and as a result all of them are dead. Now he's slipped through the cops' hands and gone missing so there's a big push on to find him. Initially, it seems he was being held captive by some

Loyalist thugs that he owed money to but, before the cops could get to him, someone else scooped him up." He laughed heartily. "You couldn't make it up! Sounds like the stuff of murder mystery fiction."

Alice could imagine the pressures on Burrows, McVeigh and Pradić to bring in the killer and, in Caroline's absence, DS McCluskey would be feeling angsty. He didn't like when things appeared less than perfect to the public eye.

Hugo continued. "Tonight in the group they wanted to discuss what had happened on the Shankill. They had a hotch-potch of supposed facts from radio and TV news broadcasts and some more salacious stuff from the internet that they'd accessed on their phones. I let it run for a bit and then stepped in and suggested a bit of structure. It was hot and heavy and you were missed – especially by Rae."

Rae was the only young woman in a group of eight who were either offenders or at risk of becoming so. Alice rebalanced the gender count just a little when she was there. They had all been working together several times a week for over a year and had developed genuine friendships and sophisticated group work skills. Managed by Hugo and more recently assisted by Alice, they were all involved in restorative-justice programmes where they met and dialogued with people against whom they had offended. Now, they wanted to know who was accountable to them for the harms they experienced. With Hugo and Alice they were preparing to invite and critically interview political and community figures responsible for policy and practice across the range of areas that impacted on their lives. Once a week with Alice they were also learning Tae Kwon Do in the context of alternatives to violent and adversarial relationships. They had become a savvy group of young people concerned about social inequalities and determined to change their lives and their communities for the better.

"Once I'd managed to get them to shut off the images of the alleged killer handcuffed to a wall in a Shankill lock-up, the conversation became more interesting. Rae and Gary had done a bit of research on the stats for violence against women in the North and that was a good focus. They were interested in the small number of women who reported rape and sexual assaults and the even smaller number of convictions. Inevitably we got onto gender roles, and masculinities surfaced as a focal point in the discussions."

"No surprises there," quipped Alice who was fascinated by the account of the session. She loved the work and could imagine the buzz in the room as they started to unpick what had happened and why. Many of the group had past experience of violent relationships in their families and peer groups and could speak with great insight. Some had committed violent misdemeanours themselves. To be part of the EXIT group they had to be 'clean' not just in terms of drugs but also the lifestyle that accompanied them, including theft, dishonesty, carrying and using weapons and all kinds of violence. They had learned to care for themselves, support each other, to be open in their assessment of their progress and clear in their life goals. One of the young men was helping another with learning the literacy he had missed at school. Another was working with Rae to decorate her newly acquired independent accommodation. The group was an example of what well-resourced social practice could do to rescue young people at risk of wasting their life potential and becoming prison statistics.

"Anyway, someone announced that there was a vigil earlier this evening outside the home of the murdered woman and her children," Hugo went on. "They would have liked to go but didn't fancy going across to the Shankill in the evening when they might not be safe. Then Jed said that his ma was going to a Reclaim the Night March at the weekend with some of the people in her group of survivors of clerical and institutional abuse who were volunteers with the Falls Women's Centre. Jed said that the organisers had said it was time for men to step up as allies of women who bore the brunt of violent assaults."

He sounded tired, Alice thought, and she knew how an energetic two hours with eight dynamic young people could be exhausting, as well as uplifting.

"That sounds like a very positive way of showing solidarity," she said. "When is the march? Will you go with them?" She had lots of questions but didn't want to overwhelm Hugo, who was already worn out. "I'm sorry not to be there to be part of the action – and to share the load, of course."

She laughed and Hugo joined in her positivity and enthusiasm.

"Well, it's in the city centre on Saturday night. There will be groups setting out from different areas in the city and meeting up outside the City Hall where there will be speakers and some music. A local group is meeting outside the Fall's Women's Centre to march into the City Hall. It's being well coordinated by the women's community sector. The town will be full of Saturday night revellers so it should be an interesting mix. In the meantime, the group is planning to get together tomorrow and make an EXIT banner. They have some great ideas. You'd have loved it!"

"I'm surely enjoying your account of it all," Alice said with genuine appreciation. She loved working with the group, especially when they became motivated by new ideas and applied little or no restraint.

Hugo had relaxed into the story of the evening and Alice stretched out in her comfortable reclining chair and watched the clear night sky as she listened.

"The idea for the banner is to have EXIT full centre of a large rectangle made from somebody's mother's old curtains. Then a strapline: 'Against all forms of violence against women'. And then, around the edges, will be single words like, physical, emotional, economic, sexual, verbal and whatever else they come up with. Their graffiti spray-painting skills will be useful!"

"Sounds like a great idea. Send pictures! I'm glad that at least I'll get to admire it when I get back." Alice heard the genuine regret in her voice and didn't try to disguise it. She knew that Hugo would empathise and maybe even be pleased that she missed them and would like to be a part of the outing. "It will be the inaugural outing of the new banner – and hopefully the beginning of a new phase of activism for the group. I think it's a really positive development." She could hear him agreeing with her in a series of low sounds a little like purring. She had noticed that he did that when he was contented about something and she smiled to be a part of all this. "Let's keep in touch, Hugo. Maybe I can be supportive at a distance?"

"I'd like that, Alice," he said gently and they ended the call with a strange mix of regret and satisfaction.

CHAPTER 23

After a somewhat unexpected conversation with DS McCluskey, Bill Burrows said goodnight to Zara Pradić and headed for home. In actual fact McCluskey had been quite understanding and told him he had every confidence in him and to call him if he wanted to discuss any aspect of the case. Burrows had felt guilty that he had misjudged his superior and determined that tomorrow would be another day when he gave the task his all … but first he would sleep. McVeigh had called it a day a little earlier, after he had finished up at the vigil outside the home of Donna Nelson and her sons. Burrows could hear that he was exhausted by the draining day and knew they would do better tomorrow if they got some rest and emotional sustenance from being at home. Every uniformed officer in the city was on the lookout for Marshall or any news of his whereabouts and Burrows felt his best option was to ensure to be his best self the next day.

Pradić would remain vigilant about what was going on about the case in the vast world of the Internet. Sammy Marshall and his alleged murderous assault on his ex-wife and his two small sons was generating floods of chat and analysis that Pradić was scanning for elements of interest to the case. As he put on his coat and headed for the carpark he couldn't help but wonder about Pradić's personal life. Of course she had a home to go to and clearly chose to keep her private life to herself. Suggestions that she lived in the Station smacked of racism, he thought, and he determined to be more vociferous in challenging those types of comments when they surfaced. He wasn't a man who noticed things about women's fashion, but he had started to observe that Zara did actually change her clothes although her basic look was always the same. He had noticed too that she had a signature smell of some herbal type of aroma that was at once relaxing and refreshing. He didn't want to pry but he hoped that she had more to her life than work, although she never gave any hint that this was the case. Most people made some reference to a partner or a pet or a blocked drain or something that suggested a home life but so far Pradić remained an enigma to them all. Security issues meant that PSNI staff had more than usual privacy around their personal details and Burrows respected that protection completely. His curiosity remained just that.

When he arrived home he paused in the garden to inhale the scent of the new blooms and felt himself wind down a notch immediately. He and Myrtle spent nearly all their free time together digging and weeding in their flower garden. They lived in a modest semi that was built when garden allocations were more generous than nowadays, when every square centimetre was counted and gardens were a costly luxury. He breathed the satisfying smells of home and, as he turned his key in the door, he heard his wife coming out of the kitchen into the hall to greet him. He had texted that he was on his way.

In her arms he heaved a sigh of relief and saw, over her shoulder into the kitchen, that there was a cold beer waiting for him on the table beside his carefully reheated evening meal.

"Myrtle Burrows … you are the best woman in the world and I am a lucky man to come home to you every evening."

"Oh, Bill, I've been listening to the news so I know you're up to your neck in this horrible new case. Did you have to go to the autopsies?" She knew that even after all these years he still hadn't got used to being present for the invasive forensic examination of the murder victims.

"Boylan had a backlog to clear today so that's tomorrow's delight. I can't expect anyone else to do this one but you know I have my ways of coping."

"I'll go and put some lavender oil on the hankie in your coat pocket, now while I remember."

He sat down, carefully poured his beer and slowly savoured the first cooling mouthful. Then he lifted his fork to attack his home-baked beef pie, carrying with him all the time an awareness of the utterly different familial scene he had witnessed the previous morning.

* * *

In the Four Winds suburb of Belfast, Ian McVeigh sat beside his wife, Sally, on the sofa and watched the late evening news. The report of the Murder Squad's latest case was brief but horrifying. The bald facts of the triple murder and the identity of the victims made chilling listening. Sally and Ian had put their young son to bed together. They had played with him as they gave him his evening bath, singing silly songs that he loved and filling the bath with all manner of toys and waterproof books. They both wanted the best for him and the fact that not all that far away someone had killed two children the previous night sharpened their urgency to protect him from all harm.

"I've really been thinking about your question as I've been working today, Sal."

"What question is that, darling?" She was half listening to the rest of the local news and he waited until he had her full attention.

"You asked me what sort of a man I wanted our son to be. I didn't really know what you were getting at but today the penny dropped." And he explained about his evening visit to Sharon and Jack's house and how she had wondered out loud how an innocent boy could grow up to be a killer. "I realised that we have to work consciously to make sure that our son does not become a sexist man ... and that begins with me."

There were tears in his eyes when he explained about Jack's picture for his dead friend and she held him in her arms and told him she was sorry that he had to look at the handiwork of disturbed, angry men and that she was happy to be raising her son with a kind and gentle man.

"I do think that maybe soon we'll try for a sister for our boy." She kissed him on the nose and pulled back to study his reaction to her suggestion. "I need to make sure that we even up the gender balance in this house."

She laughed roguishly and his heart swelled with happiness, while in the same moment he realised with horror that if something ever threatened to take all this away from him, he too might find a 'disturbed, angry man' lurking within him. He would have to make it his business to eliminate any shred of that possibility.

* * *

Constable Zara Pradić loved to get the office to herself. Most of the time, even if there were others present, she was able to become completely absorbed in her many computer screens but there were always interruptions. She didn't mind the challenges she was allocated. In fact she relished the problem-solving and contributing to catching killers through doing what she loved best but she loved the silence of the empty office. The building was never empty and in fact there was often more commotion at night as drunks and rioters were brought in and processed and taken to the cells for the night. Here, however, in the Murder Squad HQ, there was peace and hours passed while she became immersed in this alternative world where she felt she could most be herself.

Zara knew that she was a subject of curiosity in the PSNI in general and in her new position on the Murder Squad to a certain extent. However, here there was a sense that she was most respected for her digital acumen. Her unusual appearance and behaviours were a very peripheral issue.

The current case was intriguing for her in that it had particular echoes of her homeplace. There, the macho culture also tolerated violence against women and gangs operated drug and protection rackets in some communities. Pradić had known many Sammy Marshalls and many Bull Nelsons and like other women had first-hand childhood experience of control being enforced with aggression and violence.

She had saved herself by developing her highly valuable digital skills which allowed her to earn money, find protection from the worst thugs and finally to negotiate her escape to Brussels. There she had found an education collective that helped her accredit her technical know-how and acquire the papers she needed to become a legal and employable resident in the west. Northern Ireland was not high on the list of destinations of choice for migrants and she had chosen it because of that very lack of attraction. When she arrived ten years previously she had discovered that it suited her very well. She had radically changed her appearance, done some higher level qualifications through schemes for new residents and developed an admirable employment record. She hoped that the unpleasantness of her past had been consigned to history although memory was a more difficult beast to silence.

She was scanning various chat rooms and online newsfeeds for comments about Sammy Marshall. His face was everywhere and she wasn't surprised that he had been easily identified and picked up as soon as he was released. She was absolutely certain that the fact his location had been discovered had been leaked by someone within the PSNI. She had been cautious not to broadcast it more widely than was necessary for local uniformed response to be activated. Their systems were well firewalled and so it could only have been an insider. Betrayal was a characteristic she despised and she would pursue the culprit with all her digital savvy, when the issue of finding Marshall was resolved.

She was considering heading home, taking a shower and getting a few hours' sleep when an email dropped into her inbox from Alice Fox and she opened it immediately. She liked the American woman and they had worked well together on a previous case. Here was a mind not unlike her own – someone who took nothing at face value and thought further outside the box than most. Of course she could see that she and DI Paton were an item but that was no concern of hers. Get your pleasure where you can was her motto. Life is short. The email was brief but interesting. Already this afternoon, Pradić had sent DI Paton all the case files on Jordan Campbell. Now, 'off the record', Alice Fox was looking for any info, in English, Catalan or Spanish, on one Jordi Campbell, the same person but in his Catalan reincarnation. Suddenly, Pradić lost her interest in sleep.

* * *

Paula and Grace and their counterparts, May and Tina from the Shankill Women's Centre, sat in the car outside the disused mill on the Lower Falls.

May and Tina had known a good number of the women at the vigil and they had introduced Paula and Grace to Sharon, next-door neighbour of the murdered woman and her two young sons. The murdered woman's neighbour had spoken freely to them about Donna and the abuse she'd suffered with Sammy Marshall.

"The crazy thing is you wouldn't have thought he would ever snap like that. He was just a big child really who needed to get his way." She spoke quietly, all the time checking her son who was holding her hand tightly, his small brow furrowed in anxiety. "I despair of what we can do to raise sons that aren't potential killers." She looked at them expectantly as if they might hold an answer.

Paula had shaken her head and replied for them all.

"It's not that straightforward, Sharon. We can't change men, no matter how much we want to. Men have to change themselves."

And they had all looked glum, considering the unlikelihood of that happening.

The four women had spent an hour in Goliath Row and been careful to talk to as many people as possible. Better still, they had ensured that they had been in the forefront of shots taken by press photographers that had turned up to get some poignant images of the latest case of femicide that year. There would be a few days of media hype and analysis and then it would all fade from public interest until the next woman was harmed. The momentum needed to make a difference was never reached and the women had spoken amongst themselves many times about what was needed to bring about real change.

For these women, now in their sixties, there had been decades of protesting, organising vigils and marches and lobbying politicians. They had shouted themselves hoarse with slogans that despite their ongoing relevance seemed somehow empty of hope now, after all this time. They all remembered their younger selves striding through the evening streets with candles and torches shouting: "*However we dress, wherever we go, 'yes' means 'yes' and 'no' means 'no'!*" And then there was, "*Not the Church, not the State, women will decide their fate!*"

"Over four decades later," said Tina despondently. "It's the same issue, the same slogans and little progress to speak of. I think we need to take a more creative approach to all this hurting of women. How can we change the message to being about men changing rather than women learning self-defence or staying at home? I'm just so tired of it all. There's no sign that the State is doing anything worthwhile. Sure, it's the biggest bastion of patriarchy there is!"

In the north of Ireland, even during the Troubles, women of all ages had gathered together to demand an end to systematic aggressions against them whether in their homes, in the streets, in prison or anywhere else. They had created refuges for women violently beaten in their homes. They set up Rape Crisis Centres for women and girls sexually assaulted, often by someone they knew and sometimes by a stranger. They accessed funding and created a network of women's centres in both urban and rural areas. They studied and trained and professionalised their work and still the numbers of violent attacks on women grew as if there was a plague to which there was no antidote.

When they named their common enemy as the patriarchy and clarified that their fight wasn't with individual men but with a system that belittled, reviled and denigrated women, things still didn't get much better. A small number of men who had done women's studies in prison, or who were partners or sons of these women began to get the message. They stopped participating in sexist banter and some even challenged other men about such talk. A very small number began to organise to support each other in how to be a different kind of man and how to become real allies of women in their war against patriarchy. The White Ribbon Movement and the Men's Development Network were good examples of how men could change but their influence remained slight in comparison to the size of the problem. Progress was slow. It was much too slow for the women and children on the receiving end of men's violence, like Donna Nelson and her boys.

"How many times have we said that this is enough?" said Grace, lighting a cigarette and opening the car window.

Paula closed the window again, using the dual control. "That's just blowing the smoke back in again, Grace. Put it out. You gave them up years ago! Let's deal with the business in hand." She turned towards the women in the back of the car. "So here we are with a chance to do something that makes a direct impact on how the news about violence against women is presented." She sighed deeply. "We have this guy at our disposal and my boys will have cleaned him up by now and given him something to eat. He was a total mess when we got him and my car will need more than a deluxe valet before I can sit in it again. We don't want to hurt him. In fact, we've probably saved him from becoming really ill from dehydration and hypothermia." They all knew that was a bit of a stretch but let it pass. "We just need to be clever here and see what we can make out of this moment in the cause of women's rights."

Tina placed her hand gently on Paula's shoulder. "We're agreed that we have an opportunity here, Paula. You don't need to convince us. It's a bit of a wild move but if we're careful we've nothing to lose … aside from a few charges like kidnap and obstructing police business that we'll try to avoid. May and I have talked it through carefully while we were waiting for you to pick us up. Let's not dilly-dally any more and get inside now and down to strategy. I don't want this to go pear-shaped before we can make some use of it."

They all knew Tina to be a sharp planner and, without further delay, they left the car and headed into the historic redbrick building where they would decide their next steps.

Grace and Paula's sons were waiting inside the Mill, having supervised Marshall's clean-up. The Women's Centre had accommodation there for when a woman needed to flee a violent home situation and there were no refuge places available. It wasn't luxurious – it reflected the use it had been put to in previous times – but it had served its purpose and provided no-frills safety when it was needed.

"Hiya, lads!" Tina and May greeted the young men that they had known throughout their lives.

May looked at the two young men admiringly. "Yiz both look very fit. Are ye still mad gym bunnies?"

They laughed and one of them responded with mock gravity.

"When yer ma has brought yeh up as a non-violent, radical feminist, Auntie May, yeh have to look as if yeh could do damage to someone even though yeh wouldn't hurt a fly."

The women laughed and Tina chipped in, "You're our hope for the future. You're the proof that men can be real allies of women and maybe even make a good cup of tea too." She winked and continued dramatically. "We're gasping for a cuppa. Figuring out how to use some shock tactics on attitudes towards violence against women gives yeh a terrible thirst."

"The meeting room is all ready for ye. There was a request in from the education project but we told them there was a plumbing issue and they rebooked for next week. If they'd got a whiff of yer man they'd have been sure the drains were blocked."

"How's he doing, son?" Grace asked, touching her son's arm affectionately.

"Smelling sweet, fed and watered and tucked up for the night. He won't be any bother. He thinks he's landed in Fenian hell. I'd say he'd leap into the arms of the nearest peeler if he got the chance. We'll stay over and make sure he's ready for a bit of self-development with us in the morning. I'll get the tea and then we'll get out of yer way. We've a game of chess started that will probably take all night." And he winked at the women. "Our brains are just as fit as our bodies, Auntie May … We'll get the tea now."

The four women, showing only a few signs of wear despite their age, moved into the small meeting room and saw that there was a clean flip chart and water and biscuits on the circular table.

The four women, two from the Falls Road and two from the Shankill settled around the table and, when they'd taken delivery of four mugs of steaming tea, turned their attention to the serious business in hand – how to use their chance acquisition of a violent woman-killer to heighten the public's understanding of male violence.

Tina dunked her digestive into her mug of tea and began to speak slowly and thoughtfully. "The way I see it, there's no point in even considering whether or not the acquisition of Sammy Marshall as a non-paying guest was wise or not. He's here now and we need to see what we can make of that. We need to think of this as a PR exercise. Not the kind we're used to but, nevertheless, we are able to make this work."

May had worked with Tina for almost four decades and in all of that time they had been supporting women who were abused, mostly by men that they knew and often by men that they actually loved. May touched a small scar above her right eyebrow. She had been one of those women who needed rescue and Tina had been there, an unlikely hero. Tina was short and solidly built. She looked ordinary enough but May knew her to be one of the most extraordinary people she had ever met. She had a brilliant mind that she used to fight for the rights of the women who lived in the grubby streets that were crowded behind the bustling shopping front that back in the day was the Shankill Road. Before the Troubles, Catholics from the Falls Road would have walked across Northumberland Street to shop for the bargains on offer in the shoe shops and drapers on the Shankill. That trade halted abruptly when the Troubles unleashed new phases of sectarian violence and the activities of the Shankill Butchers spread terror throughout the community.

When May had first met her, Tina's hair had been jet-black and then it went suddenly grey. She always joked that the cause was the shock of the horror stories she had to listen to every day in the Women's Centre and the everyday trauma of living on the Shankill Road in Belfast in the seventies. She had never coloured it and for all those years May had watched her friend age without really physically changing very much. She had the kind of face that didn't wrinkle and her eyebrows had remained black. What changed was her skill at manipulating situations to benefit the women that she had worked tirelessly for all her life.

"We need to be quick and we need to be very, very focussed," May said quietly as if speaking to herself. She raised her head then and looked at her companions. "We need to make the whole country sit up and take notice of the harm that men do daily, often to women they are supposed to love. Let's face it, they also do it to each other." May picked up her pen and readied herself to make notes.

"Let's agree some boundaries, will we?" Paula began and the other three nodded. They were all used to working together and knew to trust each other's priorities. "I think we're agreed that we will cause Marshall no harm. He's not our concern really. The cops will deal with him when we hand him over."

There were grunts of agreement.

"Actually, we don't need to concern ourselves with him at all," Grace chipped in. "The lads have an awareness-raising programme planned for him." She laughed. "He'll be the best-informed prisoner about violence against women in Maghaberry Jail. Let's just agree that we can leave him to the two boys."

Paula continued. "I think we should establish a time limit for ourselves. Say, we hold him here until after the Reclaim the Night March is under way and then have him delivered or we let the peelers know some scenic spot where they can collect him. Does that give us enough time to do what we want to?"

Grace looked up from the page that she was doodling on. "Once we put the word out that Marshall is being held by women who are unhappy about how the state deals with violence against women, I'd say that we will well and truly have everybody's attention. I'd say forty-eight hours will be ample. We won't be disturbed here as I've put the word out that the refuge is in use so let's see how we can make best use of our time."

"Right. So I'd say our primary target with our message is social media. The mainstream press, TV and Radio will pick up the word there and run with it. Let's agree some initial messages to grab attention and then we'll set up a few bogus accounts to get started with. We have a fund of links to violence-against-women sites that we can include so that the media use up-to-date, well-researched data. I also have lists of women who will talk to the media and take part in interviews and chat shows at short notice. If we work through the night I reckon we can go live tomorrow afternoon."

She assumed the look of absolute concentration that they all knew meant she was ready with a plan.

"Pen at the ready, May? Let's get this show on the road!"

Good Friday, 18 April 2014

CHAPTER 24

DI Caroline Paton was not in the best of shape the following morning when she woke to the sounds of the new day in Hotel Aiguaclara. Someone closed a door rather loudly in a nearby room and the sound of gentle jazz music floated up from the breakfast room below. She turned over on her side and saw that the French windows onto the balcony were open. Alice's running gear was in a heap on the floor and the shower was thrumming in the bathroom. There was a chilled bottle of water beside her on the bedside table and Caroline took this as a token that she was not in the doghouse. Peace reigned. It was a long time since she'd overdone the wine to that extent but she had clearly needed to switch off. She would catch up on her reading this morning and see where that got them to with the Campbell case.

"Good morning, sunshine!" Alice said a little too heartily as she emerged from the shower. She kissed Caroline on the end of the nose and stepped back to gauge how she was. "Are you feeling under the weather?"

"Nothing a good Catalan breakfast won't sort out," Caroline replied bravely. "However, I will take it easy today … just read some files on the terrace and maybe a walk along the beach at Pals later.

Alice had hatched a plan of her own during her run and wasn't ready to share it just yet.

"I want to do some searches about the AHIGE group and maybe even arrange to meet up with them. I guess I might as well get on with that this afternoon until you need my help with the translation of the files from the Mossos."

Late the previous night while Alice was still sitting on the terrace contemplating the stars, Zara Pradić had sent through a number of interesting files about Jordi Campbell that she had helpfully put through Google Translate. Alice had thanked her for her rapid response, downloaded them to a new desktop file named 'Jordi' and planned to read them in the morning. One newspaper headline had particularly caught her attention: **WHO ARE THE NEW MEN?** The subheading said: **Irish thief, rapist, murderer and wife-beater joins Catalan branch of men's equality group.** The smiling face of Jordi Campbell sat incongruously beneath the headline.

Campbell had shoulder-length, light-brown, curly hair that was held back from his face by a brightly coloured hair band. His soft, freckled complexion gave him an air of youthful innocence. He was wearing an open-necked shirt and had a black stud-earring in his left ear. There was a brightness in Jordi Campbell's eyes that wasn't a match for the person described by Hugo as naïve, slow-witted and unable to understand the consequences of his actions. This was an alert and dynamic man with an alternative image and a sense of having eschewed the more aggressive forms of masculinity. She was fascinated to find out more about him. Alice had looked at that face for some time before deciding to leave reading the text until she had some sleep and some exercise.

While Caroline showered, Alice couldn't resist reading the newspaper article that had captured her attention the previous evening. The journalist has done a lot of research and had clearly first encountered Campbell in the Spanish criminal justice system. It seemed from what she read that Campbell and his partner had come to Catalonia from Scotland where they had initially tried to set up a business and failed. Then in a small Catalan holiday town they had taken over a tapas bar and against all the odds had succeeded in making a go of it. If the business had worked, their relationship did not and after ten years in Catalonia, Campbell was convicted of serious domestic abuse and spent a number of years in prison. There he overcame his learning difficulties and became literate in his first and second language. He also completed a perpetrator programme delivered by AHIGE and through that and counselling he came to understand himself and how his early life had contributed to the violent abuser he had become. He joined AHIGE on his release and became passionate about changing the cultural and sexist legacy that he now understood had blighted his young life. Alice breathed deeply and felt the deep pleasure of understanding that change is possible and that, given the chance and access to the truth, someone can choose a different way.

She wondered what had happened to Campbell's partner whom he had badly hurt. Had she remained in Spain and what did she make now of his transformation? Alice's work gave her an interest in knowing all sides of the story. She stored those questions for another time when she might get a chance to ask them. For now she closed her laptop and prepared to have breakfast with her lover.

She had thought a lot about their conversation of the previous evening while she ran along the coastal path near the village and realised she was being unrealistic in expecting a senior police officer to be openly critical of the system that she was still working in. It was probable too that she herself was feeling under pressure about the decisions she needed to make about her future and that she was just lumping everything to do with her life into that process, whether it belonged there or not.

"I feel ready for the day now." Caroline emerged from the bathroom with considerably more energy that she had going in and Alice laughed.

"You have amazing powers of recovery, Caroline! I wouldn't have given much for your productivity level today but I'm going to have to revise my predictions." She embraced her warmly. "It's only Good Friday but I am happy to acknowledge your premature resurrection."

"Never underestimate a PSNI," Caroline bragged. "Let's get that breakfast and then I'll be ready for whatever the Mossos have to throw at me."

And they headed for the stairs arm in arm, each one intent on becoming more au fait with Jordi Campbell and his activities before the end of the day. There would be a few surprises, Alice thought, given Campbell's radical transformation.

* * *

After breakfast, while Caroline and Alice were in a small sitting room of the hotel, quietly reading files on their laptops, Alice received another message from Zara Pradić. She had asked herself why she was working secretly on the AHIGE link to Campbell and realised this was her pattern. She liked to follow a range of hunches and gather information before she openly stated her theory about a case. There was no point in distracting Caroline with her unsubstantiated conjectures until she had done some more digging and Pradić's latest message told Alice that she was heading in the right direction. She had found a piece in an online regional newspaper that suggested that Jordi Campbell was now an outspoken member of the Catalan independence movement. Campbell's social conscience was certainly wide awake since he'd come to grips with his childhood issues in prison, mused Alice. She sent Pradić the details of Xavier Duxo, the murder victim in Verges, to see what she could find out about him and also asked for whatever she could find about Campbell's ex-partner Marcella Murray. Her details were all in the newspaper accounts of Campbell's criminal trial at the time and Pradić could quickly access a lot of social-media stuff that would take Alice a lot longer. To be doubly sure that she wasn't compromising Pradić, Alice always made it clear that if her requests were inconvenient in any way Pradić only had to say so and that would be the end of the matter. However, Alice knew from some previous collaboration that Pradić enjoyed the chase as much as she did and that she relished the challenge of having lots of things happening at the same time.

Later in the day, the women had lunch at a small café beside the hotel before Alice headed to Girona, about an hour's drive away. She had secured an interview with someone from the Catalan office of AHIGE, ostensibly about their courses for young men. She also wanted to inquire into the activities of Jordi Campbell in AHIGE and if possible in the Catalan independence movement.

There was nothing through yet from Pradić about Marcella Murray so that would have to wait for another day. In the meantime, Caroline planned a recuperative siesta and said that she and Alice would consider the Mossos' file about Campbell's misdemeanours in Catalonia in the evening. Alice quietly hoped that she would have another perspective on those events by the time she returned from her trip to Girona.

CHAPTER 25

After a tortured night, Sammy Marshall woke in his barren accommodation somewhere in Catholic West Belfast and considered his situation. He was not sure that he hadn't swopped one version of hell for an even more terrifying one. At least in the first instance he had been clear that his jailers were local thugs concerned about an unpaid debt. They were undoubtedly employed by Bull who was the original source of the money and while things had been OK between Sammy and Donna there was never any suggestion that the loan needed to be repaid. Sammy knew that Bull liked him. At times he thought that there was more to it than just brotherly closeness but it hadn't ever gone anywhere beyond that … at least, not that he could remember but then he'd been off his face a lot of the time. Anyway, after the Exclusion Order was put in place, his relationship with Bull had ground to a halt completely. Zero communication. Sammy had phoned a few times and left messages but they were never returned.

Then one night when he'd been out drinking on his own he'd been given a cautionary verbal reminder that his debt repayment was long overdue and he'd better get it sorted. Yesterday was definitely a more severe prompt but then, just when he thought he was done for with the rats and all, something had brought that episode to an abrupt end.

Anyway this second place of detention was a whole other ball game. Yesterday, he thought he was free and was heading for the Shankill Road when two ould dolls had picked him up in a banger of a car and thrown a blanket over him before he could get a good look at them. What might have been a welcome rescue had turned very alarming indeed. "Let's get back to the Falls before the peelers spot us," one of the women had said and then he knew she was a Fenian. And here he was now, locked in the back of an old industrial building surrounded by notices in Irish and carved wooden Celtic crosses and harps. A framed sign on the wall in some kind of embroidery said '*You are safe now*' and all the windows were covered in green adhesive plastic that obscured the view outside. It was definitely some kind of Fenian hideaway and that was a thousand times more terrifying, Sammy thought, than a rat-infested lock-up on the Shankill.

There had been very little chat in the car – a lot of swearing about the stink of him and some chat between the women and someone on the phone in what he assumed was Irish. When the car stopped the women had moved into a different car. There were two very big lads waiting outside. They were wearing some kind of animal masks and had horsed him up a couple of floors of stone steps and into a tiled room with a shower and a toilet. He wasn't feeling the best and even now he wasn't very clear what had actually happened and what he had conjured up in his disturbed mind. They'd told him to get naked and put his stuff in a black bin bag and then they wrapped each of his fingers carefully in cling film and then inserted his hands into snugly fitting latex gloves secured at each wrist with sticky-backed tape. As they wrapped his hands, one man said to the other, "It may be a waste of time trying to preserve the evidence but at least we'll show willing." Then he turned to Sammy and warned, "Do not interfere with these or I will be very, very cross."

Then he turned the shower on and they left him alone with a bottle of cheap liquid soap and a threadbare towel. At least he'd die clean, Sammy had thought as he felt the filth fall away from his body, although the grinding fear did not lessen. After ten minutes or so, when he had dried himself and wrapped the thin towel around him for decency, the heavy metal door was flung open and one of the men handed him a grey tracksuit still wrapped in plastic.

"Get that on yeh," the man commanded gruffly. "Then I'll show yeh to yer sleeping quarters. Yeh'll need yer kip cos there's a very busy day of mental activity ahead of yeh tomarra." And he had laughed scathingly at Sammy's efforts to conceal the garish Rangers Football Club tattoo on his upper arm. "Don't worry, mate. Yer football loyalties won't be part of tomorra's proceedings." Then he had taken him firmly by the elbow and led him along a corridor where the bare brickwork had been painted in cream gloss. He'd kicked a door open and pushed him inside. Aside from a single bed and a bucket with a lid, the room was empty. The window was high up and, as it was dark now, there was little light in the room. On the floor beside the bed was a packet of egg mayonnaise sandwiches, a carton of milk and a bottle of water.

"Tuck in, Sammy," said his jailor and he closed the door and locked it from the outside.

Then everything had been quiet. He tried not to wonder what the new day might hold for him.

* * *

As dawn broke over Belfast's Divis Mountain, Constable Zara Pradić was already at her workstation. She had set up a number of links from which she wanted to receive immediate notification of new activity and was waiting patiently for what she expected to be a deluge of chat. She had reasoned that perhaps Sammy Marshall had been abducted for a second time because someone or some group wanted to make use of him to raise awareness of their particular issue. She hadn't wasted too much time speculating because Northern Ireland politics often defied logic. There was always the remote possibility that this time it might be something with which she could identify but it might just as easily be the Loyalist Poodle Protection League or some other equally worthy cause. In any case, whether or not she found the issue interesting was immaterial. The tracking element might not be as straightforward as in the past. Nowadays, there was a lot of widespread understanding about how to conceal your identity while making use of social media. She hoped the kidnappers were not too IT-savvy but suspected she was hoping in vain.

While she waited patiently for the alerts to begin, she reviewed the posts about the Reclaim the Night March the following evening. This latest episode of so-called domestic violence had really captured public attention and debates, both personal and political, were raging across social media. Survivors retold their own stories and sympathised with the family of the latest attack. Women's groups called for a reinstatement of their funding that had been cut during a period of austerity and cited statistics of the numbers they were unable to support because of lack of resources. There was the usual backlash from men who felt aggrieved that their victim status was erased from the debates. Then there was support from the small number of men who wanted to be allied to the feminist side of the argument. It was a messy enough pool of participants.

The fact that there were children involved in this killing generated additional sympathy. Countless women were harmed without much notice being taken and here there were abundant references to 'innocent children' as if the woman's culpability was always in question. Pradić nodded at her screens, affirming that she knew this to be almost always the case. It might be her clothes, how much she had to drink, her level of confidence or just the fact that her views differed from a man who wouldn't tolerate dissent. As in the case of Donna Nelson, it might be that she paid too much attention to her children and left her husband too much to his own devices. The truth was, Pradić mused, that even in this day and age it was easy to discredit a woman and thereby excuse or at least explain a man's violent behaviour.

* * *

The case review in the Murder Squad that morning produced little in the way of new ideas about how they might go about tracking down Sammy Marshall. Wherever he had been taken there was no trace to be found, despite a full-scale alert being in operation throughout the force. They were convinced that he was still alive but the other hand, it was always possible that someone just wanted him dead and had executed him and buried the body somewhere secluded. Even if this was the case and they located Marshall's remains, they would just be shifting to another murder inquiry with the goal of finding his killers.

It was agreed subsequently with DS McCluskey that they would try appealing to the general public. A press conference was planned for early that evening to coincide with the local evening news bulletins. As well as the usual progress statement from DS McCluskey, Burrows would be present to answer questions and there would be a live appeal from Donna Nelson's parents for their ex-son-in-law, or his captors, to give himself up and allow the family to grieve in peace. Burrows would meet with McCluskey before the meeting with the press to agree the parameters of the information that they would disclose. They would do their best to avoid any discussion of paramilitary or gang activity or the detail of how Marshall managed to elude police capture. That was a separate issue.

Burrows' morning would be taken up with the autopsies on the three victims while McVeigh would liaise with the uniformed officers doing house-to-house calls in the Shankill area. He would follow up on any leads they might uncover as well as keeping in touch with the Nelson and Marshall families. Bull Nelson had grudgingly given Burrows an undertaking that he would pass on any pertinent detail that he discovered about just what had become of his brother-in-law. McVeigh would keep Nelson's activities under close scrutiny as one potential source of information in an otherwise fairly spartan field of inquiry. They had not ruled out the possibility that Bull Nelson was still controlling Marshall's detention albeit from a safer distance and so his phone and whereabouts were still being kept under close scrutiny. They knew he undoubtedly had any number of phones and so he would be careful to reveal nothing in that way. He was staying very close to his parents' house for the time being but they were prepared for that to change at any moment.

Pradić continued to be absorbed in her screens, occasionally turning her swivel chair in McVeigh's direction to pass on some detail she had uncovered. "There's a lot of activity online, Ian, around tomorrow night's Reclaim the Night March. It's turning into a major policing task but it's also attracting comment from a wide range of parties. Feeder parades are coming from across the city and buses from further afield. The women's sector is mobilising across the country and there are even solidarity groups coming across the border. There's a good deal of speculation too about who might have Marshall now and what they should do with him. Some of it is highly creative and extremely painful." She swivelled back to her screens.

And they lapsed back into a diligent silence.

* * *

Pradić was busy collating the morning media coverage of the Goliath Row killings and placing them in a file on the shared drive. Unsurprisingly, the double abduction of Sammy Marshall took precedence over the case of the murder of Donna Nelson and her sons. *WHERE'S SAMMY?* was one front page, that replicated the *Where's Wally* children's books where the goal was to locate a character in a striped bobble hat and jumper in a crowd of hundreds of figures. The text exposed how unsuccessful the plan to keep the detail of Marshall's kidnapping secret had been. The story was light on facts but indulged in as much speculation as journalistic standards allowed. **MYSTERY OF THE DISAPPEARING MURDER SUSPECT** read one of the main dailies that asked how the PSNI had managed to both find and lose Marshall at the same time. Another paper that led with: **FAMILY KILLED IN A DOMESTIC EPISODE GONE WRONG** would anger at least fifty per cent of the readership. When did a domestic ever go well, Pradić wondered?

One local daily hit a more sensitive note with **WOMEN TO PROTEST AGAINST INCREASE IN GENDERED VIOLENCE** with a strapline highlighting the Reclaim the Night March the following evening. It was unashamedly a call for women and their allies to demonstrate their impatience with an intransigent problem.

And then the predictable debate about male victims of domestic abuses was raging in opinion pieces despite the statistics showing that women were the group that are predominantly abused and assaulted by intimate partners and in almost all cases by male intimate partners.

Radio and TV channels and websites had gathered some information about the murder victims and some footage of the previous night's vigil. There were interviews with the little boys' crèche and schoolteacher, highlighting how innocent children got caught up in adult problems.

A statement made by a woman from the Shankill Women's Centre said that it was despicable that a woman and her children had to die for the media to take any notice. "You will all be there with your cameras and your reporters at the funerals of this woman and her boys, but where are you when women's refuges are closed because of lack of funding or there aren't enough women to answer the helpline phones?" The woman's anger was palpable but she held it together. She quoted statistics about rising numbers of attacks on women. "And, yes, some of this is because more women are reporting experiences of male aggression but that's not the only reason. Violence against women is increasing and convictions of perpetrators remain shamefully low. If you are not punished for wrongdoing you have no incentive to change your behaviour." She paused for a moment and then continued, "And who in government is doing anything to make this matter a priority? Where are the suggestions about law reform and funding to protect women from male violence? We are sick and tired of the same old tribal politics that offer nothing to transform the dreadful reality of violence and assault in women's lives. Really what is attracting attention to this story is not that a man may have killed a woman and his two children. That is one-day news. The fact that he has been abducted before being taken into police custody is what is holding media attention."

CHAPTER 26

Girona was a big and bustling city with the River Onyar flowing majestically through it. Driving in from the coast, Alice was struck by the huge cathedral that dominated the skyline and seemed oversized in proportion to the surrounding buildings. It must have been even more disproportionate when it was first built in the eleventh century, she thought. Already it seemed to her that Spain was full of churches and it was hard to imagine how such elaborate ancient buildings came into being especially in times when the entire process was done manually. It said something about the wealth and the power of the church, she supposed. No change there really.

The perfect place to park presented itself on the city's left bank and she took a phone photo of the location in case she lost the way back. She crossed the river by a faded, narrow, red bridge and was surprised by the old apartment buildings on either side in soft earthen colours of terracotta and ochre and the occasional touch of Moroccan blue.

Now she was headed for the ancient Jewish Quarter where AHIGE had their premises. Her brief scan of the Internet that morning had told her that Girona's thriving community of Jews had been expelled in the fifteenth century after decades of persecution and forced conversion to Christianity and Catholicism. Some of the Jews who fled Spain back then had actually introduced this blue to North Africa where it became an iconic colour in that part of the world as well as also remaining part of Girona's colour palette. She liked that kind of insight about how the world evolved.

Long, narrow, stone stairways wound their way upwards through a labyrinth of narrow streets with high, honeyed stone walls of four and five-storey buildings on each side. An array of aromas of lunchtime meals seeped out of homes and small cafés and mingled with cigarette smoke and occasionally something else that Alice thought might be incense and marijuana. Frequent stone archways crossed these slender passageways overhead with the result that she naturally moved from light to shade as she followed the historic paths. The stone steps underfoot were polished to a shine from the footfall of ages and their irregularities in height and width were a testament to the hands that had hewn them so long ago. The city felt ancient and with no noise of traffic there was a sense of being transported to medieval times … until the host of people using cameras and mobile phones and drinking water from plastic bottles interrupted that illusion.

When she found her meeting place the plaque on the door read *AHIGE – Asociación de Hombres por la Igualdad de Género*. Alice translated for herself – Association of Men for Gender Equality. It was an exciting concept, she thought – a group that gathered together men who wanted to give up power over women, and all that entailed. She smiled as she pushed the buzzer below the name plaque and waited to be admitted.

The guy that met her was in his forties and called Raoul. He led the way up a flight of stairs and they took their seats in a relaxed area of the main office space. A few other men were working quietly at office stations around the room and they smiled in greeting to Alice when she came in. There was an air of calm and industry. She and Raoul spoke in Spanish and she found him easy enough to understand. They talked first about the awareness-raising work AHIGE did with young school-age boys and with groups of older men too. Alice asked about the training they did with men convicted of violent crimes against women. She wanted to know how receptive to change they found these men.

"Well, to be honest, Alice, we are learning all the time about what makes men violent and it is a complicated scenario. It would be foolish to think that one programme of training alone would undo a lifetime of conditioning. It's a big task to ask people to give up power over women when in other areas of their lives they are social underdogs. It doesn't seem to imbue them with empathy." He looked at her searchingly.

She decided that he was trying to gauge if she had any idea what he was talking about.

"Yes," she said, "I understand that and I realise from my own experience that a much more holistic approach is called for. Most importantly, the man himself needs to decide that he wants to escape from the patriarchy and that isn't something that very many violent men understand. So what is AHIGE's approach?"

Raoul was smiling, now that he realised they understood each other. "Well, that is constantly evolving and we are, of course, obliged to work in tandem with the Criminal Justice system. They have recruited us to do this specific work with perpetrators of gender violence and they are constantly examining how effective it is." He wrinkled his nose as if there were a troublesome insect inside it.

Alice knew the nature of that bug intimately. "I'm familiar with those struggles too, Raoul." She nodded encouragingly at this earnest man who near enough to her own age. "After all, the 'do nothing' option is not a runner." It was comforting to find that there were people everywhere, ardently working for just change and yet constantly disappointed by the pace of progress.

Raoul inhaled deeply as if getting ready for some great exertion. "We know there's no quick fix to the issues caused by toxic masculinities. So many people think an anger management course is all that's needed and everything will be resolved. The trouble is that the state wants a sticking-plaster approach and we know it has to be long and slow and holistic." He was smiling sadly now.

Alice had been nodding in agreement and spoke with fervour from experience. "Exactly. For the funders it's 'give us the cheap version'… and we know it won't work. They can claim every offender has been through a rehab programme but we know we might as well have taken them all on a package holiday. It will have as much impact on their gendered behaviour."

They talked some more about the potential for working together with groups of young people and agreed to check out EU funding opportunities. As this new work began to sound possible, Alice could feel her decision about remaining in Belfast and working with the EXIT group shifting towards a positive response. She agreed to discuss this conversation with Hugo on her return and moved on to the delicate matter of Jordi Campbell.

"I wanted to ask you about something else I'm involved in here as part of some work I am doing with the Belfast Murder Squad." Alice paused to see the impact this had on Raoul and when he didn't seem spooked she pressed on diplomatically. "I know that normally this type of information would be confidential but I have seen it discussed at length in the local papers and thought it might be OK to raise the issue. It's about a man called Jordi Campbell."

Raoul's face darkened a little but he did not shut down the discussion. "I know Jordi well and, in fact, I have had an inquiry from the Mossos about him this morning. I guess it's the same situation that you are referring to. They want to talk to him about a current murder case they're investigating. I told them that Jordi Campbell is a changed man and I would be very surprised if he was of any interest to them. In the light of our previous discussion topic, I can say that he is the best example of how our work with offenders can be most effective. As you say, most of the detail of his case has been explored in the public domain so I have no problem talking to you about it."

Alice learned that Campbell had indeed been convicted of violent assault on his partner and early on during his stay in prison had participated in a number of adult education courses. He was fortunate to be paired with an older prisoner who had taken part in a peer-learning training initiative where men serving long sentences were trained as literacy tutors to work with fellow prisoners. Jordi Campbell formed a close bond with this man and learned not just literacy but experienced, for the first time, what it meant to have a caring adult in your life. He seemed transformed by that relationship and by the time he took part in the AHIGE perpetrator programme he appeared ripe for absorbing their message about becoming a different kind of man.

On his release he joined his nearest AHIGE group and became an ardent advocate for alternatives to violence and the men's ongoing campaign against gender-based violence.

"His violent criminal past attracted a lot of attention, and newspaper headlines," said Raoul, "but he spoke openly and made a strong connection with men who were struggling with some of the same demons he had known." Raoul looked intently into Alice's eyes. "I would stake my life on Jordi's innocence in terms of this murder. His whole way of being changed when he became literate and learned about how society had neglected him and mismanaged his childhood. Jordi has formed a whole new set of life goals and things that he is passionate about. He isn't just involved in AHIGE but also in the Catalan independence movement. No movement for change is perfect and there are messy disagreements between members in that movement but, like us, it is egalitarian in its value base and I promise you that Jordi Campbell is no longer a person who sees violence as a solution to difficulties. He is too committed to making things better. I am sure of this."

Alice silenced her inner sceptic and smiled at the sincere man across from her. "Do you know how I might get in touch with Jordi? Or his ex-partner? I would like to talk to both of them if I can manage it." It was worth a try, she thought, although she doubted Raoul would give out private addresses to a total stranger.

"As I told the Mossos about an hour ago, Jordi was booked on the early flight out of Girona to Belfast two days ago. He goes home for a few weeks every so often during the year. His father is still alive and he's been trying to build a new relationship with him. It's a trip that has been planned for months."

And, of course, you've called him, Alice thought, and let him know what's happening here.

"I called earlier and left a message for him to let him know the Mossos were asking after him but I haven't had any response yet. I'll give him your number if that would be of any use."

Alice gave him a card with her contact details.

"Although they are not together any more, his ex-partner Marcella and he still run a tapas bar together in Calella. I'm sure you'd find her there if you dropped by."

Alice recognised the name of a coastal town on the running route that Joan had prepared for her. She might even call by there on her way back to Begur.

They said their goodbyes and promised to stay in touch about the joint youth project.

Outside, Alice sent a quick text to Pradić: **Heads up. Jordan (now Jordi) Campbell is back in Belfast. I'd say the Catalan police have been on to you already. Any info re his location there, or his business here would be useful. Thanks, Z. A**

The reply came instantly: **Yup. It's suddenly got very multinational around here! Z**

There followed an address on the Shankill Road where Jordi's father lived and an image of the interior of a traditional bar with menu and Catalan bunting. Pradić had added a comment: **Bon profit!** Alice had already learned that this was Catalan for 'enjoy your meal' and she smiled at Pradić's multilingual wit.

There were several missed calls from Caroline so she headed back towards the car to return her call as she speculated what the next twist in this fascinating holiday trip would be. Caroline's phone went straight to voicemail and Alice left a message to say she would be back in a few hours and switched her phone off.

CHAPTER 27

The autopsies on Donna Nelson and her two young sons took place in the basement pathology department in the Grosvenor Road police station. Burrows did not take long to travel the two short flights of stairs from the Murder Squad HQ to the underground domain of the Chief Pathologist.

Cynthia Boylan was widely known for her apparent cavalier attitude to those who came, however briefly, into her care but Burrows knew this to be a protective front. On the far too many occasions when he had attended autopsies in her lab, he found her to be respectful and meticulous in what she did. He could not fathom how anyone would choose dissecting dead bodies as their daily work but for those who did he could not begrudge them the odd flippant remark if it helped them to cope. Today's task was particularly onerous in that it involved a mother and her two children aged just two and five.

Despite acknowledging the necessity to gather evidence about their death from the bodies of the deceased, Burrows could not suspend his fragility about the invasive process involved. He moved the hankie soaked in lavender essential oil around in his jacket pocket, passed it reassuringly beneath his nostrils and took up a position at as great a distance from the gurneys holding the three bodies as he could manage. Then notebook and pen in hand, he waited for the procedure to begin.

"Dr Boylan will be a few minutes, DS Burrows," said George, her assistant. "She just got a call from the lab about some of the bloods they collected in Goliath Row. She'll update you when she gets here." He was in his green scrubs and carrying his camera, ready for recording different aspects of the dissecting process. He looked more serious than usual and shook his head at Burrows. "I have boys myself," he said quietly by way of explanation and placed his camera on the side table where his equipment was waiting for the autopsy to begin. "Some days in this job are harder than others," he added.

Burrows just nodded and they stood together in silence for a few minutes, each lost in his own reflections until Cynthia Boylan made her energetic entrance through the swing doors into the lab.

"OK, my men! Let's get going with our day's work. We'll start with the mother and do the children afterwards." She looked from George to Burrows to gauge their response to this and when there was no comment she assumed her position beside the remains of Donna Nelson. "Things may not be as clearcut as we assumed. The forensic lab boys have turned up two different blood groups at the scene – in addition to the victim, that is. We may have a choice of two perps in this one. One is a match for the husband's stored in the Criminal Records Office. No surprises there. The other is a fifty-two per cent match with the deceased and therefore likely to be a sibling. Two sets of prints too so the scene was more crowded than we initially thought."

She raised her eyebrows enquiringly at Burrows. "That make any sense, Bill?"

Burrows muttered an expletive, excused himself, moved out into the corridor for a moment and called McVeigh. "Ian, some incriminating evidence had been turned up by forensics that might link Bull Nelson to the murder scene. Get uniform to pick up Bull and bring him in for additional questioning and send someone round to that gym of his. Look at the CCTV for Tuesday evening and, if the two heavies are there, grill them and get any vehicles taken in for close scrutiny. Also, Ian, have a look at the uniforms' account of Bull's alibi for the Tuesday evening. If he had time to be in Donna's, I want to know about it. I'll be here for a few hours so take Pradić with you to the interview room and see what you can get out of him. I'll join you when I get away from here. The report should be with us any time now. For the moment we haven't anything else to go on but better to have him on the spot and see what he had to say for himself."

"When you're ready, Sarge?" Boylan stood with her scalpel in hand, poised to begin.

Burrows nodded his assent and Boylan switched on her recording machine and began her familiar incantation that would give a full account of the final sad moments of Donna and her boys.

* * *

While Burrows stoically assisted at the three autopsies, Pradić and McVeigh made their way to an interview room in the basement of the Grosvenor Road Station to interview Bull Nelson. Nelson was accompanied this time by his solicitor, a young woman in a sharp pinstripe suit and carrying an expensive, soft-leather document folder.

She stood when they came into the room and introduced herself. "I'm Jane Carruthers, Mr Nelson's solicitor. I hope that we can clear up this misunderstanding as soon as possible and allow my client to return to the task of supporting his parents in their bereavement." She spoke with only a slight hint of a local accent and exuded entitlement in every aspect of her demeanour.

"I am unaware of any misunderstanding, Miss Carruthers," McVeigh responded curtly as he sat down opposite them and spread his notes in front of him. Rather than formal introductions, McVeigh immediately switched on the recording machine and announced, "Friday 18 April 2014 at 12.32pm. Interview in relation to the murder of Donna Nelson and her sons with her brother, Robert Nelson also known as 'Bull'. Present are DC Ian McVeigh, Constable Zara Pradić, Mr Nelson and Mr Nelson's solicitor, Jane Carruthers."

The formality of the situation always introduced a degree of gravity to proceedings and McVeigh had learned to use these moments to the maximum. He fixed Bull Nelson now with his most penetrating stare and spoke calmly and directly.

"Forensic evidence that we have just received in relation to the remains of Donna Nelson and her murder scene has shown that Sammy Marshall was not the only person present on Tuesday evening when she was fatally injured."

Pradić watched Bull carefully and noted the pulsing nerve below his left cheekbone.

"From analysis of samples at the scene," McVeigh continued, "we are able to say that a sibling of Donna's was also present and that blood samples taken at the scene came from that sibling."

Bull Nelson's expression tightened, as he made sure that he registered no obvious response to McVeigh's statement.

"In your statement to the uniformed officers that called at your parents' home on Wednesday, Mr Nelson, you said that you had not seen your sister since Tuesday morning in your parents' house. You said that you had spoken to her on the phone but not been to her house or met her elsewhere."

Nelson remained tensely silent and avoided making eye contact with either of the officers. McVeigh allowed the silence to extend and after some uncomfortable moments, Nelson's solicitor spoke in a condescending manner.

"DC McVeigh, I am wondering if you intend posing any questions to my client or if you expect us to sit here while you make a series of statements. Might I remind you that Mr Nelson has been recently bereaved and that this … this excuse for an interview is a very untimely intrusion on his grief." She all but snorted her disdain for the two officers before her. "It would not be surprising, DC McVeigh, to find evidence of a brother's presence in his sister's house. You would need something much less circumstantial before anyone would consider your assertions as having any merit."

McVeigh was confident about his facts and immediately, and with some satisfaction, he called the solicitor's bluff. "The presence of fresh blood at a murder scene is not quite like the remains of a family tea party, Miss Carruthers. I have, as yet, made no assertions in relation to your client, but the tests to identify siblings through DNA are one hundred per-cent accurate. We are already arranging for a supplementary DNA test to be carried out with Donna and Robert's father that will confirm the family link. Only two offspring are registered to the Nelson family and so we are confident that the second samples gathered at the murder scene must belong to Robert Nelson. I assume that when we are finished here Mr Nelson will also voluntarily provide us with whatever prints and samples we require."

He turned to Pradić now and signalled to her to continue the questioning. She began without any pleasantries.

"What were your movements on the evening of Tuesday the fifteenth of April, Mr Nelson? Let's be quite specific. What were your movements between six and ten o'clock that evening?"

Nelson looked at his solicitor for guidance and she nodded that he should answer. When he spoke, his voice was uncertain and barely audible.

"I'd ask you to speak louder, Mr Nelson, so that the recorder can register your voice," said Pradić. The point of her pen was indicating the sound register on the recording equipment, which was barely responding.

Bull coughed and began again. "As I said before, I ate dinner with my parents and then went out in my car to do some business calls. I have a number of clients who primarily operate in the evenings and so I am often out late. My parents will confirm this."

Pradić made some type of sound in the back of her throat that might have been interpreted as a disparaging response but she also might have been clearing her throat.

"Do you wish to maintain your previously stated position that you did not call to your sister's home in Goliath Row on Tuesday the fifteenth of April?"

Again, Nelson looked at his solicitor. She affirmed that he should continue but it was clear that the police had something on her client and she was losing confidence in the account of events that Nelson had given her.

Nelson nodded and Pradić asked him again to speak audibly so that the recorder would register his response.

"I do!" he said brashly, reached for the plastic glass of water in front of him and drank deeply.

Pradić persisted without hesitation. "I must tell you, Mr Nelson, that data gathered from your phone records suggest that you spent twenty minutes in Goliath Row on Tuesday evening and we know that while you were there Sammy Marshall was also on the premises."

Bull's mouth formed the beginning of an expletive but, before he could articulate anything, his solicitor moved her hand across as if to hold him on the seat.

"I would like to request a break for lunch and a consultation with my client before we proceed with any further questioning." Her tone was less arrogant and she was clearly beginning to realise that she was not in full possession of the facts.

"Interview suspended at the solicitor's request." McVeigh recorded the time, stopped the recording device and he and Pradić withdrew, feeling that they had made some progress.

CHAPTER 28

On her walk back to the car Alice reflected on what she now knew about Jordi Campbell. He seemed to have made a remarkable transformation in his life and she would like to find out more about that. It was useful for her own research but also for the work with the EXIT group. The biggest surprise was that he was actually now in Belfast and not in Catalonia and, as had been originally planned, imminently going to be interviewed by the Mossos, Caroline and herself as interpreter.

She wondered where that left his status as a potential killer of Xavier Duxo. He would still have had time to kill him, go home and clean up and catch the early flight to Belfast from Girona. She was not sure that was a likely scenario and felt mostly inclined to trust Raoul's view that Jordi was no longer someone who sorted out differences of opinion by using violence. She wondered where the collaboration with the Mossos would go, now that the suspect was back in Ireland. Might their holiday be cancelled altogether while Caroline went home to assist the Mossos' investigation of Jordi Campbell or would that be added to Burrows' already overcrowded agenda? She would have to wait to get Caroline's verdict on all that. For now she turned her sights onto Marcella Murray who must have her own fascinating story to tell.

Calella was only a short drive from Begur so Alice made the detour on her return from Girona. Tapas del Mar, referring to both its owner and its proximity to the sea, was in a pedestrianised area of the town that ran alongside the Cami de Ronda, the Costa Brava coastal path that she had already been introduced to by Joan for her morning runs.

Calella was a charming Catalan seaside resort that had managed to preserve its front line from high-rise building and had a pleasant bustle about it. As she made her way to the bar, Alice heard a lot of French being spoken by families around her and deduced that it was a school holiday period in France and this was a popular resort not far from the border.

As she had hoped, Tapas del Mar was empty and the evening rush wouldn't begin for another few hours. She sat up at the bar and waited for the woman who was skilfully slicing a large leg of local cured ham with a large, sharp knife and placing appetising, bite-sized snacks into the chilled display cabinet along the counter. She cleaned the knife and added it to several other impressive knives on a magnetic strip mounted on the wall and, wiping her hands on her apron, she turned and smiled at Alice.

"*Que quieres?*" She asked Alice in Spanish what she would like.

"If you're Marcella, I actually wanted to have a chat with you, if that's possible," Alice said in English, "but I will have a sparkling water and a few tapas while I'm here."

"Yes, I am Marcella. Help yourself," the woman said, indicating the plates at the end of the counter. She still spoke with a significant Belfast accent. "Everything is on some kind of a stick and I'll count what's left on your plate when you finish, to calculate the bill."

Marcella had the tanned complexion of someone who lives in the sun all year round. An impressive scar ran along her left jaw that did not detract in any major way from her open, beautiful face. Jordi's handiwork, Alice deduced, before his ideological reconstruction. Marcella's thick, dark hair was tied back and held on each side with red combs. When she moved, she limped slightly, almost like she was doing a well-practised dance step.

She smiled broadly at Alice as she placed her water in front of her. "You want to talk to me? How mysterious! It's been quite the day of surprises. My brother will be here later this evening but for now I'm on my own so if I get busy I'll have to abandon you … but fire ahead. What do you want to talk about?"

Alice nodded sympathetically. "I'm Alice Fox and I already know a little about those surprises today. I know that you are in business here with Jordi Campbell, your ex-partner, and I know he is in Belfast at the moment."

Marcella registered her surprise at Alice's candid statement but said nothing so Alice continued.

"I'm actually from Massachusetts but I'm working in a college in Belfast for this year and I'm in Begur for a week's holiday with my partner. I've been asked to act as an interpreter in talks between the PSNI and the Mossos d'Esquadra and that's where I learned about Jordi and you and your business. I work with young people, mostly young men, both in the States and in Belfast. They are either in trouble with the law, have been in the past or are likely to be in the future and I like to think I'm on their side, trying to give them a better chance in this very unequal world." Again Alice paused and thought she could see Marcella thaw a little towards her. "I've been talking to AHIGE today and the guy there told me, and the Mossos, that Jordi was in Belfast. The youth group I work with in Belfast is interested in working with AHIGE to learn about their courses and how they support men to become less invested in violent behaviours. I'm impressed at what I hear about Jordi turning his life around and I want to know more about that."

"So, if you know Jordi is back in the North, and it's him you're interested in, how come you're here wanting to talk to me?" The smart, defiant character of a street-smart Belfast kid flashed at Alice from behind the smiling face of Marcella Murray.

"Good question, Marcella," Alice said with a smile and they both laughed.

"Neither Jordi nor I are the greenhorns we used to be. He is not the only one who has learned a thing or two since we discovered Catalonia and made a new start here."

Alice could feel Marcella sizing her up and she met her appraising look without wavering. "I do want to talk to Jordi whenever I can but I am also interested in your side of things. It's unusual for someone who has been hurt by a partner to still be working with them almost every day. I am curious about how that came about. To explain why, I suppose I can tell you a bit about my own story." She paused, sipped her water and looked directly at Marcella. "I used to be a cop in Lowell, Massachusetts. My father was a cop too and my brother is a firefighter. That will give you an idea of the kind of family we were. My dad was killed in a car smash where the other driver was a young man high on drugs and – short version – I took part in a restorative justice project where I had to listen to that young man's side of things.

It was life-changing. I left the police force and went back to study and I am interested in how we can make the justice system fit people's real lives better than it does now."

Marcella laughed a little ironically. "You really should be talking to Jordi. He loves all that stuff and he has strong opinions on it too. I've always been the practical one – trying to keep the wolf from the door, make sure we had the rent money – and that kind of thing. Even before he caught up on all the missed schooling, Jordi was the one with the longing for things to be different."

Alice nodded her head several times in rapid succession to show she was gripped by the woman's words.

"It's actually amazing how much both Jordi and I have changed since back in the day. The teenage me was like most girls of that age … easily drawn into romantic notions of a future away from the horrors of life on the Shankill. There was a lot going on in the North then and we didn't have anything resembling a normal life. I was always a bit fascinated by him, even when we were teenagers, before he killed Maudie Prior. Other people thought he was some kind of monster but I could see he wasn't able to explain himself. His eyes were wild with all sorts of messages but he didn't have the words to articulate things."

Alice could see she was caught back in the past now and waited quietly for her to continue.

After a few moments Marcella sighed deeply and wiped at the counter surface with a clean cloth. It was clear she was someone who kept busy and maybe liked the undemanding day-to-day exchanges across the counter with customers. Jordi was perhaps the more complex character.

"He had a very rough time as a young fella," Marcella continued.

"He has had to work hard to overcome all that. I have had some work to do too, especially after the last time he hit out at me and I had to have my jaw and my leg rebuilt." She touched her scar gently and again was pulled towards the past. "We nearly lost the business but some women friends here stepped in and helped me get things back on track. My brother, Kyle, has always been there for me too. He left Belfast as soon as he could and he has been my rock. Jordi was in prison by then and the trial had been a complete nightmare. I wasn't long out of hospital and still hadn't much use of my jaw. I was only able to manage liquidised food through a straw and I had a leg and wrist in plaster."

Alice winced at the extent of Marcella's injuries.

"You're probably wondering why I continued to have anything to do with someone who treated me like that. People are always surprised when women go back to men that have abused them but it happens a lot. Maybe we're too conditioned and can't imagine life without them even though their presence can be almost entirely negative. Anyway it's complicated." She looked inquisitively at Alice, trying to gauge where she stood.

"He had caused you a lot of hurt, Marcella, and not just physical I'm sure. The worst wounds are often the ones that can't be seen."

"That's true but we had come a long way and I wasn't done with him, even then when he had hurt me repeatedly. I went ahead with the charges against him because he deserved that. He needed to see that violence makes nothing any better and I needed to finally find my self-respect and stop believing that I owed him anything. Not loyalty, or love or even kindness."

She wiped away the tears that suddenly welled in her eyes. Alice responded quietly.

"It actually sounds to me as if you did him a favour. He needed intensive support and sometimes prison is the unlikely place that such help is made available."

Marcella smiled. After all this time she still showed her relief at not being judged harshly. She continued her story with determination.

"I waited for over a year before I went to see him. He was in jail up near the French border and I had no car then. Kyle had his motorbike but he needed to look after the bar when I wasn't there. It was a trek in the bus to get there but that's not what stopped me. I was so angry and disappointed in him that I wouldn't have been able to speak to him. I was busy trying to keep the bar going during the season and I got counselling through the court system here and that kept me sane. Eventually, like yourself, Alice, we got into a process of restorative justice that lasted several years. We both had a lot of hurts and harms to bring to the table. I don't think that many men are able to make the changes that Jordi has but, once he filled in some of his other gaps, he was able to actually manage his anger. He learned alternative ways of coping. "

Marcella looked tired with the effort of retelling her story but Alice did not break the silence between them. The sound of holidaymakers calling to each other outside was incongruous against the sombre mood inside the bar. Marcella sighed deeply and finished her account with what sounded like resignation.

"I decided eventually that even though I loved him I would never take him back as a lover. I would not be able to repair the damage to my trust in him. He had to accept that. We are friends now and I can't believe the progress he has made. It makes me really happy that he has overcome so much but my faith in him will always be limited. Does that make sense?"

"It surely does." Alice felt great respect for this woman who had managed to rebuild both her business and her friendship with her abuser, in a foreign country, far from home and family. She was conscious too that Marcella, who probably knew him better than anyone else, would not give him her unmitigated trust. "It sounds as if you have both made massive changes in your lives and somehow kept a relationship going despite everything, against insuperable odds. I'd say that is a very rare achievement and speaks volumes about your generosity and determination."

Marcella shrugged her shoulders and accepted the praise without any hint of triumphalism. She went back to her organisation of things behind the bar.

Alice stood up and reached for a small plate from the far end of the bar. She helped herself to some tapas from the display case in front of her.

"Marcella, do you know this guy Xavier Duxo, who was killed the other night after the event in Verges?" Alice watched her reaction to the man's name, which was one of barely concealed distaste.

"I'm afraid I did know him." She grimaced. "He is well known locally as a member of a right-wing group called Vox. They are very vocal in their opposition to Catalan independence amongst other things. In fact they are committed to ending the autonomous status of Catalonia if they come into power."

Alice had noted the Catalan flags that decorated Tapas del Mar and assumed that Duxo had found several reasons to be at odds with this feisty woman who had come from another country and who clearly supported independence.

"As I told the Mossos, Jordi was actually trying to build some kind of relationship with Duxo. I thought he was being naïve but he recognised something of his old self in him and thought he could reason with him about becoming a different kind of man. Duxo has form for violence against both men and women and he didn't take kindly to someone from Ireland telling him what was what – but Jordi was like a dog with a bone."

Her laughter maybe lacked conviction, Alice thought.

"You know what converts are like," Marcella said. "They preach with much greater passion than those of us who are not such recent arrivals at the party."

"I can be guilty of that myself," Alice replied, recognising some of her own tendencies for enthusiastic proselytising in the accounts of Jordi Campbell.

"Look, Alice, Xavier Duxo was a bad lot. His own mother would have a hard time finding something to like about him. He certainly had brothers and cousins who didn't share his political enthusiasms. Last time he was here I told him not to come back again after he picked a fight with two Romanian guys who did some of the heavy lifting here when Jordi wasn't about. He accused them of taking Spanish jobs from Spanish people when I know for a fact he rarely did a genuine day's work. He's been agitating to get back into the bar and I didn't want that under any circumstances. He has threatened me in the past and I didn't want him any where near me, or the bar. For that reason, I didn't want Jordi making friends with him and I told him as much. I guess that's why he met him some distance away. Now the Mossos have him in their sights and he'll have to talk his way out of that now too. I knew him having anything to do with Duxo would lead to grief one way or another."

Alice absorbed this outburst against Xavier Duxo, surprised by the depth of the woman's feelings against him and wondering if she and Jordi had fallen out about it before he headed back to Ireland.

An English couple had come into the bar and taken a table by the window. "Sorry, Alice, I'll have to get back to work here. Nice talking to you. I'll let Jordi know you called."

Alice left a card with her contact details and made her way back to the car, wondering how many others shared Marcella Murray's deep dislike of Xavier Duxo. It was ironic, she thought, that with so many people against him, the man who was apparently trying to befriend him was now the number one suspect in his murder.

CHAPTER 29

When Constable Zara Pradić returned to her workstation there were a number of flashing lights. They signalled that she had received messages on certain networks where she had requested alerts to new activity matching particular criteria. These included new posts in the Belfast locality about violence against women, data and/or proposed actions against femicide, reference to men held captive for alleged crimes against women and mentions of the forthcoming Reclaim the Night March in Belfast the following day. Pradić hoped earnestly that Marshall was being held by some pro-feminist activists but she was prepared to be wrong and also had eyes on Loyalist and Republican extremists who might wish to use Marshall for less worthy political motives.

She understood that the vast territory occupied by the Internet could not be kept under surveillance by a single individual and so she was a member of various collectives that supported each other in their tracking activities. Searching for the needle in the digital haystack was a nerd's idea of a good time. Not all of them were completely legitimate in their approach to scrutinising private accounts but they got rapid results and sometimes that was just what Zara needed. It was a mutually supportive grouping and they fed each other challenging opportunities whenever they could. Early feedback suggested that her hunch was correct and that those holding Marshall wanted to provoke attention to the seemingly low state priority area, in fact the often fatal neglect of harm done to women.

Early in the afternoon, a statement had been posted on the Internet that went viral within minutes. It was headed **Good Friday Agreement Plus – Ending Harms Against Women**. The text was brief but clear in its meaning. It read:

Exactly sixteen years on from the signing of the Good Friday Agreement in Ireland, while a welcome peace process is taking hold, the record of governments in both parts of the country, in tackling all forms of violence against women, is abysmal. We ask for evidence and comment supporting this assertion of neglect to be made public throughout the next twenty-four hours by women's groups and others active in this area. At the same time we call on government representatives to account for their poor record and give undertakings as to their intentions to do better. Our fight is with systems rather than any individual perpetrator.

Sammy Marshall is safe and being well looked after and will be handed over to the PSNI in due course. But will that ensure that justice is done?

NO MORE PATRIARCHY! Enough patriarchal harm to women and girls, boys and men. Enough male violence. We can do better than this!

The message was signed with the initials 'NMP' followed by a palm-print coloured orange and green in equal parts. Acronyms were a familiar element in Northern Ireland politics and it was a moment before Pradić realised that this was not one of the usual references to the pope or to Protestants but an abbreviation of the kidnappers' No More Patriarchy slogan. She smiled at the ingenuity of these people. She suspected that they were probably all women.

As might have been predicted, the statement was encrypted and entirely untraceable. It had been bounced practically around the globe and there would be no chance of tracking down the source. Pradić disseminated the text to her colleagues and settled down to see what the response from the wider media might be. She didn't have to wait long.

* * *

Burrows had returned from the post-mortems and his phone rang within seconds of the message being disseminated. He subsequently reported that DS McCluskey was very clear in his response to the communication about the kidnapping. In fact McCluskey had practically exploded in Burrows' ear.

"Find Marshall and shut this circus down immediately! This is a murder inquiry not a bloody soap opera. We will need to make a statement saying that this is not the way to go about achieving social change. They may think that they are capturing people's attention but if Marshall does any more damage, we will be the ones hauled over the coals in the media. Find these crackpots, bring them to book and put the lid back on this can of bloody worms!"

In a slightly calmer tone, McCluskey had also informed Burrows that he wanted Jordi Campbell brought in at ten o'clock on Saturday morning for questioning. He said that Dr Alice Fox had already been acting as interpreter between the Catalan police and DI Paton and he planned to arrange for her to continue this role in Belfast. The Mossos had opted for a video call and they might then ask for a further interview with Campbell on his return to Girona on Monday.

When Burrows informed Pradić that she would be needed to interview Campbell, possibly with Alice Fox the following day, she wasn't at all surprised and smiled at how slow her hotshot detective colleagues were to see what was under their noses.

Meanwhile, on social media, Pradić constantly scanned the flood of comments in response to NMP for any insights they might give on Marshall's whereabouts. There were none apparent as yet and her contacts confirmed that view. It was too easy to remain anonymous online nowadays and it was unlikely that the hostage-takers would reveal themselves in their posts.

The fact that some pro-feminists were holding Marshall hostage, to highlight their concerns about the increases in harm done to women, had rapidly captured the attention of people. Interest was peaked not only in Ireland but much further afield. The action of taking an alleged woman-killer hostage had tapped into a deep well of impatience globally with all things patriarchal. Pradić was not easily overwhelmed but in this case, the magnitude of the Internet attention was truly astounding and not unsatisfying. She hastily drew up a new, tighter list of criteria for her fellow net-watchers to apply to their viewing and settled back to scan the posts to date.

There were those of a very rudimentary nature that asked, "And what is patriarchy anyway?" immediately accomplishing the kidnappers' goal of beginning a public conversation about the very roots of violence against women. The number of people, in Ireland and beyond, coming to grips with a new 'P' word was not insignificant. The media had immediately taken on the educational task and was full of verbal explanations, cartoons, links to YouTube videos and more. Pradić could imagine families sitting down to Friday evening fish and chips debating the meaning of NMP and its relevance to their lives. She found it hard not to smile at the images conjured up in her mind but then she realised that there was an expectation that she would be doing everything she could to locate the offenders and she became suitably subdued.

As Pradić had anticipated, opinion was divided on the issue of holding someone captive, irrespective of the circumstances. For some, the illegality of the action made it wrong, regardless of the cause. Nevertheless, a surprising number of people, women and men, thought that as the State did relatively little to protect women against male violence, the action designed to create dialogue was at least understandable if not admirably creative. There were startling statements of statistics about all forms of harms done to women close to home and further afield.

The European Institute for Gender Equality (EIGE) highlighted their comprehensive report published only the previous month and gave a few shocking quotes from the Europe-wide findings. They had surveyed forty-two thousand women aged eighteen to seventy-four across all twenty-eight EU member states and the results had initially caused a flurry of well-intentioned promises of action.

Even Pradić, who considered that she was savvy about violence, was shocked at the evidence that just over one in five women reported that they had experienced physical or sexual violence from a current or previous partner. The patterns across all twenty-eight EU countries told the same story and, whilst not commenting on the hostage situation, EIGE called for all member states to end their lethargy in relation to this issue.

Broadcasters and bloggers and members of the public who wanted an easy piece of information to hold on to, in commenting on the hostage situation, latched onto the one-in-five statistic. Within hours it was written and painted on walls and windows, along with a stencilled circle with a cross on the outer lower edge. This was the scientific sign for a woman and widely used by feminists as an icon. Leaflets and posters were produced and distributed in the streets and at Easter events. Throughout Ireland, recent research was discussed across the media and local women's and men's groups, that were active in the field of violence against women, were brought onto radio and TV discussions to explain the local situation.

The timing of the capture to coincide with the anniversary of the Good Friday Agreement was taken up by many who felt aggrieved at the dysfunctional record of the NI Assembly. The Executive was based on mandatory power sharing and old sectarian divides surfaced frequently in the day-to-day business of attempts at democratic government. Time spent on tribal bickering left many problematic aspects of the social infrastructure neglected and, although sectarian violence was mostly a thing of the past, violence against women remained as a durable and relatively unpunished atrocity. Elected representatives were asked to account for the lack of funding, services and awareness training about sexual and domestic violence.

On a personal level, more women began to speak out about their experiences. A tide of heartrending stories was unleashed that filled the airwaves and social media and added instant credibility to the new wave of discussions about gender inequality.

The arguments raged. Could the kidnappers be trusted to release the man to the police unharmed, as they promised? He hadn't been charged or found guilty of anything and didn't deserve this infringement of his human rights. Each position ignited another. Would any man be safe if women took the law into their own hands? How come there was outrage about one man being retained, allegedly in safety and well looked after, and women could be beaten and killed with a fairly negligible response?

The Irish mother came in for her share of blame too. She spoiled her sons, waited on them hand and foot and encultured them into expectations of women which were untenable, particularly in times where women worked outside the home almost as much as men. After work, research showed that women did a 'second shift' that meant they also took responsibility for the work that needed to be done in the domestic sphere even though both partners worked outside the home.

As well as all the doom and gloom, Pradić noted that there were rays of hope in the posts from men talking about being allies of women in the struggle against male violence. They called for the focus to move from women needing to change and become about men facing up to their need to find different ways of being masculine in the world.

In all of these posts that came from the island of Ireland there was a call for groups to mobilise and attend the Reclaim the Night March on Easter Saturday. Pradić emailed colleagues who she knew were preparing to police the forthcoming march and alerted them to these indications that there would be significant traffic issues and that the gathering itself would bring the city centre to a complete standstill. The prospect of a massive turnout to the march made her personally happy even though it produced a policing challenge about which she needed to provide evidence for her colleagues.

What was interesting was that there was no obvious coordinating point to any of this. Existing women's networks were stepping in and assuming responsibility. They were able to use extensive mailing lists and the word about the Saturday protest march was passed around the country with the flick of a switch. There were volunteers to act as stewards, drummers and banners made available, transport being organised and women making their availability to speak to the media known. Others had already been contacted by chat shows and special current affairs discussion programmes and were sharing the information across existing networks. What was clear was that the hostage-takers had succeeded in capturing the attention of those already committed to ending violence against women. Pradić could see that these numbers would swell with the additional coverage that seemed to be forthcoming in the time up to the march. To what extent they would succeed in extracting information or a meaningful promise from lawmakers and funders was another question.

As she reflected on all this Pradić was putting together a short report that Burrows could draw on in the evening press conference. She knew he wouldn't get pulled into discussing the core issue but he would be better prepared if he knew the range of opinion and the extent of the interest out there. He needed to appear knowledgeable and empathetic both to the family of the murder victims as well as those impacted by the core issue of gender-based violence.

And then this was only what was reported on the Internet. The print and visual media were clamouring for comment from the Murder Squad about what was happening. Burrows instructed those fielding the calls to say that the early evening press conference would respond to all these matters. He hoped that this would indeed be possible although they were making slow headway despite all PSNI stations throughout the north being on the lookout for possible locations where a hostage might be secreted. The territory was such that this was an almost impossible task. There had been no signal from

Marshall's phone since he had been taken from his parents' home the previous day and to date they had received no useful information in response to a call for people to contact a confidential telephone number. On the contrary, it was possible that there was a great deal of misinformation being sent through in an effort to confuse things even further. The organisers of this affair had come up with a strategy that made tracking them seemingly impossible.

"Maybe we should just focus on Bull Nelson for now and deal with Marshall when they hand him over." McVeigh said this quietly to Burrows as they took five minutes to eat a filled roll that Eileen from the canteen had been inspired to deliver to their desks. He could read the pressure on Burrow's brow and was looking for any ray of hope to put in his direction. "Nelson's car and the one used by his henchmen are both over with forensics for a thorough scrutinise. The uniforms questioned the men who were quite cocky so we'll wait to see if anything turns up in the car and then bring them in."

Burrows felt quite weighed down. "All we needed was this Jordi Campbell issue to be landed on our plates as well as a triple murder with sizeable complications." He ran his hand across his balding head and gazed at his palm as if expecting some loose human matter to have lodged there. He sighed deeply and smiled at his young colleague. "I just keep thinking that it's like digging a hole in the garden. Sometimes the earth you've just removed falls back in again and seems to set you back but with perseverance it all comes right in the end."

McVeigh nodded more enthusiastically than he actually felt and placed the last piece of his roll in his mouth.

"Let's dig holes," Burrows said as he stood and led the way back to the interview room where Nelson and his solicitor were waiting.

CHAPTER 30

When Alice returned from her visits to Girona and Calella, Caroline was sitting on the terrace of their hotel room, drinking coffee and reading files on her laptop.

Caroline smiled broadly and said, "There you are!" as she opened her arms and raised her face expectantly to be kissed. "There've been some developments here … we need to talk."

Alice pulled the second reclining chair over beside Caroline and stretched out, kicking off her shoes and pulling at the end of her socks so that her toes felt free. "OK. Let's hear the latest in the saga of the very surprising un-holiday in Begur. I am prepared for anything, I think." She reached for an orange in a bowl on the small table and began to peel it. "I'm all ears," she said earnestly.

"That's good." Caroline laughed a little nervously. "I won't beat about the bush so." She took a deep breath and looked steadily at her partner. "I've had the Super on the phone with a suggested change of plan. Now that Jordi Campbell has turned up in Belfast there has been a shift in how to accommodate the Mossos' request for help. McCluskey thinks it's appropriate that this support comes from the Murder Squad based in Belfast."

Alice tried not to leap ahead and tried to listen as Caroline revealed the latest twist in their holiday plans. Her discussions with AHIGE and Marcella Murray meant that she was actually engaged in the investigation now so she didn't mind if the holiday was put on hold.

"I can see that makes sense," she said, making it easier for Caroline who visibly relaxed.

"He suggested that I fly home and continue the contact with the Mossos from there." She paused to gauge Alice's response to that idea.

Alice maintained her calm expression to show she was open to all suggestions.

"I said to him that I didn't agree with the idea of my flying back as it would disrupt the murder investigation and it might seem as if he didn't have confidence in Burrows to complete the task."

Alice wasn't sure now where this was going and decided to interject. "If it's of any use, from my meetings with AHIGE and Jordi Campbell's ex-wife and current business partner, I would say it's quite unlikely that Jordi is the person who killed Xavier Duxo. The role of the Murder Squad might be smaller than anticipated if a new suspect comes to light between then and now." She waited to see how that view played into the forthcoming plan.

Caroline was nodding in agreement. "Well, McCluskey agreed that it was a bad idea for me to queer Burrows' pitch, so to speak," and she smiled mischievously at her own choice of words. "In fact, he thought it would be better if you went, Alice. Officially you would be the interpreter there to assist the Squad provide the promised support to the Mossos."

Alice was taken aback by this turn of events and her forehead wrinkled in surprise.

"Think about it," Caroline prompted. "Pradić and you can interview Campbell and allow Burrows and McVeigh to concentrate on the murder inquiry. I can be available on video if there is any issue to be resolved. You can also be the interpreter between the Mossos and the Murder Squad during the interview and in any discussions afterwards. My understanding is that Campbell has a return flight booked for Monday and there will be an opportunity for another interview here if the Mossos deem it necessary."

Caroline closely watched Alice's reaction to this proposal and was relieved when her eyes showed she wasn't opposed to the idea.

"I guess that could work," Alice said. "It would also mean that I could attend the Reclaim the Night March with the EXIT group which I would really like to do." She twisted a strand of blonde hair around her finger and smiled at Caroline. "I could come back on Monday and maybe we could start our holiday again." In her head she began planning what she would need for a two-day trip to Belfast.

"Sounds like a plan to me," said Caroline. "I'll get Pradić to do your flight bookings and then we'll have a chat with the Mossos and let them know what's happening. You can fly from Girona to Belfast direct tonight and that will give you time to interview Campbell and be with the EXIT group by mid afternoon. How does that sound?"

"Fine," said Alice who was wondering if she should phone Hugo or just surprise them all with her arrival. She opted for the latter in case the interview dragged on or there were complications. Better not to disappoint.

Alice glanced at her phone and saw an alert for a WhatsApp message from Pradić. Caroline was already busy calling McCluskey to update him and Alice opened Pradić's message.

Rapid developments here. Initial contact from Marshall's kidnappers demanding engagement from government around Violence Against Women. Wider response growing by the minute. Also – seems that Jordi Campbell and Sammy Marshall were at school together. Interesting.

CHAPTER 31

There was a decidedly different atmosphere in the interview room when Burrows and McVeigh made their way there after their very late and hurried lunch. Burrows was feeling a little indigestion and rubbing his chest.

Jane Carruthers was looking less confident about her position and Bull Nelson had assumed a hardened expression that suggested he was not planning to cooperate with her or anybody else.

Burrows had seen it all before. A solicitor assured of a generous fee, for what she has been told is a mere misunderstanding, discovers her client is lying through his teeth and things begin to get very uncomfortable. *If you lie down with dogs you get up with fleas*, Burrows thought, remembering one of his father's frequent comments as he and McVeigh took their places and prepared to restart the recording device.

The fact that Burrows was replacing Pradić added to the influential weight of the interviewing team. When Burrows met with Bull the previous evening he had found him to be reticent and decidedly tense. The experienced detective had put that down to the grief and the stress of having to ID your sister and nephews and at the same time trying to hold your self together. Now it was clear that Bull had also been worried that Burrows might discover he had more to hide than his fragile masculinity.

Burrows started the recording device.

"Interview with Robert, alias Bull Nelson, on Friday 14th April 2014, resumed at sixteen twenty hours. Present are Mr Nelson and his solicitor Jane Carruthers, DC Ian McVeigh and DS Bill Burrows in the chair." Burrows paused and looked enquiringly at Bull and his somewhat crestfallen legal representative. "Mr Nelson, when you spoke with my colleagues earlier there seemed to be some miscommunication between you and Miss Carruthers. I expect you have had time to sort that out now and will stop wasting police time and explain your movements on the night of the murder of your family members."

Jane Carruthers looked expectantly at Bull and waited for him to make the response that they had agreed during the pause between the interviews. Nelson remained mulishly silent. He rolled his eyes upwards, clamped his lips together and examined the yellowing ceiling that had not been repainted in the seven years since the smoking ban in workplaces had been introduced.

"Let me phrase that a little differently," Burrows continued reasonably. "When was the last time you were in Donna's house in Goliath Row?"

The nerve in Bull Nelson's cheek twitched and he moved his lips back and forward as if trying to remember how speech was actually produced. This quest produced no results.

Burrows persisted. "As well as telephone trace records, which might arguably be inconclusive in terms of your actual presence in Donna's house on Tuesday evening, the blood samples collected give us to believe that you were actually there in person. Furthermore, the other forensic evidence suggests that you were at least present, and in all likelihood an active agent in your sister's killing."

Bull's body shuddered involuntarily as he struggled to suppress any visible response to Burrows' questions. Beside him, his solicitor looked almost helpless as she tried to maintain a blank expression even though the proceedings were taking a turn that was clearly not to her liking.

Burrows allowed the silence to continue uninterrupted for an uncomfortable amount of time, as both Nelson and Jane Carruthers sat immobile and looking decidedly awkward.

Finally the solicitor attempted to salvage some face and made a somewhat insincere plea on behalf of her client.

"Detective Sergeant," she intoned rather sweetly, "I think we can agree that my client has suffered a huge emotional upset in the death of three of his family members. He is clearly much too distressed to be subjected to your insensitive grilling in this time of personal trauma for him. I would like to request that we defer this interview to a more appropriate time and allow Mr Nelson to sufficiently be able to support your inquiry in the way that he would wish to."

As this request was delivered, even Bull Nelson found it difficult to react appropriately. Carruthers' audacity beggared belief and yet both detectives understood it as a vain attempt to salvage something from the situation and perhaps ensure some fee would be forthcoming.

Burrows played along, conscious of counteracting any claim of insensitivity on the part of the Squad. "I can assure Mr Nelson that we are extremely sympathetic to his loss and our intention is to do right by his family in bringing the perpetrator, or perpetrators, of this truly heinous triple murder to justice. That is our goal and we will do our utmost to deliver on it, as I'm sure Mr Nelson would wish. So Mr Nelson will remain in custody until he responds to our questions."

Carruthers' expression was one of not unexpected defeat and she nodded half-heartedly and studied her silver fountain pen intently. Bull's head was bent so low now that his expression was not visible.

"At the same time, Ms Carruthers, you will understand that until the presence of Mr Nelson's blood and prints at the scene of the murder and the indication from his phone records that he was in the precise area at the time is satisfactorily explained, we will be holding him in custody." He looked at Bull. "When you are ready to talk to us, Mr Nelson, we will be happy to hear your explanation. In the meantime, you will understand that we must devote our energies to more productive areas of evidence."

Burrows and McVeigh ended the recording and stood to leave. McVeigh told the uniformed man outside the interview room that Nelson was to be moved to a holding cell and Jane Carruthers gathered her papers and preceded her client out of the room.

Burrows stopped by the front desk and asked the man on duty to doublecheck that DNA, prints and blood samples had been taken from Nelson along with photos of any cuts on his hands and face. He asked for the results to be returned to the Murder Squad as soon as possible.

"Now, Ian," he rested his hand on his young colleague's shoulder, "before I accompany DS McCluskey to the press conference, let's have a well-earned cuppa and see where Pradić has got to in her surveillance of the brave new world of the Internet."

* * *

While Sammy Marshall reviewed his strange day as a captive of the two young body-builders with the animal masks, Bull Nelson contemplated his own bleak surroundings. He had been taken to a holding cell in the Grosvenor Road Station and placed on suicide watch as a matter of course. There was no way that Burrows was going to risk losing another suspect at this stage. He could see that Nelson was so tightly wound that he was capable of anything. His belt and shoelaces had been removed and the cell furnishings amounted to a wooden platform on which he could lie and a stainless steel toilet fixed to the wall in the corner. The smell was nauseating.

Not very far away, Sammy was also feeling immersed in a darkness of his own making. His hands were still wrapped securely and he had been given tea and toast for breakfast and then placed on a hard chair in front of a screen loaded with a series of videos. It was as if he'd been at some kind of a tortuous college course for the day and he had never been one who was open to learning.

The men had explained that they were not going to hurt him. They were just passing the time with him and then he would eventually be handed over to the police. He was to think of this as a small detour for him on his way into the justice system and in the meantime his kidnap was being used to stimulate discussion about violence against women.

"You might as well make some good use of your time here so we've prepared some educational materials for you. We've stuff to do so we won't be spending much time with you but don't even think about trying to get out. This place is a fortress and actually you're safer here than out in the open. You're public enemy number one and you might get a nasty shock at what social media are suggesting should be done with you."

And they had chuckled to themselves.

"In actual fact, Matey, you may even come to think of your time with us as a bit of a gift."

And they'd gone and left him with a remote control, a bottle of water and a metal cup.

His viewing had been a variety of recordings of women talking about their experiences of domestic violence, sexual assault and various forms of harassment by men. Sammy had struggled to avoid engaging with the content but it made uncomfortable watching and he found himself increasingly horrified by the reality of his own actions. He was just about to switch it off when a series of discussions between groups of men had kicked in. They were ordinary-looking guys and, despite himself, he had been drawn into listening to what they were saying. It was as if they were talking about his life and he had started thinking about Donna and the kids and Bull and the time he had spent with him. He had made a real mess of his life, he thought, and the sense of living in a nightmare intensified. He sat with his head in his hands and tried to shake off the image of Riley's puzzled look as his own father, covered with the blood of his mother, began to lower a pillow over his face.

Sammy felt a wave of nausea and began to pace the room in a frenzied manner. A pervasive panic coupled with a sense of choking on his own breath left him gasping and banging his head off the painted brick wall in a frantic act of self-hatred. As he slid down the blood-smeared wall an all-enveloping blackness finally gave him the release he was craving.

* * *

As night fell and the sky darkened, the slamming back of several heavy bolts roused Marshall and his captors returned carrying a filled baguette and a bag of apples. They were unfazed as they registered their captive's obvious distress and lifted him onto the chair.

One man examined his injuries not unsympathetically and commented almost kindly. "I see the viewing gave you some food for thought, Sammy."

As they opened a first aid kit and began to wipe his wounds, Sammy noted that the bigger guy had a smear of pillarbox-red paint on the palm of one of his hands and he picked up the tang of white spirits. Very strange, Marshall thought, that he had been doing some home décor at the same time as holding a killer hostage from the police.

CHAPTER 32

As Alice waited for Caroline to collect the car from the Hotel Aiguaclara carpark around the corner, she sat in the foyer and reviewed what they had been reading before it was time to leave.

The two women had looked at the detail that the Mossos had sent on Jordi Campbell's convictions in Catalonia. His attack on Marcella had severe consequences. She had fallen awkwardly and after the damage caused to her hip she had been obliged to learn to walk again. She had a steel plate in her lower leg to hold it together after multiple breakages. As Alice had deduced, he was also responsible for the scar on her face.

The detail of Campbell's second recorded violent attack, this time on a woman who had been his friend and lover for years, was such that Caroline had seriously questioned the solidity of his reformation. "I doubt that was the first time he had hurt her – just the first time the authorities here became aware of it."

Alice was also shaken in her earlier conviction about Campbell's absolute innocence and the credibility of his rehabilitation but she determined to keep an open mind until she spoke to him the following day.

Caroline articulated what they both were thinking. "It would be unusual to move from no violence to such a brutal attack. I'm sure there had been violent behaviour in the relationship before this."

Alice reflected and wondered if she was being foolish to hold on to her conviction that change was possible. She thought that the crucial factor here was that Campbell had actually been through a holistic process of change, not just a single perp programme that could leave the participant impassive and unaffected.

"It's important to remember that Campbell's issues had never been addressed. That only happened when he was in prison in Spain and so I think we can be pretty sure that Marcella Murray has experienced his frustration on occasions before this most devastating tale of aggression took place."

While she abhorred the trauma Campbell had caused to Marcella, Alice was also conscious of the chaos and hurt in him that had contributed to his behaviour in his most intimate relationship.

The Mossos' file that Alice and Caroline read detailed the injuries caused to Marcella and her testimony to the police had been clear and uncompromising. Some members of Marcella's family had been visiting at the time of the attack and, while they were mostly staying in a B&B nearby, her brother Kyle was staying in Jordi and Marcella's two-bed-roomed flat and had totally corroborated his sister's evidence.

Their telephone conversation with the Mossos had been brief. They reported that they were following up on some other conflicts that Xavier Duxo was known to be involved in and were happy to wait for the outcome of the video interview in Belfast the following day before taking up the possibility of speaking directly to Jordi Campbell on his return. They had confirmed airline records that Campbell was due to return to Girona on Monday and they could probably wait to talk to him then if he was still of interest. Alice considered the likelihood that she and Campbell might well be travelling together and wondered how she would manage that.

The honking of a horn outside interrupted her reflections. She shouldered her small backpack and went out to make the forty-minute journey to Girona Airport. Her head was full of detail about the two murders but she would keep them to herself until they made more sense to her. Maybe Jordi Campbell would provide some of the answers she was looking for about the Belfast case but she needed to delay talking to him about those things until after her role as interpreter in the interview in the Murder Squad HQ the following day was finished.

* * *

In the small Girona Airport departures' lounge, Alice reviewed a series of emails and texts from Pradić who, at Caroline's suggestion, was keeping her in the loop about what was going on back in Belfast. She could understand that Caroline didn't want to crowd Burrow's investigation but she suspected that through her own closer involvement, Caroline also became involved by proxy. She would have to be careful about that and not become a stooge for the absentee Detective Inspector or her anxious Chief Superintendent. She would adhere to her role as interpreter and preserve her distance in that way. At the same time, she had respect for Burrows and McVeigh and she was increasingly admiring of the skills that Zara Pradić brought to the Murder Squad. She would see how things were on her return in just a few short hours and manage her participation accordingly. She saved the report about the Belfast case and Pradić's findings about Xavier Duxo and Marcella Murray to her documents file to read on the flight.

The potential explanations to both cases were churning around in Alice's head. She took out the small notebook she always carried with her and began to formulate some questions for herself.

How did Jordi Campbell and Marcella Murray meet when they were teenagers living in Belfast? If there was a link between Campbell and Sammy Marshall going back several decades, was there also a link between Marcella Murray and Marshall or Marshall's deceased wife?

Was Marcella Murray's brother, Kyle, who had been in the apartment the night that Jordi broke her jaw and her leg, a person of interest? How had his contact with Jordi evolved since he had become a reformed character? Were they on good terms? Had he any connection to Sammy Marshall or Bull Nelson? There had been several mentions of Kyle as a constant, protective presence in Marcella's life and Alice wanted to know more about that.

What was the true nature of Bull Nelson's relationship with his sister and her husband? Did he have any contact with Jordi Campbell back in the day or with Campbell's father then or now? They lived in a close-knit community and if they knew each other when they were younger, it wouldn't be unusual for there still to be connections between them.

Was there any link between VOX and Loyalist extremists in the north of Ireland? VOX wanted to stop the disruption of Spanish unity whereas Loyalists wanted to preserve links with the British union and oppose Irish unity. These seemingly different goals had somehow a common political thread, Alice thought, in that both wanted to preserve the status quo.

Finally, she thought, both the Catalan and Irish crimes had links to violence against women. In the case of Xavier Duxo both the victim and the suspect had convictions for domestic violence. In Belfast, an ex-partner and a family member were suspects in the killing of Donna Nelson and her children in their own home. Was male violence the only common factor? Was the common factor as much about 'why?' as 'who?'?

There appeared to be a growing connection between the murder in Verges and the triple murder in Belfast's Shankill Road. It wasn't just that both seemed to be an extreme expression of male violence because, in fact, a woman might have committed the murder in Catalonia. Xavier Duxo sounded like the kind of man who might have enraged a large number of people. The Mossos knew him for previous misdemeanours related to his right-wing politics and Alice hoped the information from Pradić would be illuminating in that regard. Marcella Murray had told her the story of his aggression towards some men who had worked for her and that had caused her to exclude him from Tapas del Mar. She had admitted to being against Jordi's contact with Duxo and might this have been a situation that her brother was motivated to protect her from … and might he go to the lengths of killing Duxo to ensure his sister's peace of mind? Duxo's political leanings meant he was at odds with feminists, Catalan independence supporters and foreigners and that was just the obvious group of adversaries and amounted to a sizeable number of potential grudge bearers.

The Mossos were understandably suspicious of Jordi Campbell. He had robbed, sexually assaulted and slit someone's throat in the past and he was known as someone with a history of extreme violent behaviour. Alice had witnessed Marcella's knife skills too on her visit to the Tapas Bar and she wondered if, aside from her own grievances with Duxo, Marcella might still be protective of Jordi and want to make sure that Xavier Duxo did not lure him into any more trouble.

Then there was the fact that Pradić had found a link between Jordi Campbell and Sammy Marshall, the primary suspect in the Belfast killings. She would have to see if there was any point in following up on that. It seemed as if it was just happenstance that these men had been at school together but she was wary of what seemed like coincidences and often turned out to have been more contrived than that. Enough speculation, she thought, and closed her notebook.

Alice was strangely looking forward to being back in Belfast and spending a few hours in her flat there but she also was curious about a lot of elements of both of the current cases and wouldn't mind spending a bit of time with Pradić and her screens.

She sent off a text. **Landing in Belfast around ten o'clock. Will you still be at your desk and could you bear a visitor?**

The reply was instant. **Will there be turrón?**

Alice laughed and headed to the airport shop that had a big stock of the soft nougat filled with nuts.

But of course, she replied, stashing the sweets in her backpack, and then headed to the departure gate in the hope that she would not have a talkative passenger beside her and could return to her unread files and notes.

CHAPTER 33

The press conference that took place that evening was one of the most animated that anyone present could remember. There was a sense that something momentous might happen. Good Friday was not usually the most lively news day and so the function room in a Belfast city centre hotel was crammed with hopeful journalists, photographers and camera crew. Rain had been falling steadily and the overheated room smelt of damp clothes, lingering stale cigarette smoke and fried food.

As ever, DS McCluskey began proceedings precisely on the dot of six o'clock. To begin with, he gave his update on the investigation and included the fact that they now had two people of interest to them. One person was in custody pending further questioning and the other, as they were aware, was being sought by the police. He declined to name the second suspect at this point in time and did not respond when someone in the room actually named Robert (Bull) Nelson. This caused a flurry of interest and urgent muttering into mobile phones and an increase in the attention paid to Bull Nelson's parents seated on the platform.

After Bull had been taken in for questioning, Burrows had given Mr and Mrs Nelson the option of withdrawing from making an appeal at the press gathering. He didn't want them to be further upset by a tirade of questions about their son but they said they wanted to give every chance to the killer of their daughter and grandchildren being made to answer for his crimes. It was agreed that Burrows would answer questions after McCluskey's update and that the Nelsons would make a prepared appeal at the end. Then there would be no further questions.

Burrows had been as well prepared by Pradić as was possible given that every element of the media was alive with speculation about the whereabouts of Marshall, the issue of hostage-taking and debates on the subject of violence against women. He had determined to keep his responses strictly to matters of police concern. It was inappropriate for him to be drawn into the wider debates. Managing the barrage of questions was a task in itself but Burrows maintained his calm exterior and tried to select questions from a range of those present. Most of the local media reps were well known to Burrows and those from further afield were used to wearing the obligatory press ID.

A woman from a local daily asked the first question. "DS Burrows, can you shed any light on how Sammy Marshall managed to avoid being apprehended by the police and fell into the hands of hostage-takers?"

Burrows consulted the list of points he'd prepared for various predictable questions. "As you already know, Angela, we were aware that Marshall had been taken from his home on the morning after the killing of Donna Nelson and her two sons. We had a description of his abductors and worked with a number of agencies and all the PSNI personnel at our disposal to locate him and bring him in for questioning. Unfortunately, at the moment when that search had produced results, he was freed by his captors and missed being apprehended by our officers by a matter of minutes. We arrived a few moments too late and have now increased our efforts to find Sammy Marshall so he can help us with our inquiries. As you know, we are asking for any help the media can provide in that regard."

An older journalist standing at the side of the room shouted his question without being selected. He was from one of the more controversial dailies. "Was there a leak from within the PSNI that warned the men who were holding Marshall?"

Burrows could see behind the table draped in green baize that McCluskey's leg started to bounce in an agitated manner even though his expression remained calm. Burrows answered with more assurance than he felt.

"There is no evidence that this was anything other than an unfortunate coincidence. Of course every aspect of our inquiry will be subjected to the closest scrutiny but for now I can assure you that the PSNI are doing everything possible to resolve this case."

McCluskey turned over the page in the notebook before him and raised a hand to signal that he was going to speak. Burrows took the opportunity to drink some water from the glass in front of him.

"As most of you will be aware, our Murder Squad has an unparalleled success record in solving murder cases across the communities in this jurisdiction. You have full details of those figures in your press pack. This case is no different but it has become complicated by the unlawful interference of some elements in the community. We are here to appeal for the support of the media in bringing some peace of mind to Mr and Mrs Nelson who have suffered a multiple and heart-breaking loss of three family members." He paused to gesture towards the Nelsons who were sitting to his right and then continued firmly. "This is a time for the community to respect the family's needs and fully support the police efforts."

Burrows pointed to a young man from the BBC who was standing beside a colleague who was shouldering a camera.

"What is the PSNI position on the holding of Marshall by those wishing to generate attention towards the issue of violence against women?"

Burrows knew he had to choose his words carefully and was aware of cameras rolling and recorders being held aloft to capture his statement. He internally thanked Pradić for the quality of her preparatory notes.

"The Murder Squad is well briefed on the issue of violence against women. We are aware of the recent EU research that gives us the one-in-five statistic for women across the EU who've been sexually and physically harmed. Of course this is a dreadful indictment of our societies and the PSNI are trained to deal with these crimes as they arise. However …" he paused to emphasise his point, "I am leading a multiple murder inquiry and that has to be my priority. Any illegality that impedes our investigation will be dealt with within the parameters of the law without any preference or favour. Nothing excuses criminality and those guilty of criminal acts will be prosecuted under the law."

A young woman in a leather jacket raised her hand and Burrows nodded to her. She was holding a Channel 4 microphone and spoke in a cultured English accent. "DS Burrows, are you aware that the actions about violence against women are escalating at a great pace and the statement from those holding Marshall has gone viral on the

Internet? Women are responding to the situation here in Northern Ireland from across the globe. How can the police possibly hope to control what amounts to virtual insurrection by those campaigning against gender-based violence?"

"Insurrection is your word and may not be judiciously, or even accurately chosen." Burrows was managing this difficult situation well and conscious that McCluskey's leg was now at peace and he was nodding sagely in support of Burrows' response. "People have a right to peaceful protest and we are not novices in this regard, here in this part of the world. Colleagues in other sections of the PSNI are taking responsibility for tomorrow evening's Reclaim the Night March in the city centre. The organisers of the event are cooperating with my colleagues about the marshalling of the event and your reading of social media will no doubt have shown you that calls from everyone for peaceful protest are abundant. The Murder Squad will be pursuing its objective of finding the killer of Donna, Riley and Timmy and we will not be distracted from that duty regardless of the wider circumstances. I am sure that you will all see that is our proper course of action and allow us to get on with it."

He looked around for other questions.

A clean-shaven, middle-aged man in a tweed jacket raised his hand and received a nod from Burrows. He was standing at the side of the room and not wearing any press identification.

Before the man posed his question, Burrows intervened. "Can the questioner please identify himself and his allegiance?"

Burrows was keen to know if there was anyone suspicious in the room. He had staff observing those who came into the gathering but there was always the possibility that someone intent on disruption could slip past unnoticed. The man looked slightly taken aback but responded with the confidence of one accustomed to being the butt of some criticism.

"I am Roger McGloin and I am the president of the 'Men Too' group."

This provoked a few camera flashes and some sideways deprecating remarks.

"And your question, Mr McGloin?" Burrows felt the pressure dissipate as the issue of men's rights lost the interest of the majority of those present. There was a good deal of groaning and eye-rolling from the audience. Now wasn't really the time for the 'What about us?' question but McGloin was a zealot and not to be deterred.

"I'd like to remind those present that physical and sexual violence is also perpetrated against men and to ask them to reflect this in how they report the current situation."

His voice sounded petulant and there was some sniggering and sneering remarks from the ranks of the old-school journalists.

Burrows raised a hand to quieten the crowd and smiled paternally at those present. "I am sure, Mr McGloin, that the gentlemen and ladies of the press will display their usual sensitivity in these matters."

Burrows allowed the amused response to this to quieten down and then he turned to Mr and Mrs Nelson and indicated to them that it was their turn to speak.

"Please, folks," he said, "I'd ask you now to give your full attention to Mr and Mrs Nelson as they make their appeal."

As they had waited their turn to speak it was clear to Burrows that the Nelsons became increasingly intimidated by the press gathering. It was larger than any Burrows had attended since he joined the Murder Squad and there were a number of foreign press teams there which always raised the tempo a bit. The taking of Sammy Marshall hostage had captured the attention of the international media at the end of a week that was known for being quiet in terms of news. Belfast had an historical attraction for the media and there was a legacy of that still remaining. Now the cameras and recorders were focussed on the parents and grandparents of Donna and her children in the hope that their statement would be newsworthy.

Mr Nelson spoke quietly and without the aid of any notes.

"I am speaking to you all today from my heart," he began and immediately got the attention of all those present. "I don't need anything written down to remind me of what I want to say. Donna was my lovely daughter. She was a good person. She was kind and she was a good mother to her two boys … to our grandsons. She wanted them to have a nice home and no hassle in their lives and she had to struggle to get that but she did and that was all credit to her courage not to accept second best. Donna is dead now and …" Mr Nelson stopped as the next words stuck in his throat. He took a large cloth hankie from his pocket and blew his nose noisily.

His wife patted his arm and looked at him encouragingly. He shook his head and moved the microphone until it was in front of her. The media waited in silence as the woman took in the fact that the rest of the message was up to her. She continued with an air of resignation as if it wasn't the only time that things were left to her to finish.

"Our daughter Donna and our grandsons Riley and Timmy have been taken from us without warning. The shock is hard to bear but that's the hand we've been given. We know that it's not right for any woman or child to be hurt in their home and we understand why people are angry that more isn't done about it. But right now we only want whoever is responsible for killing our precious daughter and wee grandkids to be found and charged and we want them to pay for what they've done. We know Sammy Marshall well. He is our son-in-law and it's hard to believe he would harm Donna and the boys but we need to find out if he did … or anyone else did … and so we appeal to them that has him to hand him over and let the police do their job." She looked at her husband who was watching her with wonder at her ability to put words together and make sense. "We have nothing more to say than that. Nothing can give us back our daughter and those wee boys. Our job now is to lay them to rest and try to get some justice for them, if that's even possible."

Burrows waited until it was clear that the Nelsons were finished and then, as cameras continued to flash he took the microphone back and faced the assembled media.

"Thank you to Mr and Mrs Nelson for that intervention. Let's call it a day there, folks, and we will be back in touch with any developments as soon as possible."

The Nelsons shook hands with DS McCluskey and then Burrows shepherded all three out of the room by a side door where a uniformed officer made sure they were not followed.

"Well managed, DS Burrows." McCluskey rested his hand on Burrows' shoulder. "Let's get this wrapped up now as soon as we can. I know you're doing everything possible."

And he headed out to his waiting car and left Burrows to make his way back to HQ and a busy few hours before he could call it a night.

CHAPTER 34

As the plane bumped its way across the Pyrenees and along the Bay of Biscay, Alice immersed herself in her reading. There was a vacant seat between her and the man at the end of the row but she was still conscious of his agitation and his white knuckles as he tightly gripped the armrests. She was not without sympathy for the nervous flyer but she had watched him compete with another man to stow his bag in the last remaining space in the overhead bin and smirk when the man's bag was taken away to be placed in the baggage hold. He was smug and she hated that kind of petty one-upmanship and was not moved to be kindly towards him now, as he struggled with his fears.

The story that Pradić had unearthed about Xavier Duxo did not make pleasant reading but then Alice hadn't expected it would be. His far right political allegiance led directly back forty years to this father's membership of the Peoples Alliance and subsequently the Peoples Party that had formed in the wake of the Franco era. Vox was established in 2013 and Duxo, already at odds with those in the PP, had joined the new party and become a vocal and sometimes aggressive supporter.

Pradić found an article that named Duxo as one of a number of Vox members who had been visible in a counter protest against a Pride march in Girona. When a young trans woman had been brutally beaten that evening, Duxo and his associates had been questioned by police but had been provided with alibis by a restaurant owner who was also a party member. The group were subsequently cited as suspects in a local LGBT journal but the accusation had been withdrawn when legal proceedings were threatened. The woman who had been attacked had reported that during the march, Duxo had taken her photograph on his phone and said, "I'll be watching for you later when you're not with your queer buddies." She was reportedly scarred by the event both physically and mentally. Demands from the LGBT community for it to be treated as a hate crime did not get any traction.

Duxo was also named in a piece that reported on court proceedings in a family court in Palamos. He was charged with acts of violence against his then partner who had been hospitalised in the wake of an assault and subsequently spent time in a women's refuge. Despite her brother and refuge staff making submissions in support of her claims, Duxo was able to present evidence that he was attending a two-day Vox conference in Barcelona and could not have committed the alleged attack. Alice noted the parallels with Marcella Murray's case and could see how Jordi had found reason to identify with Xavier Duxo.

Alice thought people must have been queuing up to have a go at Duxo – fascist colleagues he had alienated in various political parties, family and community members of the LGBT and women's community, foreign workers like those he had bullied in Marcella

Murray's bar and, without doubt, a long list of others he had aggrieved. Really the Mossos were spoiled for choice, and if they were thorough in their investigation, Jordi Campbell would be only one amid many lines of inquiry. Nonetheless it was interesting and not very fortunate that he had been with Duxo and recognised by DI Caroline Paton so close to the time of Duxo's killing.

The refreshment trolley stopped beside Alice and she ordered a black coffee and a cheese roll. It looked fairly synthetic but would keep her going for another few hours until she and Pradić had spent some time looking at the two cases. The coffee was less mediocre than anticipated and as she sipped she switched to the information that Pradić had uncovered about Marcella Murray. In the Irish context she had featured only in the reports on the aftermath of Campbell's release and compensation after the rape, theft and murder of the older woman on the Shankill Road. She was pictured smiling by a youthful Campbell's side in several Belfast papers. One headline read: **COMPENSATED FOR BRUTAL ATTACK** while another took a different tack with **NEW START FOR A HAPPY COUPLE**. Neither spin made satisfactory reading. Marcella was either presented as having a predatory eye for money or alternatively as a potentially stable influence with whom Campbell might be expected to make something of himself. The couple left the country as soon as they could and were rapidly forgotten.

As Alice had predicted, during Campbell's trial in Spain, Marcella had reported a history of violence as part of their relationship but she had also said that his remorse in the aftermath of each episode was so great that she believed each time to be the last. Because the consequences of the final beating were so severe, plus the fact that family were present from whom she could not hide what had happened, she had pressed forward with charges. She stated that she knew that Jordi needed help and that she hoped that he would get it in prison. The phrase 'cruel to be kind' appeared in several pieces of evidence, as if she needed to excuse what she was doing. For his part, he had pleaded guilty to the charges against him and the judge had recommended that he be given full access to the various educational and corrective programmes on offer at that time in 'ordinary' Catalan prisons. There were also 'closed' and 'open' prisons where regimes were stricter or more relaxed, but the recommendation was that Campbell be sent to a prison where his rehabilitation be taken in hand and regularly reviewed.

Marcella had told Alice that some local women had helped her keep the bar going while Jordi was in prison. Pradić had found social media posts that made it clear that her integration into the local women's community was not just a passing thing. She was part of a local feminist network that lobbied for greater awareness and action on the issue of violence against women and organised activities to include migrant women in the community. Marcella's was one of the more moderate voices on the site that urged people to try to understand the pressure men could be under too.

One of her posts read like a quote from AHIGE: **Patriarchy is the enemy of men as well as women. We need to help each other to bring about real change for all of us.**

Some of the responses to this in the group were less than sympathetic: **Men are hurting us and killing us and you're asking me to be patient and reason with them. Dream on, sister. They have had centuries to cop on to their mistakes. I'm out of patience now.**

There were other examples of Marcella recommending that women accept their male allies and work alongside. Alice found it hard to reconcile this level of moderation with the action of slitting a bully's throat and she set aside her suspicions about Marcella for the time being.

When they landed in Belfast, Alice received several phone messages. One from Hugo brought her up to date on the EXIT group's plans for the following day. The banner-making was a longer process than they had imagined and they would be busy in the Centre all the following day. She was pleased that she would be able to surprise them and join in the creativity when she was finished with Jordi Campbell. There were several messages from Caroline wishing her '**Safe journey**' and '**Happy landings**' and one from Pradić apologising she wouldn't be free that evening as there was an unprecedented online response to the hostage taking and she was fully occupied monitoring that. She finished with: **Turrón for breakfast?** Alice sent her a thumbs-up emoji.

In the heel of the hunt, Alice was glad to grab a taxi and head for home. She needed to try to still the noisy activity that her review of the information about the two cases had generated in her head. She would watch some mindless TV and then maybe even get some sleep.

CHAPTER 35

With the TV providing some company in the background, Alice scanned the latest documents sent through by Pradić. She couldn't resist. They were certainly not wasting any time in Caroline's absence. Pradić had sent an account of the day's interviews with Bull Nelson and the fact that he was refusing to answer any questions or explain how he had come to be in his sister's house around the time when she and her sons were killed. She wondered if Bull and Sammy had arrived at Goliath Row coincidentally at the same moment and, if so, how it had led to Marshall being held captive the following day. It was hard to make sense of that move.

Another paper gave an account of a row raging between Vox and a Catalan Historic Memory group about the alleged singing of an anthem with fascist lyrics at the party's recent conference. The text of the article quoted a Vox member as referring to their political opponents as 'the single brain cell left' and suggesting that they had missed the obvious irony in the lyrics. A photograph of the platform at the annual event showed two lines of men participating in the musical rendition at the end of the day's events. On the extreme right of the image, Duxo was clearly visible with his right hand on his chest in some kind of patriotic gesture. Here was yet another strand of evidence that would make Duxo unpopular with those working for a sensitive treatment of the civil war atrocities. Alice copied it and sent it to Caroline with a note explaining its relevance.

The mention of Sammy Marshall's name on the television caught her attention and she raised the volume slightly to hear what was happening. The presenter of the *Late Night Debate* outlined the context of the evening's discussion as the recent tragic murders of Donna Nelson and her sons and the subsequent disappearance of her ex-husband who was wanted for questioning in relation to her murder. An overview of the news headlines prior to the debate beginning showed a range of photographs of actions taking place across the country. The NMP group's demand for a mobilisation on the issue of gender-based violence had provoked a massive response at home and further afield. Government buildings had been daubed with blood-red paint depicting women's signs incorporating a clenched fist, the one-in-five statistic and the word ENOUGH in large capitals. The running red paint was a clear visual reminder of the fact that violence and bloodshed was the core issue.

A gently spoken male presenter, who commanded attention effortlessly, introduced the panelists. There were three women and two men. One of the women, grey-haired and possibly in her sixties, was from the Shankill Women's Centre, the second was a local councillor and the third was from a Women's Aid Refuge. A middle-aged man with a white ribbon attached to his chunky sweater was representing the Men's Development Network. The second man was younger and came from the Men Too group and his expression articulated his sense of unrecognised victimhood. It was easy to discern the panellists' ideological position even before they spoke, and Alice settled back to hear how these age-old arguments would play out here in Northern Ireland. The invited audience of about a hundred was asked to refrain from interrupting the speakers and was promised a fair opportunity to speak later on.

The presenter said that each speaker had been allowed two minutes to make a prepared statement about the current situation and he asked the elected representative to begin.

The woman talked about the low priority given to women's issues in the City Council and seemed to suggest that this was understandable given the number of more pressing things the Council was asked to look after. She cited the poor state of the city's water pipes and perennial matter of flags and marches, the city's housing shortages and lack of youth facilities that led to anti-social behaviour and damage to property.

Alice could feel her hackles rise but she waited patiently to hear the full range of opinions.

Next to speak was the guy from Men Too. He was diplomatic enough to lament the murder of a woman and her two sons but argued that for as long as men's experience of gender-based violence was ignored there would be no progress for anyone. This sounded a little like a threat. He quoted statistics about male suicide and violent attacks on men and received a round of applause from the audience.

The camera panned across the rows of the invited guests and it was clear that the presenter's chosen order of speakers, planned to generate friction, was working well. Alice decided that he was probably sympathetic to the feminist viewpoint and watched with even greater attention.

The older woman from the Shankill Woman's Centre was impressive. She began, "Let's not manipulate the data to make self-interested arguments on the back of a murdered woman and her children." There was an outburst of loud applause and some whooping. "Research clearly shows that most men are hurt or killed by the violent actions of other men or by women acting in self-defence. Our focus here needs to be on femicide and infanticide." The woman modulated her voice, resisting the temptation to be critical of the previous speaker's viewpoint. She quoted the European research that produced the one-in-five statistic in relation to physical and sexual violence against women by someone known to them. "This is what 'domestic' means," she said. "These hurts happen in the places where we're supposed to be safe, where we are supposed to be with those that love us and have our interests at heart." She touched her forehead lightly with her forefinger. "The following data come from research entitled *Counting Dead Women*. In the UK in 2012, men killed one hundred and twenty-eight women. In 2013, the number of women killed by men rose to one hundred and fifty-four. Forty-nine women aged between twenty and eighty-four have been murdered so far this year by a man who was a partner or ex-partner. They were killed in a range of ways: raped and stabbed, in one case sixty times, shot, smothered, strangled, set alight, drugged and thrown from a block of flats, decapitated. Faced with this kind of uninterrupted killing of women, we have to conclude that our lawmakers' inaction can only mean that they do not care. In many cases these deaths are not even recorded and they are labelled accidental death or some other obfuscating term. Alongside these facts, there was recently an outcry when members of a local council had insufficient places to park their cars. The situation was remedied almost immediately. The relentless killing of women does not engender the same urgency." She paused and let the impact of her words magnify in the shocked silence. "We have files of data recording these acts but the silence from those in power is deafening and their inaction is indicative of the lack of importance with which these facts are received." She nodded abruptly to show she was finished.

The Men's Development representative began by expressing his sympathies with all those impacted by the recent killings. He made the point that we were all diminished by living in a climate where violence against women appeared to be an acceptable blood sport. "Like others," he said making a clear reference to those holding Sammy Marshall hostage, "my aim is to be shocking. As a man I am ashamed of the harm that is done to women with apparent impunity. I don't subscribe to the idea that strength and courage are measured in how much hurt we can cause, but actually the opposite. We need to teach boys and men how to escape from this identity and become their better, humane selves. A real man is not a brute. A real man is kind, empathetic, respectful and loving. Spreading this new gender culture is the goal of the Men's Development Network and we will be proudly marching as allies of women in tomorrow evening's Reclaim the Night March."

Alice was suddenly very tired and switched off the television and did her evening routine of locking doors and making sure everything was safe. Her father's gentle face smiled at her in her memory. She was grateful not to have lived in a home where violence or abuse was present and she was glad that tomorrow she would spend time with some young people who were prepared to take to the streets to defend this right for everyone.

Holy Satuday, 19 April 2014

CHAPTER 36

Alice ran her familiar route along the towpath on Saturday morning and, despite having appreciated the beauty of the Costa Brava, she enjoyed breathing the fresh Irish spring air. She was on familiar ground and somehow that was more relaxing than trying to absorb the detail of a new route.

By nine o'clock she and Pradić were amicably sipping strong black coffee, chewing sweet turrón and considering a number of images on Pradić's multiple screens. There was the Vox conference image that showed Duxo as a zealot and then an interesting school photo where Zara had located Jordi Campbell and Sammy Marshall in the same class. They were about fifteen and possibly in their final year at school. It was an old picture of boys, dressed in shirts and ties, seated and standing with arms folded, in two lines around their form teacher. The name of each boy was printed below and Alice caught the name of Kyle Murray out of the corner of her eye, located at the extreme end of the front line.

The young Kyle Murray closely resembled his sister, and Alice realised that no one had mentioned before that they were twins. That would explain their close relationship. He was well built even then, with a shock of dark hair and a winning smile. Had he been instrumental in his sister meeting Jordi Campbell or did that come independently because they all lived in the same area? Alice was thinking that Kyle Murray merited a little more investigation to see what that threw up but, before she could suggest it, Burrows and McVeigh bustled in and greeted her in their usual open, friendly manner.

Alice wondered what they made of the unusual circumstances of her being there in the role of interpreter at one of the Squad's official meetings, but if they found it odd they neither did nor said anything to make her feel uncomfortable. In fact, Burrows proposed that Alice should join them in a quick review of where they were in the Belfast case and said that it would be a good chance to see if there were any overlaps between it and the Catalan murder.

"It seems as if there are a few common threads," he said, "so no harm in checking that out in case there's something more to it than first appears."

Alice shared what she knew about the Mossos investigation into the death of Xavier Duxo and included some of the information she had gleaned from her own inquiries.

Burrows contributed some background on Campbell's original case which, like Caroline, he remembered from his earlier days in the Force. He was also interested to hear that Kyle Murray now lived in Catalonia with his sister.

"I'm sure there was a Murray from the Shankill who was involved in paramilitary crime back in the day, " he said. "I think he was in the Maze Prison for a stretch. It's worth digging that detail out, Zara, in case it becomes relevant."

Pradić reported that there were reports of women's groups and their allies across the globe writing statistics in public places and debates about the pros and cons of holding someone hostage to highlight an issue that is otherwise overlooked. Burrows reported that the PSNI had been instructed to robustly pursue the hostage-takers and those found to be breaking the law in defacing public buildings and Alice could see this just fed into the argument that everything was more important than addressing violence against women. She remained silent.

It seemed there was no town or city in Ireland that had not made some response to the call for action on violence against women. In many instances the names of women physically harmed by men were written on the walls of public buildings with the statistic 'one in five' and the word *ENOUGH* in emphatic capitals. In one village a clothesline had been stretched across the main street hung with women and children's clothes daubed with red paint. On the Black Mountain overlooking Belfast, fires had been lit in the form of large numerals 1:5. This was visible across the city night sky and would no doubt leave a scorched imprint the following day. Zara said she had made a complete file of all the reports but only presented a sample now to save time.

There was some discussion about the fact that Campbell, Marshall and Kyle Murray had all been in the same class at school and Pradić agreed to see if there was anything of interest about that to be dug up in the Internet archives. Burrows said that Redgrave Secondary School had been known as a tough place as long as he had been in the police force and that there would certainly be some history to be uncovered there.

"They were reputed to play tig with hatchets there," he said, smiling a little sadly.

There was no progress to report on the possible whereabouts of Sammy Marshall and Burrows suggested that he and McVeigh would make another attempt to interview Bull Nelson and see what that might produce. He did not appear very hopeful. The international attention on the case was increasing the pressure on everyone. Uniformed officers from the Station had been drafted in to respond to phone calls and emails. Enquiries about the case were flooding in from global news agencies and much of Burrow's time was taken up with updating press statements to satisfy these requests. They all agreed that they would report any useful outcomes from their interviews and in less than an hour Burrows had declared the meeting at an end.

* * *

Zara showed Alice into the video conferencing room where they would meet Jordi Campbell. She checked that the Mossos were online and went to the reception area to collect Campbell in time for a ten o'clock start. Alice wondered vaguely how he would respond to meeting such an unusually dressed police constable with gleaming green hair.

When they arrived he seemed to be entirely at ease. He was dressed casually in jeans and a sweatshirt – a style that Alice recognised from her brief stay in Catalonia. A suit, especially accompanied by a tie, was a rarity there and signs of power or status were more illusive than in Ireland. Jordi had an abundance of freckles and his shoulder-length curly hair was streaked by the sun. When he smiled at Alice it was a broad, unfiltered smile that didn't appear to hold anything in reserve.

Pradić explained that their interview with the Mossos would be recorded and that Alice would translate from Spanish to English for her benefit and to facilitate any other members of the PSNI who needed access to the conversation. She also said that if there was any difficulty with the connection she had agreed to put the remaining questions to Campbell and, with Alice's translation, this information would be forwarded to the Mossos d'Esquadra.

He said he had no objection. "I'm here willingly to help however I can." His accent was soft – a little Belfast and a little Catalan.

Pradić then explained that he had been asked to come in and help with the inquiries of the Mossos into the death of Xavier Duxo in Verges some time late on Wednesday or early on Thursday morning.

He nodded that he understood the reason for his being there.

"The Mossos want to put certain questions to you and, based on your responses, they may ask to talk to you further when you return to Girona on Monday."

"I should say that I am also returning to Girona on Monday but that is purely coincidental," said Alice, thinking it better to make things clear from the outset.

Pradić introduced Alice to Campbell and he smiled at her.

"I've already received two phone calls from Catalonia telling me to expect to meet you, Dr Fox."

Alice felt herself instinctively limit the degree of friendliness in her exchange with Campbell as she realised that she was there in an official capacity and she didn't want to compromise the investigation.

"Alice will do nicely," she responded coolly and wondered if she had picked up a slight hint of irritation in Campbell's reaction.

This reflection was cut short as there was some electronic rustling on the line and the familiar faces of José Mantego and Carlos Tapia Rodriguez, from the Mossos d'Esquadra, Criminal Investigation Division, filled the large screen in front of them. After hasty introductions, they established a process for question, response and interpretation and immediately set to work.

Mantego asked Jordi to give them an account of his meeting with Duxo in Verges before the Danza de la Muerte. Campbell responded in fluent Castilian and Alice translated for Pradić. His explanation was very much along the lines that Raoul from AHIGE and Marcella Murray had outlined. Campbell had a gentle, direct manner and as he spoke he fiddled with a curl that was falling across his forehead. He had clear eyes and made easy eye contact as he spoke.

He seemed altogether comfortable in his skin, Alice thought, and she found it hard to reconcile this charming person with the man who had raped and savagely killed Maudie Prior and gravely injured and disfigured his life partner.

As if he could read her thoughts, he explained how he understood that it was difficult to believe he was now a peaceful person. He addressed his remarks to the Mossos who maintained a totally formal attitude despite Campbell's casual manner.

"I understand why you would conclude that I was a fair cop for the murder of Duxo, given my past and the fact that I was seen there with him. I was seen because I had no reason to hide. There are always lots of police around those local fiestas because they bring in wealthy strangers and that's interesting for thieves and scammers who are drawn to such events for the rich pickings they offer. If I was going to kill someone I wouldn't choose to do it in a busy place with lots of cops around." He smiled at them as if the point that he was making was entirely logical.

There was a pause as Alice relayed his response to Pradić.

"And yet," said Pradić, "someone did think that Verges on that busy night was just the place to cut Duxo's throat."

Mantego smiled wryly at Zara's astute comment and continued

questioning. "Why don't you tell us why you went to Verges on that night and exactly what happened?"

Despite being preoccupied with translation, Alice could feel the atmosphere intensify.

Campbell appeared unperturbed by the shift in the mood. He explained calmly that Duxo was known to him and had been a customer in Tapas del Mar until Marcella had barred him. "Duxo has a fiery temper. I sometimes talk politics with him. He believes very different things to me and I disagree with him but I am able to do that verbally, now that I have the use of words."

His use of the present tense was striking, given that they were discussing the murder of Duxo, but Alice continued to relay the information accurately.

"I had problems learning at school," he said easily. "I lived with my father who was mentally ill and wasn't the chatty kind. My mum left when I was a baby. I was told it was because of my father's illness but she didn't take me with her so I can't fully accept that explanation."

There were still a few demons left for Jordi to contend with, Alice observed, but he was open about them and that suggested that he was dealing with them.

"When I was in prison in Catalonia, after I hurt my partner very badly, I learned a lot of things I had missed out on … educational things and important things about feelings and relationships. I am different now but I understand that is hard for some people to swallow and so I accept that I often have to explain myself. I suppose it's part of my ongoing payment for the harm I did. I don't think it's unfair."

Alice thought it was difficult to believe that he could be this adept at presenting information in a manner designed to deflect from his role as a potential killer.

The Mossos made no shift in their tone despite this quite emotional input from Campbell. They remained intent on getting the answers they wanted.

"Why did you want to meet Duxo on that particular evening?" Mantego bullishly asked. "You were going to Ireland the next day and maybe your talk with him could have waited until you got back after your trip home."

Campbell answered with ease. "I had arranged it before I realised that the Danza de la Muerte was the same night. I was waiting until our bar was less busy because Marcella was driving in for a women's group meeting and I was getting a lift. I haven't learned to drive yet. Anyway, I wanted to talk to Duxo because I can see he is digging all kinds of holes for himself. Sometimes people just need to realise that they don't have to be going around aggressing everyone. There's another way to be that is much easier to live out than the bullyboy routine. I understood that he has been up on charges for violence against his wife and others and I wanted to share some of my own experiences. Again, I think I owe it to society to do that to pay off some of my wrongdoing. It shouldn't be women who have to explain what's wrong with acts of aggression against them." He paused for a sip of water and looked fleetingly at Alice to see how she reacted to his response.

Mantego's next question came rapidly. "How did that conversation go?" The detective's tone suggested that he didn't give much credence to someone holding out hope for the Duxos of this world who belonged to alt-right groups, hated foreigners and beat up women.

Alice could also see that Duxo wasn't a likely candidate for salvation and she wondered at Campbell's willingness to invest in such a mission. Was he naïve or was he so driven that he wasn't put off by the diehard cases like Duxo? Campbell seemed undaunted by the implication that he was on a fool's mission with someone like Duxo.

"He wasn't very receptive, I'd have to say, but I didn't expect anything else. I just wanted to plant another version of the truth in his head that might begin to ring true at some stage in the future. He was only really interested in asking if he could come back to the Tapas Bar but I told him that was non-negotiable. He started to bad-mouth Marcella and I said I wasn't listening to that and he laughed at me and called me a pussy. I'm used to that line of argument: your wife sent you to jail and now you're back working there even though she won't let you into her bed and her brother is installed as her guardian angel. My life is an open book, I'm afraid, and those guys can only see weakness in my situation."

Mantego paused and looked hard at Campbell as if to gauge whether he was as genuine as he seemed. Campbell didn't break eye contact with the Mosso who seemed to soften slightly as he continued to put his questions.

"Where did Marcella go while you were with Duxo? Did you meet her after that to go back to Calella?" Mantego tracked the detail like a well-trained bloodhound.

"Marcella's life is her own business now and I don't want to be reporting on her to anybody. As I said, she was meeting some women friends and she texted me when she was finished and collected me down the road from the café. I didn't arrange to meet Duxo again but I did leave the door open if he wanted to chat some more." He waited and then added, "It is fascinating for me to see that kind of mental stubbornness up close. It's a bit like being able to watch an old reel of film of your former self." He laughed easily. "Marcella made a very wise move when she pressed charges against me all those years ago. I don't like to think what I would be like now if she hadn't."

"Do you know where Duxo went after you left?"

Campbell shook his head. "He walked to the end of the road with me ... which must be what you guys caught on the CCTV but while I waited for Marcella he turned right back in towards the town centre. I would guess he was going in search of another drink and hoping to pick a fight with someone. We drove straight back to Calella. We had left Kyle, Marcella's brother, to lock up but he wasn't there when we got back. If business is slow at this time of year, we just close up. I left Marcella at the door and headed off to my own place about ten minutes' walk away."

"Did you meet anyone on your way home? Could someone verify that part of your story?"

By this stage Alice thought that Mantego sounded almost hopeful that Campbell would be proved to be a man of his word.

"I was getting up at four the next morning to catch the early flight to Belfast so I didn't dilly-dally but I did shout goodnight to a few mates still grafting in their bars along the sea front. I'm sure they would remember, although one night is pretty much like another in Calella. Anyway, that area has loads of security cameras so it wouldn't be hard to check them out."

Campbell's replies were confident and definitely had a ring of truth about them. Nothing in what he had said or in his manner suggested that he might be implicated in Duxo's death and Mantego sat back, apparently satisfied that he had told the truth.

"You can be sure, Mr Campbell, that we will crosscheck every element of your evidence. For now I am happy to leave things there. Thank you for your cooperation."

Alice thought this appreciation was excessively positive in terms of the Mossos' style of inquiry and, as she relayed the final remarks to Pradić, she could see that Jordi was feeling quite pleased with himself and how he had managed the situation.

When the video link was switched off, the audio recording was still operating.

Alone with Campbell, Pradić looked towards Alice and gestured to her to put any further questions if she wanted to.

Alice smiled at Campbell who was examining the rows of beads on his wrist and showing no sign of pressure or discomfort.

"Jordi, I just have a few questions. You said that you didn't have much luck at school and I understand from Raoul and Marcella that you were badly bullied there. Is it OK if I ask a bit about all that?"

"Sure. Fire away."

"I think that you were in class with the guy who is the centre of the hostage-taking story that is in the news here in Belfast at the moment. Do you remember Sammy Marshall from back then?" Alice could see the uneasiness Marshall's name caused for Campbell and she smiled encouragingly.

"He was quite the hard man back then. He wasn't one of the smart guys and so he used a lot of physical bully tactics to keep his profile up – if you get me."

Alice nodded that she did.

"I was totally lost back then. I was skinny and stupid and didn't know much about anything. Most of the time I didn't even know what people were talking about. I mainly remember being hungry and on my own – not part of any gang that would have offered me any protection. Marshall was the one that christened me 'Florence' after the little girl on the *Magic Roundabout* programme that was all the rage on the telly. I guess I did look a bit like her." He smiled at this. "I used to cut my own hair and it was a bit of a mess and my jeans were probably too short and showed my skinny ankles inside my ankle boots. When I look back with what I know now, I can see that I was continuously and mercilessly taunted about being a girl and all the stuff that teenage boys do to each other. Anyway, it was thanks to Marshall that Florrie became how I was known."

Alice could see the shadow of the lost boy in Campbell's eyes as he revisited the past but she sensed he had told this story many times before and could cope.

"When I say all that, it's just that it is the way it was for me back then. I am not excusing what I did partly as a reaction to that but also because of all the other shit in my life. None of it excuses what I did to poor Maudie Prior but it is all connected."

He stopped and Alice nodded to show she understood what he was saying.

"We don't need to go there now," she said reassuringly. "I was wondering if you have had any contact with those people from your schooldays now that they are men. When you are home with your dad, for example, have you caught up with any of them?"

Jordi vigorously shook his head. "I'd be going out of my way to avoid them, believe me. It was nearly worse that they put me on some kind of a pedestal when I killed Maudie Prior. That was almost harder to live with afterwards than being bullied. It was like I had joined them and been accepted into their gang and I didn't fit there either. The best thing for me was getting away from them all. As for Sammy Marshall, I can believe the stuff about him only too well. He had a very fragile ego and I'm sure that didn't improve over the years. From what I hear, he lived very much in his brother-in-law's pocket and was off his head most of the time."

"How did you hear that, Jordi?" Alice asked as if out of simple curiosity. The conversation was heading where she wanted it to go now.

"I didn't mention that Marcella's twin brother, Kyle, was in class with us too and of course I've seen him pretty constantly since Marcella and I got together. In many ways, Kyle has always been there in the background. I was talking to him since I got home this time and he filled me in about Marshall so he must be in touch with somebody here who keeps him up to date. His da maybe? He's still active in the Shankill area and would know what's what." Jordi said this as if it was a new insight. "In fact, it was Kyle who first introduced me to Marcella when I got out of jail the first time. He has lived in Calella now since before I went into prison. He helped Marcella with the business when I was away and has always watched out for her … I guess twins have a special thing going on that keeps them close …" Campbell's thread seemed to peter out as if he was uncertain about where to go next.

Alice could see there might be something more to find out about the relationships between Kyle, Jordi and Marcella but it could wait until she had a little more time to think that through. She tried another tack.

"Was Robert Nelson also in your year at school? I think he's often known as Bull."

Jordi sipped the water in front of him and continued pensively. "Bull was always smart, always a few steps ahead of the pack. He went to the grammar school and studied business at college. He was always going to be higher up on top of the pile than any of the rest of us. The Shankill was known then, and still is in many ways, as the area in the North with the lowest educational achievements for young men. Bull bucked that trend but I don't think he fitted in the grammar school either. There were murmurings about Bull's sexuality back then but never more than that. Being gay was still very much a no-go area in that community but Bull was always into bodybuilding and could have floored anybody who annoyed him. We all knew that."

Alice could see the Jordi who liked to understand his world getting into his stride now and she didn't interrupt although she could see Pradić checking her watch.

"Protestants traditionally left school and got a job in the shipyard or the aircraft industry. Their places were more or less assured by their fathers before them and they didn't need to rely on education to get work. Catholics were excluded from many areas of work through discrimination and they grew to see education as a way of changing their unequal lot. Even after equality legislation was introduced these educational trends continued but back then, we were part of all that. There was no culture of education for young lads on the Shankill. My case was more complicated, but the overall context didn't help."

"Were Marcella and Donna at school together?" Alice wondered just how many links she could track between these two murder cases.

"They were, actually, but Donna was younger and they wouldn't have been friends. Marcella did hairdressing for a year at college when she was sixteen but then we left for Scotland so there was no time for studying after that. I'm not sure about Donna. She would still have been in school when my shit hit the fan."

Pradić was getting a volley of texts on her phone and she indicated to Alice that she would need to finish up the interview. She thanked Jordi and switched off the recorder, excused herself and headed for the door. Alice agreed to show Jordi out and was pleased to get the chance for a chat on the way. There was one more piece that she needed to clarify and this might allow the opportunity for that to happen.

She asked how he and Kyle got on and Jordi explained that Kyle was a solitary person who demanded very little other than a peaceful life. He had been traumatised by some of his father's activities and he had learned early on to look out for his sister. "When we first went away to Scotland he did a spell in the army but he didn't last long and when we moved to Catalonia he visited a lot and eventually moved there."

Jordi said that against all the odds he and Kyle got on quite well but he realised that Kyle would protect Marcella before everything else and he knew not to do anything to disturb that peace.

CHAPTER 37

As she settled easily in a black taxi in the city centre, Alice texted Caroline with an update on the interview with Jordi Campbell. She said that in her opinion, supported by Pradić, it was unlikely that Jordi had harmed Xavier Duxo. His weakness was perhaps his zeal in attempting to persuade a hardcore fascist that there was another way to view the world. That aside, he seemed entirely innocent. She told Caroline that the same CCTV footage that identified him might later on confirm his claims and left her to speak to the Mossos about that.

Alice did not mention her interest in Marcella's twin as she wanted time to check some issues out for herself. She had texted Pradić to ask if she would check out Kyle Murray in relation to any dealings with Vox or the Catalan Independence Movement.

Pradić responded with a voice message that they were dealing with an avalanche of international press teams arriving to cover the march that evening. With six hours more to go before the local area gatherings that would make their way to the City Hall, already there was a large press presence at the scene. DS McCluskey was refusing to hold another press conference but she was putting together a statement for distribution and, alongside the weight of Internet posts about the hostage situation, she was at full stretch. She agreed to look at a profile for Kyle Murray as soon as possible, probably when the march was over.

As Alice's taxi meandered slowly up the road through the Saturday lunchtime traffic the talk was all about the murder, the hostage and the evening's march.

"I'm making all my lads go," one older woman said. "They usually go out drinking on a Saturday night but I've told them nobody goes anywhere until they've supported the march. This has to be really big or no one will take any notice. I have a gigantic sign in my front window: one in five, enough and NMP. That says it all."

And there was general agreement from the other passengers.

"Will you be going yourself?" the woman asked Alice directly.

"I will indeed," she replied. "Actually I'm just going to make a banner with the youth group I work with." She was pleased to feel she belonged to this collective effort and the woman's clear expression of approval was most rewarding.

Outside the Falls Women's Centre there were women on ladders painting an enormous billboard with glaring red letters. The one-in-five statistic, ENOUGH in massive red letters and beneath it the NMP slogan that seemed to have captured the imagination.

"It means 'No More Patriarchy,'" the older woman explained gently to Alice. "We've had enough of men making decisions that don't take our views into account. It's not good for women and it's not doing men much good either. We've had enough."

Alice loved the wisdom that was shared in the Black Taxis where cultural change was rehearsed and disseminated without the need for anything more strategic than the twenty minutes free time it took to arrive at your destination.

She tapped the taxi's glass partition with a coin as they neared Milltown Cemetery. The EXIT project was across the road and along a narrow entry and she wanted to ensure that there was no one about to spoil her surprise. The alley way was clear and as she opened the red door into the project she could hear the noisy excitement from inside.

"*Surprise!*" she called out as she did an athletic Spiderman jump through the doorway.

There were a few seconds of astonished silence and then whoops and laughter as they bombarded her with questions.

"What are you doing here, Alice? Hugo said you were in Spain!"

"How did you get here so quickly, Alice?"

"On my electronic broomstick," she joked. "I knew you would need some extra hands with this banner and couldn't stand the idea that you would all do it without me."

She was already hanging up her coat and getting ready to leap into the middle of the very messy preparations. She could see Hugo sitting on the floor, hammer in hand, attaching some sturdy poles to the frame that would hold the banner. He waved to her and stayed seated in the midst of the group. For now there was no sign of the actual banner but there was a lot of material and a sewing machine and stencils and some very loud rock music coming through a large speaker rigged up at the side of the central space.

Hugo mimed mopping the sweat from his brow and called out to her. "Are you just going to stand there smiling or are you going to help? Rae is the Commander in Chief so she'll allocate you your role in the banner collective! I must be psychic. I even got an extra T-shirt from my secret contact!"

He jumped up and flourished a white T-shirt with a red woman's sign on the front under NMP in capitals.

"*What does it stand for, team EXIT?*" he joked.

"*No more patriarchy!*" they responded loudly in chorus.

Hugo turned the shirt around to reveal the writing on the back. It said 1-in-5 in numerals and ENOUGH in large red letters and then below that in bullet points:

No more sexism

No more hurting women

NMP

"How has this all been organised so quickly and who's paying for it?" Alice was impressed, especially if as it seemed the T-shirts were widely available.

"It's all to do with the power of connection," Hugo said in his mock-serious voice. "But, seriously, apparently an Irish artist activist living in Berlin came up with the design and sent the artwork to women's organisations all around the EU, and beyond. The 'ENOUGH' varies from country to country where it is translated appropriately. So local groups are getting the shirts made nearby and paying whatever is needed. I purchased ours from the local women's centre under the course-materials budget heading. Apparently they can't get them printed fast enough." He tossed Alice the shirt, saying, "Now you have to work for it so talk to Rae," and he went back to hammering poles.

Rae was ready with the instructions. "I was counting on someone reliable turning up to make the EXIT letters. I've made a stencil of the exact size and you need to cut them out in material, sew the edges neatly and then stick and sew them in the centre of the banner. The other stuff is being prepared and will go around that. OK?"

And so Alice was in at the deep end and happily seated on the ground amongst the group. They were singing along to the music and obediently doing what Rae told them. Some were making placards and the smell of spray paint filled the air. "No sniffing now," Rae warned those entrusted with the cans. Others were actually constructing the banner – an enormous cream rectangle made by sewing three double duvet covers together.

"I hope my ma doesn't recognise her spare bedclothes," laughed Liam.

And someone else quipped, "It's all for the cause, Liam. She'll only ground you for a few weeks."

The banter was all good-humoured and interspersed with serious chat about things people had read online and the many heart-wrenching images of the small boys and their mother on the front of all the papers.

Alice watched as Hugo sat in the middle of it all, keeping an eye on those he knew had their own demons that were resurrected by all this talk of violence in the home.

When Alice crawled towards him in search of a decent pair of scissors, he said, "I should tell you that we actually have a plan. Hopefully we will be finished the creative stuff by half past four and then we are going to clean up both ourselves and the space here. After that we will have a serious half hour to chat about protest etiquette and how we expect everyone to represent EXIT irrespective of what else is happening. Then we have tins of sandwiches and cake that the local Italian chipper has sent down and we will prepare for marching on our stomachs like any army would."

Alice noted how much Hugo seemed to be relishing the buzz of the whole process.

"Word from the Women's Centre is that this is going to be massive," Hugo continued. "I phoned in our numbers earlier on and it sounded as if they were very busy indeed. There are busloads coming across the border. The platform speakers are from the Falls and the Shankill Women's Centres and the Federation of Women's Aid Refuges. I think there will be some music too. So, I think it's good to let off steam now as the emotions later will be more serious." And he raised his eyebrows to seek her agreement.

She could see that as usual he had it well thought through and she nodded positively.

"I should say too that I am very glad to see you back, Alice. I feel less like the old woman who lived in a shoe now."

And Alice chuckled at the image that conjured up. "That's a relief," she said and got back to making the letters for the banner.

* * *

Sammy Marshall had long since been left in the hands of his two custodians. The women wanted to be seen in their women's centres, enthusiastically organising the sector's response to the demand for action. May had participated in the Friday evening late-night debate on TV and Tina, Paula and Grace had been busily organising the printing of T-shirts for the march. They were charging ten pounds each for them and hoped that would cover the costs incurred in the purchase of materials for the protests and the march itself. There was a generator, sound systems and lighting and the covered platform itself to be paid for. Of course a lot of things had been provided free of charge by local groups and businesses that willingly supported such ad hoc activities but the four women liked to be prepared for all eventualities and there were many aspects of this event that were unpredictable. Already the hotels were stretched to cope with the international journalists and film crews, and bars and restaurants were expecting Saturday evening before and after the event to be extra busy.

"I remember a time when we would have billeted foreign journalists in our own homes," Grace reminisced, "but that's not the way nowadays. It's all expense accounts and fancy hotels."

The women had asked for groups to give them an idea of how many people would be attending the march so that they could gauge the number of stewards they would need. They wanted the police to keep a distant eye on proceedings and so they needed to show they were as in control as was possible. The network of women's centres around the country were collating local numbers and feeding them through to either the Shankill or Fall's centres and they in turn were organising high-vis vests for women who would act as stewards.

The four women had also been looking for an appropriate way to deliver their hostage to the PSNI and the answer had come on Saturday morning as they worked with local women to pepare for the day ahead. As women do when they get together in groups, Brenda, a local woman, had been recounting some extraordinary events that had happened to her when the body of a priest had been found in a confessional of a Belfast Chapel. Brenda's name and address had been found in the priest's diary and she had become implicated in the subsequent murder inquiry that had been national news for days afterwards. The name Alice Fox had emerged in Brenda's story as someone who had gone the extra mile to support Brenda and her son Jed and who had acted as an intermediary between them and the PSNI.

Paula and Grace had exchanged a knowing look and consequently Paula had made a call to the EXIT project and spoken in confidence to Hugo. She knew his father and took it on trust that his son would behave honourably in the situation.

* * *

After the banner was completed to everyone's satisfaction, it was rolled carefully and placed to the side of the room. The group then had a serious discussion about the march and how to avoid situations that might be conflictual. Then the food was put out on the side tables and everyone helped themselves to sandwiches and cake and soft drinks. The atmosphere in the group was sombre but purposeful. The young people had brought warm clothes because, even though the weather was mild during the day, it would be a chilly evening for standing around at the City Hall. The conversations were all about the hostage situation and speculation about how it would all play out.

"There is no way that any harm is going to be done to the perp," said Rae. "A promise was made that he would be treated well and handed over to the police when the purpose of holding him had been achieved. And it really has."

"Yeah, that's for sure," said Jed. "The town is full of foreign film crews and Ma has been in the Falls Women's Centre all yesterday evening and all day today. She says that the phone never stops ringing with groups calling in to give numbers of people coming. They work very closely with the Shankill and apparently it's even busier there as they're all up filming at the house in Goliath Row. Nobody's talking about anything else on the radio and TV so that's what they wanted, isn't it?"

"What they wanted was attention and that has happened, OK," said Gary, "but more than that they wanted a change in the systems so that that kind of violence doesn't happen any more and I don't know how that could even begin to start."

There was some muttering of agreement and the enormous weight of the problem seemed crushing.

"You're all correct, of course," said Alice gently, "but when I was away I met with a group in Spain whose whole purpose is helping boys and men become different in themselves and in their attitudes and relationships. It's not impossible. Look at how much you've all changed and imagine if everyone made that much progress how much better things could be."

That made sense and suddenly they could all feel hopeful again.

"Hugo and I are looking into some of the training that the Spanish group do in schools and communities," Alice continued, "and we hope to be able to work in partnership with them … and you, if you're interested."

"Cool!" someone said and immediately there was general agreement.

"We can talk about all those exciting possibilities soon," said Hugo, "but I'd say you should all relax for a bit now because the march will take more out of you than you think." He laughed. "Some of you haven't walked that far in years! Alice and I need to have a bit of a catch-up now. Let's say we're all ready to go in half an hour from now. There's a group walking down from the Felons Club and a few more coming down from further out the road to meet up. We'll walk together and meet up with everyone at the women's centre."

He and Alice withdrew into Hugo's office and settled down with cups of tea and some biscuits.

Hugo stretched out and put his feet on the desk. "You said on the phone you were getting drawn into another Murder Squad inquiry. How's that going for you?"

Alice gave him the bare bones of what she knew and explained why she had come back rather than Caroline.

"Anyway, I was pleased to have the opportunity to be back for the banner-making and the march with the group." She didn't want to sound as if she was making excuses for her involvement with the PSNI. "I've been making my own inquiries and I really don't think that Jordi Campbell, as he is now, had anything to do with killing the man in Verges that night. I believe he really has been transformed by his time in prison and the work he continues to do himself." She wondered if now was the time to say she was considering staying on and taking up his suggestion of part-time paid work with the group, but she thought there was too much happening tonight to open up that discussion.

She shared her surprise that Jordi and Sammy Marshall had been in the same class at school and had both turned out to be very violent men.

Hugo said it was hard for young men with little or no prospects, back in the day, to avoid absorbing the violence all around them. "Most people don't get the intricacies of the events that were a part of the Troubles. That name makes it sounds as if there were some minor disagreements but it wasn't really that serious. In actual fact, it was a fullscale war scene here. There was violence and collusion by the State in the name of peacekeeping and there was war waged by the Republican movement against what they saw as the occupying forces of the Crown. They were still fighting the historic treaty that established the six counties remaining under British rule. Even those in the twenty-six counties who had been anti-Treaty had moved on from that point and now classed Republicans in the North as terrorists for continuing the same struggle. And then there was violence from the Loyalist groups against Catholics in the North whom they saw as enemies of the Union. You'd actually wonder that more young men didn't learn that violence was what you resorted to when dealing with your demons. That was the model that they lived with, all around them."

Alice was quiet. She knew that she wasn't able to talk about the Irish question because she just didn't understand the depth of feelings that generated the divided culture she still witnessed daily all around her. It was historic and deep-rooted and pitted with twists and turns that were hard for an outsider to understand. The parallels with the Catalan struggle were clearer to her. Vox didn't want their country divided just as Republicans north and south wanted a thirty-two county Irish Republic – and northern loyalists did not want to be wrenched away from the UK. The shades of nationalism and loyalism in the North, in relation to the same six counties, were baffling. It was impossible to envisage a solution that wouldn't anger some faction.

"It's good then that something like tonight's march seems to attract support from all quarters," Alice said, clutching hopefully at the evidence that this was a unifying action.

"The women's community sector has always been able to transcend the tribal stuff because their common enemy is patriarchy," Hugo said easily.

Alice wondered how he had learned his feminism and from whom. She then remembered he had told her that his father had studied feminist politics when he was interned in the Maze prison. She wondered what his mother was like.

They were quiet for a bit and then Alice started to share her thoughts about the Catalan murder. Hugo was a receptive listener and she thought he might give her the nudge she needed to link the pieces together. That feeling of being very close to making sense of it all was tantalising for her, but she couldn't yet fully grasp the clear picture. She filled him in about Jordi's Emmaus moments in jail.

He laughed. "I know so many men who have had those light-bulb moments in jail that sometimes I think a spell of incarceration should be compulsory."

"Maybe," Alice smiled, "but I suppose there must be an easier way than that."

Suddenly there was shouting outside and someone knocked on Hugo's office door and called out. "*Time to go, Hugo and Alice! There's a massive crowd of other marchers outside!*"

Alice pulled her gloves and warm top out of her backpack, put them on and they made their way out into the chilly evening. As a veteran demonstrator Alice knew that demonstrating could be a cold business.

And so the EXIT banner made its proud debut and they gathered behind the others for the ten-minute walk down the road to the women's centre.

On the way, Hugo and Alice chatted again about Jordi Campbell.

"This morning, when I was walking out of the police station with Jordi I asked him about Marcella's twin, Kyle, who seems to have been a fairly constant feature of their lives in the past and still is a presence today. Jordi told me that at school Kyle had been quiet and solitary but not because he was shunned by the group or the butt of bullying and ridicule like Jordi had been. Kyle was quite self-contained, I gathered. He kept himself out of bother with teachers and the other boys too. He didn't join in the banter or bullyboy stuff but just did enough school work to get by and then got off-side at the end of the day."

"Sounds as if his priorities were elsewhere," observed Hugo. "I'd have seen similar behaviours here from young fellas who were involved in one faction or another of the Republican movement. School was not their focus but they would be expected by their commanding officers to keep up a regular lifestyle and not attract attention to themselves."

Alice nodded emphatically. "That makes a lot of sense." Then she explained. "Jordi told me that back in their school days there had been talk that the Murray family had some paramilitary involvement but he hadn't ever discovered if that was the case. He thought that might explain why nobody would want to mess with Kyle, in case they drew more serious attention to themselves."

Hugo was grunting agreement. "If the rumours about that were true, the consequences could have been harsh. There was no verification needed and there were no warnings, just a beating up a dark alley some evening or worse if you were unlucky. You could lose a kneecap or two and then you really had to leave the country for good. People used to disappear overnight and not be seen again. Then the family would talk about a new job in Scotland or the States or some fudged story like that but everyone would know what the real way of things was." Hugo talked about the reality of those days as if they were less horrific than Alice heard them to be. He was ruminating about the Murray family.

"I wonder what the Da's name was. It wouldn't take long to get that checked out." Hugo laughed at Alice's expression. "I don't have secret files on Loyalist paramilitaries. A lot of that stuff is written up nowadays as local history. It was a massive part of people's lives back then. There were few people in working class areas, of whatever persuasion, that weren't caught up or touched in some way by all of that."

Alice came up with another explanation. "Perhaps it may also be that the simple explanation is the real one. Maybe Kyle and Marcella had enough contact in their own home with paramilitaries and bullies and welcomed the escape to a peaceful life somewhere else. He has been a constant in her life, I gather, and despite everything he and Jordi have become good friends."

There were loud whoops up ahead and Alice strained to see the cause. The pace and volume of the marchers had increased as if a certain urgency to reach the local starting point had infected everyone. As they passed the Falls Park on their left the gigantic word ENOUGH, fixed on a wooden base and painted in luminous paint shone out of the dark. Along the road billboards had been commandeered and the now familiar one-in-five, enough, NMP message was blazoned in bright red over now irrelevant ads for fashion labels and cocktails. Each message provoked a series of whoops from the marchers.

At the bottom of the Whiterock Road they had to wait while other groups clustered behind banners and holding placards and torches made their way down the steep hill and out onto the main Falls Road. Women in steward's vests assumed control, directed the traffic and kept the pace up so there were no stragglers.

"Look how many people there are," marvelled one of the EXIT lads. "I wonder if we'll all fit around the city hall."

The excitement was palpable and the determination of the marchers magnified as the visible numbers grew. The EXIT group were keeping tightly behind their banner and exchanging those carrying the poles so that everyone could have a turn. While they waited to move off again Alice took photos on her phone of the whole group and promised to send them to everyone. There was a real sense of the importance of their being there, making history and their introduction to street activism for a worthy cause getting off to a momentous start.

Alice sent a copy of the picture to Caroline with a text to say she would be in touch when she got a moment. **Any news from the Mossos?** She checked if there was any further contact since the interview earlier in the day.

All quiet for now, came the reply and Alice felt relief that things were not moving ahead without her.

She also sent the picture to Pradić while thinking that she was probably watching live webcam footage and much better informed than anyone else. At almost the same moment a file arrived from the green-haired constable marked KM. Alice clicked on it to see how much information Pradić had uncovered. There were five pages including some data from Facebook accounts and a number of scanned newspaper articles. One was about the conviction of Kyle's father for membership of a proscribed organisation. Another article was about the conviction of a paedophile that had been employed in Musgrave Primary School, which was the feeder school for Redgrave Secondary.

Hugo was watching her closely.

"Kyle and Marcella's father's name was Alistair," she said. "He was convicted with membership of a proscribed group back in the eighties and sent to the Maze. Around the same time that Marcella headed off into the sunset with the young, newly compensated Jordi. I wonder what became of Kyle at that point. I know he tried the British Army at one point but he didn't last there."

Hugo looked pensive. "There are various possibilities but they are not infinite. He may have had enough of violence through being close to his father's activities and wanted to leave it behind. He may have been involved himself as a youth member of a loyalist group and when his father was jailed decided that he wanted no more of it. He joined the army and then got out as quickly as he could and moved to Spain and, like many others, determined never to go back to the North. Associated with either of those options he may also have been determined that he was going to protect his sister whatever else happened and that might have become his life. I'm sure you could find that out from some of his mates at the time."

And Hugo turned his attention back to the group and their progress down the road.

* * *

Outside the Shankill Women's Centre, Tina and May organised groups into a loose order for walking across the Westlink and meeting up with those marching down the Falls Road. It would have been more usual for them to walk directly into the city centre and arrive along Royal Avenue but the four women had decided to push things a little and have the groups mingle and arrive together. They always had an eye to occasions when political progress could be made for the women's sector.

Outside the Falls Women's Centre the number of people surpassed all expectations. There were women's groups from all the local areas, some schools that had made banners and then some political groups. There were banners in Irish and a large number of people with home-made placards and various depictions of NMP inked onto their faces and clothing. The T-shirts worn by the EXIT group were visible everywhere. The age range of march participants was comprehensive, including families with children in buggies and even a few elderly women being pushed in wheelchairs.

A microphone had been rigged up outside the Centre and three women were singing. Behind them, hanging from the top-storey window was a sheet on which were written the words of the Women's Army Song, adapted from the well-known African-American spiritual 'Mary, Don't You Weep'.

Oh, sister, don't you weep, don't you mourn
Oh, sister, don't you weep, don't you mourn
The women's army is marching
Oh, sister, don't you weep.
One of these nights about twelve o'clock
This whole town's gonna reel and rock
Cos the women's army is marching
Oh, sister, don't you weep!

People sang along and the large crowd of women and men picked up the melody with ease. As the crowd continued to swell, there was also a rehearsal of chants that would be led by women carrying megaphones.

What do we want?
An end to harm!
When do we want it?
Now!
What do we need?
An end to Patriarchy!
When do we need it?
Now!
What do we want?
An end to the killing!
When do we want it?
Now!

Alice watched as the crowd prepared to make a meaningful noise and wondered at the crowd management skills that were in evidence.

Here was a people used to generations of street activism and their comfort with protest was clear. They were used to organised demonstration and were ready to give it their all. The EXIT group were learning from old hands here, Alice thought as they raised their voices to the rhythm of the chants, keeping an eye on Hugo and Alice so that they all remained together.

An older woman took her place at the microphone. "When we move off shortly, we'll take our lead from the drummers at the front. No need to rush. We want a dignified, unhurried march that makes clear that we have had enough. Our message is clear. Enough violence against women! Enough violence, full stop!" She gave a signal and women in high-vis vests came out of the Women's Centre and took their places along both sides of the road. They all had whistles that they blew shrilly. "*Let's walk!*" said the woman at the microphone and the drums set up a marching beat and headed up the hill in the direction of the city centre. Torches flared and banners caught the mild breeze and carried the crowd forward towards the city hall. The air was filled with slightly acrid smoke from the torches and the shouted messages of people demanding change. Alice found herself moved by the solidarity of purpose and action.

As they waited to have room to start walking, Alice caught a glimpse of Brenda Clinton, Jed's mother, walking along the far side of the road in a steward's vest. She looked intent on her role and Alice was pleased that the shy woman had found a way of continuing her campaign against gendered harm in her own community. She thought she had seen an exchange of signals between the woman on the platform and Hugo but perhaps she had misconstrued a simple acknowledgement between two people active in community politics.

CHAPTER 38

It was a clear night and the darkening sky was sprinkled with the first stars. Long shadows danced against the buildings they passed and the pavements were full of people watching the spectacle. Some slipped into line beside a passing group while others remained as observers. The sound of the deep drums filled the air alongside the rhythmic call of the question and answer chanting. Alice watched as the young EXIT group members found their voices – shyly at first and then more confidently. She knew that feeling of finding your true voice and she was happy for them and their more open futures.

At the bottom of the road they stopped and marchers coming from the left were inserted into the parade with as little disruption as possible so that the usual demarcation of communities was blurred.

A young man, who had just joined with a group directly ahead of the EXIT banner, shouted a greeting to Gary. He smiled and waved back.

"*He's from the Shankill!*" Gary shouted to Hugo who was nearby. "*I know him from the Young Offenders Centre!*"

Hugo nodded encouragingly and smiled at Alice at the layers of the change that were happening before their eyes.

There were sizeable numbers of police in attendance but for the most part they were grouped back down side roads off the main route and keeping a low profile. There were no signs of riot gear, shields or batons and the general mood was supportive and non-adversarial. Someone had made good policing decisions about how to manage this crowd.

The number of marchers was colossal and everything ground to a halt as they neared the Belfast City Hall. There were women singing on the platform and many of those waiting were familiar with the songs and sang along. There was an evening chill in the air but nothing too bothersome. Alice noted that the chants about not objectifying women were incongruous as they passed by shop windows filled with provocatively dressed mannequins.

Hugo had a specific spot in mind for the group and he guided them along the edge of the marchers until they were safely tucked into a small street opposite the City Hall. They had a clear view of the speakers' platform and the option to leave with ease if they decided that was necessary. He had anticipated the possibility that they might get hemmed in and taken steps to avoid that. They settled down and waited for the speeches to begin. They didn't have long to wait and Alice recognised the older woman from the *Late Debate* on TV as soon as she took the microphone.

The woman had a commanding presence that defied the usual attitude towards older women. Within moments of beginning to speak, she had the massive crowd listening in hushed silence. "Let's remember that it is the killing of a young woman and her two small sons that brings us onto the streets this evening. In our protesting and our campaigning for radical change to the way we deal with patriarchal norms in our society let us never forget the bottom line. We are here because women are hurt and killed with alarming regularity.

Women are repeatedly harmed here in Ireland, all across the European Union and the entire globe. We have the facts. These are not just our vague impressions of what is happening. We know now that a male partner has physically or sexually assaulted one-in-five women across the twenty-eight countries of the EU. The numbers of women killed is harder to quantify because often the figures are not collected. This is not a succession of random killings that just happen to involve men harming women. There is a pattern here and it's the pattern that we need to understand and it's the pattern that we need those in power to take action on. The pattern is called patriarchy and we want no more of it." She paused and the crowd chanted '*No more patriarchy!*' until the woman raised a hand to ask for silence. "Patriarchy is not just a word. It is a system that gives men power over women at home, at work, in our places of government and throughout society. Patriarchy makes the achievement of women's rights impossible and it needs to be understood and replaced with real gender equality … in every aspect of our lives. I am no spring chicken …" She paused and allowed the crowd to laugh with her. "I have been demonstrating about violence against women for over four decades. I have tried to reclaim the night so many times so that it would be safe for women, but without success. There is no safe time for women. No time when she need not be afraid, neither day nor night, with strangers or loved ones, out in the world or in her own home." She paused again and allowed the words to sink into the minds of those present and then she seemed to grow taller and more powerful as her anger became obvious. *"And I have had enough!"* Her voice rose into the word. *"Enough! Enough! Enough!"*

And the sound echoed from the crowd as they took that word and roared it into the night sky.

"In the Shankill Women's Centre we are experts at dealing with women's hurt. Our sisters on the Falls Road have the same expertise. Women the world over have learned these skills because the amount of violence against women is relentless. We can do that care work even though we don't want to have to do it. Women know that they will get support from us but what we cannot do is stop men's violence. That is up to men. Men have to make those changes for themselves. We are glad of our male allies who have already learned these lessons. We support their work with boys and men to become their best, most human selves, capable of using words instead of fists to sort out their conflicts.

It starts with us in our homes. Can your sons talk about their feelings? Do they learn to challenge sexism amongst their friends? Do they see their sisters and their friends as equals? Do the men in your family share the care work equally? All these everyday challenges to sexism are important but we need change at a systemic level. We need to see that our elected leaders make ending sexism and all forms of oppression of women a priority and this change has to begin now. Enough empty words and promises. We want to see resources put into women's refuges and help lines. We want to see funding for programmes that enable men and boys to learn alternatives to violence. Men who hurt women must be punished and learn to behave differently. We need to see the harming of women eliminated from our society and we need to see the will for that to happen demonstrated in programmes for government, in words and also in actions."

There was loud support for all of this from the crowd and Alice almost dared to hope and to overcome her belief that the ears of those in power did indeed have walls.

"There has been a lot of discussion about the holding of Sammy Marshall by those who want to draw attention to this pattern of male violence that has never generated the action needed to make it stop. I wish Mr Marshall no harm and I am sure that he will soon be handed over to the PSNI and given justice before the law. But what I want most of all is that women also have access to justice and that those in power make sure that women's justice, true gender justice is their priority."

Again the woman's words met with the crowd's approval expressed in applause and cries of "*Yes!*" and "*Enough!*" and "*No more Patriarchy!*"

"I'm nearly done!" Again she laughed at the ambiguity and the crowd instinctively joined in. "Everyone here needs to remember that we need to speak these words to those in power. Next time a politician comes to your door you need to ask: What are you doing about gender-based violence? And if they have no satisfactory response then they should not get your vote. We need an end to tribal politics that keep us divided and some new thinking that starts a war on all harm … and first of all against the needless and unrelenting harms against women. Let's take a moment of silence now to remember the senseless killing of Donna Nelson and her two wee sons Timmy aged two and Riley aged five."

As an impressive silence fell over the crowd that surrounded the City Hall and stretched as far as the eye could see in all directions, Alice became aware that Hugo was texting someone and looking a bit agitated. She hoped that there wasn't anything amiss with his son. He put the phone back in his jacket pocket and looked at her questioningly.

"What is it, Hugo? You look very perplexed suddenly."

He took her out of earshot of the group who were listening as someone from the White Ribbon Movement in Canada took the microphone.

He looked apologetic. "I got a phone call from someone this afternoon who wanted me to ask you to help them with a logistical problem. At that stage I didn't know you were on your way up to us."

"What are you talking about, Hugo?" Alice laughed at his uncharacteristic hesitancy. "Just tell me what this is all about."

"OK. Someone who learned about your support for Brenda and Jed, in the PSNI inquiry into the death of the clerics back in March, has contacted me. They want to place Sammy Marshall in safe hands so that he can be handed over to the Murder Squad in Grosvenor Road Station. They thought you sounded like someone who could carry out that task and respect their need to be anonymous."

Alice's eyes opened wide in surprise.

"Don't ask me who the call was from, Alice. Clearly there was no name and protection of the hostage-takers' identity is an issue here. I don't want you implicated in something that could lead to you being compromised. This would only work if you were to happen upon the person in question accidentally, as it were." He made a face to show that he was unconvinced about the whole situation. "Like, I'm conscious that this may well be a murderer I'm putting you in touch with."

Alice thought quickly and decided on her response. She had dealt with her share of violent men and they didn't intimidate her.

"What's the suggested plan?" she asked. She felt a certain sympathy with the hostage-takers and their desire to return their captive now that enough attention had been generated about their campaign. "Just tell me where and when and I'll get on with it while you get the guys home safely after this is all over."

Hugo nodded and sent a thumbs-up emoji to his contact and smiled gratefully at Alice. He had seen enough of her during their Tae Kwon Do practice to realise that she would be much better dealing with this situation than he would.

CHAPTER 39

As the rally continued, Alice told the group she had been called away and that she would see them after her holiday to talk about all the new ideas and plans for the future work with AHIGE. She headed off along the edge of the crowd in the direction of Jury's hotel in Great Victoria Street.

Arriving there, she made her way towards the women's toilets. There was a long queue of women from the rally, adept at finding much needed facilities wherever possible. Alice joined the line leading from the foyer and listened to the chat about the march and the events of the past week.

As she finally got inside the door of the toilets she looked around and, not knowing exactly what to expect, she took a moment before smiling and recognising the kidnappers' ingenuity. Women were often invisible and older women even more so. An elderly woman was sitting in a wheelchair at one of the hand basins, looking in the mirror with a bewildered expression. She was quite heavily made-up and her lipstick was a little askew which had the effect of making her look tipsy. A heavy woollen rug that had been placed across her lap, covering her hands, and she looked as if she might have just woken up after having been dozing in the chair.

A woman was standing behind the chair, tidying the elderly woman's hair. "Your niece will be here to collect you in no time now, dear," she said.

Alice made her way towards them.

"Oh, here she is now!" said the woman and immediately abandoned the wheelchair, walked quickly past Alice with a small nod and out the door.

"There you are!" Alice said cheerfully as she approached the wheelchair, waving a gloved hand in greeting. "I thought I'd find you in here."

She smiled at the line of waiting women as if the misplacement of her elderly relative was a regular occurrence and they nodded sympathetically. She flipped the brake off the chair and patted the older woman on the shoulder. "Let's get you back where you belong now. That's enough gallivanting for one day."

Outside, Alice looked beneath the rug and saw that Sammy Marshall was well secured with handcuffs to the arms of the wheelchair. She replaced the rug and turned in the direction of the Grosvenor Road, just five short minutes' walk away.

"You needn't worry about me trying to get away," the occupant of the wheelchair said gruffly. "After where I've been, the police station will be like a holiday camp. I'm happy to have got out with myself intact and I certainly won't be pointing any fingers at who my hostage-takers might have been. I'm sure they have eyes and ears everywhere and I don't want any more to do with them. I think they were trying to brainwash me – either into becoming a taig or some sort of feminist or maybe even both." He grimaced at the horror he had managed to avoid and added, "I hope nobody recognises me in this get-up."

"I'd say that's quite unlikely, Mr Marshall." Alice found the prospect of Marshall becoming a Catholic or a feminist unlikely but was amused at how horrifying he found both those identity elements to be. Now she saw her chance to get Marshall talking a bit and, not wanting to waste time, she launched in with her first question.

"Do you remember a few schoolmates of yours called Jordan Campbell and Kyle Murray, Sammy?"

Marshall didn't hesitate. "Of course I remember Florrie!" He laughed. "He surprised us all. We had him down as a wimp of the first order and he turned out to have bigger balls than the lot of us. I heard he did time in Spain for beating up his wife Marcella. I knew her too back in the day actually."

"And Marcella's twin – Kyle Murray?"

"Oh, I remember Kyle." He adopted a tone of mock terror. "Nobody messed with Kyle Murray – at least not twice. He was at the same primary school – Musgrave – as me, as well as at Redgrave Secondary. I remember there was a rumour that he had been interfered with by the caretaker in Musgrave who later was done for child abuse on a grand scale. By that stage the paedo was blind in one eye and walked with a limp ... and that was courtesy of Alistair Murray and associates. Kyle's father dealt with all assaults on his family with zero tolerance and extreme violence. That approach became known throughout the area and Kyle was never touched by anybody ever again."

Alice felt the last pieces of the puzzle falling into place. Pradić had uncovered substantiating information for Marshall's assertions in her

Internet searches for the relevant period in the Shankill area. However, she had found no connection between Kyle and Vox or the Catalan Independence Movement. It appeared that Marcella remained her twin's sole concern as she had been for decades since their school days.

"Kyle protected his twin sister in the same way as he had learned from his father. Punishment was sharp and instantaneous. If any of the lads so much as mentioned her, he let them have it. He broke the arm of a young fellow in my class just because he innocently remarked that Marcella was good at skipping."

They were at the crossroads nearest to the police station and as they waited for the lights to change, Alice thought about what might have saved Jordi Campbell from the wrath of Kyle over the years. Perhaps Marcella had warned her brother off interfering in their relationship or it might have been that they were both the beneficiaries of Jordi's compo money and that saved him from punishment by Kyle.

Marshall was muttering to himself and Alice tuned in to the monologue.

"You know what the funny thing is?" Marshall sounded baffled. "I've had lots of time to think and I don't actually remember killing Donna. We were arguing and I remember taking her phone and throwing it at the wall. She was threatening to call the cops."

Good plan, Alice thought, glad that she wouldn't need to listen to Marshall's self-obsessed ramblings for much longer.

"Then we struggled and I fell over and I must have banged my head. I still have the lump." He spoke as if grasping a dream that was slipping away from him. "And then she was dead. Stabbed and the knife was in my hand and I was covered in her blood."

Alice didn't engage any further with Marshall and he sat passively now in the chair and made no further comment as she negotiated the uneven footpath up the final section of road towards the PSNI Murder Squad HQ.

She was admitted to the station for the second time that day without any impediment and smiled to think that the identity of the DI's lesbian partner probably very quickly became common knowledge throughout the station. She asked the desk sergeant to speak to DS Burrows and sat down with her subdued charge to wait for the next episode in this strange case to begin.

"Dr Fox, good evening," said Burrows, looking with interest at Alice's companion.

"I think you'll find that under his current disguise, this is Sammy Marshall who is happy to have been released into your custody."

Marshall was looking sheepishly at Burrows and nodding in agreement with Alice's statement. DS Burrows response was a mix of disbelief, rapidly followed by relief and then delight as a major block in resolving this case was instantly removed. Behind Marshall's back he smiled broadly at Alice then lowered his eyebrows as if trying to puzzle out how this bizarre set of circumstances could have come about.

Alice produced an envelope with her name written in capitals on the front. Inside was a key to the handcuffs and a typed note suggesting she go to the ladies' toilet in Jurys Hotel where she would find Marshall ready to be handed over to the PSNI. "Someone pushed this into my hand at the rally outside the City Hall," she said. "I was there with my co-worker and the youth group so I'm afraid I didn't see who handed it over. There were so many people about and I assumed it was a flyer of some kind and didn't pay attention."

Burrows was overjoyed to get Marshall into custody but nonetheless he paid close attention to the detail of the handover. He slipped on a pair of latex gloves from his jacket pocket, handed the note to the desk sergeant with the instruction to bag it and to send both the note and the wheelchair for forensic testing. "Get someone to collect all CCTV available inside and on the approach to Jurys Hotel and you'll need to take a set of prints from Dr Fox as well." He looked apologetically at Alice. "Let me get him into custody and give the DS the pleasure of releasing the news to the media that we've got him. Then we can get a full statement from you and hand it over to the Criminal Investigation Department. They will be keen to follow up on tracking the identity of the kidnappers. You'll find McVeigh and Pradić at their desks if you want to wait there and we can talk later – or tomorrow if you prefer. It's been a busy day."

Alice couldn't help but be amused that he treated her like a close relative of the Murder Squad.

His pleasure at getting Marshall into custody made Alice feel like an agent in the recovery of Marshall, even though she had just agreed to deliver him. Of course she knew what the connecting pieces were that had led to her selection for the role but there was no need to speculate about that, she thought, when the result was so welcome.

Alice told Burrows she would like to spend some time with Pradić to follow up on some questions she still had about the Jordi Campbell inquiry and, given that he would have a busy evening, all things considered she was sure her paltry contribution could wait until the morning.

Marshall was unshackled and walked unsteadily in his high-heeled shoes behind the duty sergeant, who would record his arrival and process his arrest on suspicion of the murder of his wife and children.

Alice texted Hugo, saying that she was sorry to have rushed away and would be home later if he wanted to talk. She didn't want any possible digital trail to suggest that he had any idea why she had left sooner than expected.

She paused in the foyer for a few moments to text Caroline and let her know she was going to be in Murder Squad HQ for a while and had been happy to deliver a much-wanted person of interest to them this evening.

Talk later!! You're going to be very popular with the MS xx came Caroline's response.

When she went through the door of the Murder Squad offices, Burrows was on the phone to the DS and clearly very pleased to have news of Marshall's arrival to impart. McVeigh was looking as if his numbers had come up in the lottery.

"This is becoming a habit, Dr Fox," the young detective smiled. "I think we need to get you on the payroll. This is the third time in as many months that you've been instrumental in assisting us in resolving a tricky case."

"You might make that clear to my academic supervisor for me when she wonders why I'm not making more progress with my own work," Alice responded wryly.

She made her way over to Pradić who was sitting in front of her many screens, following the progress of the Reclaim the Night March and several other things at the same time. She patted the empty seat beside her to show she was open to Alice joining her.

"I was hoping the hostage-takers would be true to their word," she said. "They have made their point most articulately." She smiled and flicked to a screen that held a statement from the spokesperson in the Office of the First and Deputy First Minister with responsibility for equality matters. They announced the establishment of a cross-party group to look at educational and training programmes for boys and men and the expansion of funding for women and children impacted by male violence. They acknowledged that the response to the death of Donna and her sons had generated a seismic reaction from people across the country and beyond. They said they wanted to make it clear that they were listening to people and would act decisively to implement the promised new measures without delay.

Alice read those promises with a dubious expression. "We'll see how much of that moves beyond the level of aspiration."

"Perhaps more trustworthy …" Pradić turned to another screen where the European Union had declared its intention to prioritise funding towards developing new approaches to disturbing the culture of patriarchal masculinities so that alternatives were encouraged to the current system that was harmful to both women and men.

"I guess my T-shirt is right on message so," joked Alice as she took off her coat, hung it over the back of the chair and did a twirl to show the message on the back. "Are you picking up any chat about the brilliant minds who came up with all of this?"

Pradić was flicking from screen to screen to show Alice some international examples of the grafittied buildings, fires on mountains, banners hung from iconic buildings and pulled by small planes across the sky in Spanish coastal resorts, all citing the one-in-five statistic, ENOUGH and NMP.

"*Wow!*" said Alice. "What a lot of progress for such a short space of time! If it was only possible to hope that the system would be moved to reform itself."

There was a constant series of electronic bleeps from Pradić's monitors that Alice knew indicated incoming messages. Zara scanned them quickly without too much response until the moment when she said "*Aha!* This is the one I was waiting for!" She turned the screen towards Alice. "The hostage-takers are bowing out."

They both read silently.

As was promised, Sammy Marshall has been handed over unharmed to the PSNI so that justice, as we currently know it, may take its course. A huge number of us have responded to the wilful killing of Donna Nelson and her sons by making it clear that we have had enough. Thank you to all who acted together in solidarity against patriarchal violence. Our action was peaceful, careful and designed to make life better for women and men. We want an end to all violence, an end to gender injustice and a better, feminist future for all of us. Current gender culture and the law as it stands do not protect women and that needs to change.

We must maintain the pressure on our governments to act to enable a more gender-equal future and encourage each other with news of our successes. Perhaps someone will start a Whatsapp group where this can happen!

Now it's up to all of us to keep on pushing.

Enough. Enough. Enough.

NMP

Pradić smiled at Alice and winked. "And you know, Alice, even with all my global digital connection, there is no way of tracking down where this message comes from."

Alice understood this to mean that there would be no trail identified by Zara Pradić that led back to the hostage-takers and she felt that was fair enough.

She told Pradić about what Marshall had said about not remembering actually killing Donna and how she had interpreted it as him trying to slip out of taking responsibility for his actions. Now, having had time to digest the possible implications, she wasn't sure if it didn't mean something entirely different.

Pradić seemed a little preoccupied and she was evidently moved on to another element of the case she wished to resolve. "Hopefully, now that Marshall has been handed over, that will be the end of that aspect of the affair. I have another slug working not far from here that I want to identify. It's the same one that allowed Marshall to escape police custody in the first place. My guess is he's lurking under a stone somewhere in this very building and I'm really looking forward to bringing his double dealing to a humiliating end."

Alice had no doubt that Zara would get her man but first she wanted to clear up a few things about Jordi Campbell and Kyle Murray. Then she would be ready to talk to Caroline and hopefully put the Belfast element of the murder in Verges to bed.

* * *

Even after spending several hours checking out details online with Pradić, Alice was astounded to see just how many of the marchers were still present in the city centre as she set out for home. She walked around the City Hall to sample the atmosphere and to take a few photos to send to Caroline. Those who had travelled from a distance by coach were waiting patiently as a long line of vehicles edged its way towards the City Hall and little by little people were able to head for home. The crowd was good-humoured. Many were sitting on the grass, eating bags of chips and singing. There were group photos being taken in front of the banner that still hung from the speakers' platform and shouts of place names as organisers tried to locate their troop for the homeward journey. "Anyone for Limerick? Your bus is ready to leave in the next five minutes!" Or: "Sligo women! Time to go home! Your chariot awaits!" And there would be a flurry of activity as small groups of women answered the call.

Some foreign film crews were still at work and recording opinions from those they could find that wanted to talk to them.

Alice was relieved to see that the EXIT group were no longer present and said a silent thank-you to Hugo for being a good shepherd. She headed up Great Victoria Street towards the Botanic area and made it home in time for the late evening news.

A recording of DS McCluskey's statement to the press was the first item.

"The Belfast Murder Squad is pleased to announce that Sammy Marshall, wanted in connection with the murder of Donna Nelson and her two sons, Riley and Timmy, is now safely in custody and over the coming days will be helping us with our inquiries. Mr Marshall has suffered no obvious ill effects from his detention and maintains that he was well treated. He is unable to offer any insights into where or by whom he was held hostage. For operational reasons, the method of Mr Marshall's release will remain a matter for the police inquiry and will not be shared with the media at this point. The Murder Squad will be working intensely now and we hope that this case will be brought to a speedy and satisfactory resolution. We remember at this point the grieving Nelson family and would ask for their request for privacy to be respected by everyone."

There followed long and detailed coverage of the evening's Reclaim the Night March. Estimates of numbers ranged between 60,000 and 100,000 and were lauded as one of the biggest ever turnouts of people for any cause in recent years. The government statement promising action was also covered and all in all it seemed that the activists had made their case without overshadowing the tragedy that provoked the response.

An email from Pradić distracted Alice momentarily but she decided that she'd had enough for one day. She would read it in the morning. She poured herself a generous glass of cool white wine and made some toast. What she really wanted was some patatas bravas from the Bar de Plaça in Begur but that would have to wait until Monday evening. Finally she dialled Caroline's number and settled down for a full account of her day. She had a lot to report and she hoped her battery would last long enough.

Easter Sunday, 20 April 2014

CHAPTER 40

Burrows made his way into work on Easter Sunday morning with a lighter heart and a sense that they had all the raw material he needed now to solve this case. Marshall's filthy underwear and T-shirt had been in a bin bag under the seat of the wheelchair and Burrows had sent them off to forensics. He and McVeigh would interview Marshall first and then Nelson and he was confident that somewhere in those two testimonies the truth of what happened in Goliath Row would be uncovered.

DS McCluskey had been mighty pleased the previous evening to hear that Marshall was safely in police hands. When he had heard that Alice Fox had been instrumental in delivering the hostage he had been surprised but then began to think about her community connections and decided to leave the matter there.

"I am sure that you are meticulously gathering together all the evidence in relation to the hostage-takers and passing it on to the CID.

Of course these criminals must be dealt with by the justice system but our business is murder, DS Burrows, and we will stick to what we do well. There is a great deal of chat going on amongst the top brass about what should be done with all the graffiti artists and other protesters who've overstepped the boundary of legality. The law is the law and there is total agreement that lawbreakers must be penalised. We have a duty to protect private property and our colleagues will make that their priority. As I say, our business is murder and we'll just finish what we have begun and leave others to deal with the ancillary crimes."

Burrows had been relieved and happy to agree with that view.

Marshall had waived his right to have legal representation and so he sat alone opposite the two detectives in the interview room. He was dressed in a grey boiler suit provided to replace the women's clothing that he had been wearing on arrival at the station. He was pale and his hair hung lankly across his eyes which were full of fear and dread. He sat slumped slightly forward in the chair with his arms hugged around himself for support.

The previous evening the duty doctor had examined him and his gloved hands had been unbound and samples taken of the substances beneath his fingernails. There would undoubtedly be claims of contamination but they would follow each possible evidential trail to the very end. There were some recent gashes and a contusion on Marshall's forehead and a sizeable older bump on the back of his head. The medic had reported that although Marshall reported having been very ill while held in the lock-up, his subsequent jailers had treated him humanely and had probably prevented him from becoming very unwell.

It appeared that they had also done their best to preserve forensic evidence, which suggested that they had acted without malice and with considerable ingenuity. The forensics on the wheelchair showed it had been taken from the Royal Hospital emergency department and had the DNA of a multitude of users on it. The note to Alice Fox had given away nothing of any use.

"For the record, Mr Marshall, I'd like you to confirm that you have waived your right to have a legal representative present during this interview. We have put in a request on your behalf for Legal Aid and will ensure that a solictor will be present at any further interviews."

Burrows nodded to McVeigh that he should take over the questioning.

"Mr Marshall, we would like to hear your account of the events that took place in Goliath Row on Tuesday 15 April. You will be asked to repeat this when your solicitor is present but we are keen to hear your account now. I should inform you at this stage that we already have considerable forensic evidence that implicates you in the murder of Donna Nelson, Riley and Timmy. Your version of events and the degree to which you cooperate with this investigation will be taken into account in any subsequent court proceedings and sentencing. Do you understand that?"

"I do." Marshall looked with resignation at McVeigh and nodded his assent.

"Very well then, please speak as distinctly as possible for the recording."

Sammy Marshall described his anger and resentment at the Exclusion Order in place against him and said he went to Donna's determined to make the point that he wanted to see his kids. He said he knew that he was excluded because of his previous violent episodes but that he never set out to hurt Donna. He got frustrated because he couldn't get her to see his point of view, he couldn't find the words to make himself clear and then he lost it.

"It's like something inside me snaps and my mind goes blank. Before I know it, the red mist has come over me and I've hit her and there's no way back from that."

McVeigh waited and then, when Marshall appeared to have finished, he prompted. "And on last Tuesday evening, is that what happened? You lost your temper and lashed out?"

Marshall explained that Donna had been taunting him and said she would phone the police and have him arrested. He said he had grabbed her phone and thrown it at the wall to break it and they struggled and then he fell and must have banged his head. Maybe he had knocked himself out. Everything was confused after that.

"The next thing I remember was seeing Donna lying there stabbed and bloody and I was holding the big kitchen knife in my hand. I threw it away from me and it slid under the kitchen table."

McVeigh was nodding to show he was following Marshall's account. "Apart from Donna and the children were you the only person in the house at that time?"

Marshall looked puzzled by the question. "I don't know what you mean. Who else would have been there? It was just me and Donna and the kids were in bed."

"OK. Tell us what you remember next, Mr Marshall."

"When I think about it I'm not sure how I stabbed her because I was still lying on the ground but I stood up then and checked to see if she was breathing. I didn't think she was and so I completely panicked. My hands and top were all bloody and I wanted to wash it off. I went up to the bathroom and on the way I noticed that the front door was open, so I closed it. I would swear that I had closed it because there had been rats seen round about and I didn't want them to get in. I went into the bathroom and washed my hands under the tap and rubbed the front of my top with the towel." He looked horrified about what he was remembering.

He stopped and looked at McVeigh as if he might be granted an exemption from relating the rest of his account. McVeigh made it clear that Marshall should continue and in a lowered voice he reluctantly took up his narrative.

"I thought about the boys and how they would never forgive me for killing their ma ... so I went into their room." Marshall's eyes filled with tears and he swallowed hard in an attempt to quosh his emotions. "Riley was down beside Timmy and had his arm around him. I could see he was minding his little brother and I could also see that he was looking at me and feeling very afraid. I just wanted it all to stop." He looked at those in front of them as if hoping for understanding but they remained stony-faced. "I took the pillow from the top bunk and put it over both their faces and held it there until they stopped wriggling. Then I ran out of the house and went to a drinking place up the road and stayed there until I was drunk enough not to think. Then I went home to my ma's."

There was no sense of bluster left in Marshall and he hung his head and waited for what was to come.

Burrows spoke to him in a matter-of-fact tone. "Mr Marshall, I'd like to ask you about how your ex-wife Donna and her brother Bull got along? Were they close?"

Sammy lifted his head slightly and looked at Burrows as if he couldn't fathom what he had been asked.

"What do you mean by close?" He seemed to think about the question and shook his head slightly from side to side. "Donna didn't really have very much to do with Bull in the past wee while. When he collected me he mostly waited outside. I don't think he could stand the kids' mess. Donna used to call him my boyfriend. 'Sammy, your boyfriend's here,' she used to banter with me but for me it was water off a duck's back. Once when he did come into the house she joked with him 'Your bitch is just getting ready. She won't be long.' And afterwards Bull was furious. When I got into the car all he said was, 'She thinks she's very funny, our Donna!' You could see he was mad angry. That was the way of him. He'd be furious about what someone had said but he'd wait his time and then he'd get even. He took offence easily about things people said. You had to go very carefully around him." He looked at Burrows to see if he had answered the question satisfactorily.

There was nothing in Marshall's story that clashed with the witness statement of the neighbour and the forensic evidence except that the detectives knew that Marshall was not the only person present at the scene and they needed to make sense of that. They said that they would question him further later in the day and he was taken back to his holding cell.

Nelson and his solicitor were waiting in the adjacent interview room. Jane Carruthers had clearly spoken to Bull Nelson and urged him to be more cooperative and McVeigh thought he looked considerably less deserving of his nickname than during their previous meetings. In fact, he appeared more sheepish than anything else after a night in the cells. He was looking less well polished than usual and Burrows wondered how the reported retrieval of Marshall was influencing his mood. Perhaps, he reflected, Bull was happier when Marshall's side of things could not be reported and he considered if that wasn't the motivation for the timing of his brother-in-law's initial capture.

Burrows greeted Bull and Carruthers briskly and immediately set the recording machine in motion. "So, Mr Nelson. You have had a little time to think over our discussion yesterday. You know that we can place you in your sister's home on the evening when she and her sons, your nephews, were killed. We think that you left hurriedly, leaving the door open between the time of your sister's death and the killing of your nephews. Have you any explanation to offer for why you were in Goliath Row and what happened when you were there?"

Burrows watched the nerve in Bull's cheek contract and he was wondering if he was ever going to speak when he began. His voice was cold and devoid of emotion. He spoke as if from a script that he had memorised but felt no real commitment to.

"I was at my sister's house for a very short period of time on Tuesday evening. When I got there I let myself in with my own key. Donna was on the floor not moving. Marshall was also lying on the ground in the kitchen … I think he had slipped on her blood and banged the back of his head. I tried to take the knife out of his hand and his grip was so strong I couldn't budge it. I was afraid that he would do more damage with the knife. I cut my hands on the knife and I suppose that's where I got the cuts on my hands and how my blood was found at the scene. I didn't know at that stage that Donna was dead. I suppose I must have got some of my blood on her when I touched her to see if she was alive."

McVeigh asked the obvious question that was on everyone's mind.

"Why have you not told us any of this before so that your family's killer could be brought before the law?"

Bull raised his eyebrows. "Your record of bringing Sammy in for questioning hasn't been the most efficient so far, has it?"

Burrows held back his anger and asked brusquely, "Why did you lie to the police, your solicitor and probably your parents, Mr Nelson? You must see that your lies and your silence make your behaviour more than suspicious."

Bull met Burrow's eyes audaciously. "I was shocked, I suppose. I didn't want to be implicated in the whole mess. I have a clean record and I want to keep it that way."

Burrows could think of several reasons why Bull would want to avoid joining the prison community.

"You and Sammy Marshall were close, I believe?"

Bull's reaction to Burrows' question was difficult to read. His eyes flared, the nerve in his cheek gave a series of jumps and he ran his hand over his shaven head in what might have been panic, or an effort to suppress his fury at the suggestion that he was fond of Marshall.

His solicitor jumped in immediately. "If you are posing a question, DS Burrows, it is far from clear. You are making this process unduly stressful for my client whose family bereavement should suggest more humane treatment. I do not think that extracting information under duress is an appropriate approach to take in this day and age. My client has rights, you know."

Burrows maintained his calm exterior and responded with authority. "Your knowledge of the law, Ms Carruthers, will also have given you some insight into the rights of murdered women and children to have their killers pursued and brought to answer for their actions. I appreciate your concern for your client's fragility but I am sure that Mr Nelson must want to give every support he can to the police inquiry." He watched as the term 'fragility' clearly wounded Bull's carefully constructed masculinity and then continued. "Mr Nelson's account of the events in Goliath Row leaves a number of aspects of our forensic findings unexplained. For one thing, how did his blood and skin particles end up under his sister's fingernails if she was already dead when he arrived? We will end the interview there and allow Mr Nelson some time to reflect on that question." He nodded to McVeigh to turn off the recorder.

The two detectives left the room and paused in the corridor to exchange a few words with the duty sergeant before going into a second interview room where Sammy Marshall was waiting with his Legal Aid solicitor.

* * *

While Bull had been slow to talk, Sammy Marshall seemed to have decided to tell all. When asked to repeat his account of what had happened he spoke at length about his recollections. His anger at not being lord of his own manor any more had got the better of him. He had been drinking a lot and wanted his life back to normal. Living with his parents was not easy for him. Donna just needed to see things from his point of view and stop obstructing him coming into his own house and seeing his kids. He'd gone to the house to make that clear to her. Before calling round he had talked seriously to himself and was determined not to lose his temper and then it had all got out of hand.

He explained to the detectives that he knew he had made a total mess of everything. As soon as Donna had said she was calling the cops and that he would be arrested for breaking the Exclusion Order he had flipped. He had felt the rage coursing through his body. There was no way she was phoning anybody and he had grabbed her phone and thrown it at the back wall. It had fallen to the ground. And then they struggled and he had somehow fallen and hit his head and he wasn't sure what had happened after that.

"I know it sounds like convenient loss of memory," he said.

In fact, it came across as quite sincere, McVeigh thought, and then remembered Marshall had killed his kids and just listened to the rest as objectively as he could.

"I genuinely don't remember taking a kitchen knife from the rack on the kitchen counter and I don't remember stabbing Donna. How could you forget doing that?" He entreated them to answer this riddle for him but they remained mute and attentive.

"Then I was holding the knife and my hand and my clothes were smeared with blood and Donna was lying there not moving. The most surprising thing was the quiet because before that we had both been shouting and knocking over furniture. It was as if the mute button had been pushed."

He shook his head repeatedly as if to change the scene in his mind and repeated his account of the murder of his sons.

He looked at Burrows and McVeigh in desperation. "Maybe I thought they would be better off dead."

After a few moments Burrows asked Marshall about what he'd done when he'd left the house and what he could tell them about his time in the lock-up. Finally they asked him again about his friendship with Bull Nelson.

"We were good mates," Marshall said. "We would go out driving around the businesses he dealt with and I would wait for him in the car when he went in to collect his payments. He would come out with wads of cash and he had a lock-up compartment in the car where he stashed it. He had a great sound system and we were like young lads driving around carefree with the music blaring. Bull didn't drink much but I was usually rat-arsed or off my head on pills or both. I couldn't tell you where we went most of the time but we often finished up in his gym. Then Bull would drop a few tabs or have a few drinks and we'd hang out. We'd have the craic like." He looked to them for confirmation that they knew what 'the craic' involved. "Look, I can't actually remember a lot of what happened. "Bull was very generous with the booze and tabs and I'm not great on the off-button. I don't know when to stop." He said this thoughtfully as if getting some insight into himself for the first time.

"Given Donna's banter, did you ever feel that there was more to Bull's feelings for you than just mates?" Burrows framed the question to allow Marshall to feel beyond any culpability in its implications.

"I suppose it crossed my mind but I was getting too much out of it to be worrying about that. I was married and had kids with his sister, for god's sake. Anybody would know that I was no poof."

"Have you thought any more since we last spoke about Bull's relationship with Donna?"

Marshall nodded slightly. "You know, he sniped a good bit about women and my being tied to the house and that. He said we were free men and needed to be able to get out of an evening for a good time. I was happy to go along with that but I can see it wasn't a great deal for Donna. I suppose because it was her brother it made it seem OK. Do you know what I mean?"

Marshall's solicitor had sat fairly blank-faced through all this and now looked at his watch.

"Might I suggest we break for lunch, DS Burrows? I have something I need to attend to but can be back here by four o'clock."

They agreed that they would meet again later that afternoon at which point they would review the evidence against Marshall and he would be formally charged and arraigned. The solicitor left and Marshall was returned to his cell.

"Let's go and check in with Pradić and Dr Fox if she's here. I'm hoping that we may get something from the uniforms' visit to Bull's gym and the search of the car. Little by little we are edging forward, Ian, and it's hungry work." Burrows rubbed his tummy as if to signal that sustenance would be coming soon.

CHAPTER 41

As they had arranged the previous evening, at two o'clock in the afternoon, Alice made her way to Grosvenor Road on her bike and waited for DS Burrows at the front desk. She had spent some time both with Pradić and Caroline, considering the motives and opportunities that both Marcella and Kyle Murray had for killing Xavier Duxo and that was playing along in her head as she waited for the DS to appear.

Both Kyle and Marcella had grown up in the shadow of their father's paramilitary involvement. Kyle had learned at an early age that problems were sorted out by violent intervention. This was the backdrop to life in Northern Ireland at the time and it was especially the case in his own immediate family. At an early age, he had been abused by a man who had been swiftly dealt with by his father. Thereafter he had lived a life free from bullying and at some level he must have learned that this was an effective course of action.

The twins had always found comfort in each other's company and Kyle had followed Marcella to Spain and continued to live with her and benefit from her business. His comfortable life in Catalonia was in part due to Jordi's money and Caroline had agreed that perhaps this was why he had not intervened in their relationship when on occasion it had been violent. Alice knew that men were often silent in the face of a family member's violence against a woman. They did not think it was right to trespass on what they saw as the private business between husband and wife. Nevertheless, Kyle had otherwise assumed the role of protector with his sister and it made sense that if he felt Marcella was under threat from Duxo that he might well act swiftly to prevent that. Might the prospect of Duxo returning to Bar del Tapas have caused Marcella such a degree of concern that Kyle chose to eliminate the cause of her distress?

Kyle had been in Tapas del Mar until closing time the night of the murder but that wouldn't have prevented him getting to Verges and back in the available time on his motorbike. The pieces of this scenario fitted well enough, Alice concluded.

Alice was sure that Marcella could be ruled out of suspicion. She had been with her group of women friends and, as Pradić's scrutiny of the Facebook data showed, one of them was an officer in the Policia Locale, so Marcella was unlikely to use the group as a cover for killing Duxo. In any case, Alice thought, if women killed every man that bullied or annoyed them, the homicide count would quickly rocket.

Yes, Jordi Campbell had met with Duxo but that wasn't a crime and he was seen on CCTV leaving as Duxo went in the other direction. He was unlikely to have committed murder after having booked a return trip to Belfast and, in any case, despite how unusual such rehabilitation was, he really did seem to be a convincing reformed character.

Alice and Caroline had agreed to share these thoughts with DS McCluskey and let him decide if they should be communicated to the Mossos. That morning Caroline and Alice had a three-way video call with Mantego and he had agreed they would follow up on that line of thinking. It had also been agreed that they would no longer require the Murder Squad support as Kyle Murray was now a Spanish citizen and spoke fluent Catalan and Castilian. He could be interviewed directly without any need of interpretation.

When Burrows appeared he was brushing down the front of his shirt and tie and Alice deduced that the members of the Murder Squad had consumed yet another hasty lunch.

"Dr Fox," he greeted her and shook hands rather formally.

"Please call me Alice," she said. "I practically work here after all."

They both laughed at that remark and the awkwardness melted away.

"I thought that maybe you might come and meet with McVeigh, Pradić and myself and tell us what happened yesterday evening at the march when you were given custody of Sammy Marshall. We are going to have a review of where we are in the light of some new findings and you might like to join in that conversation. Your track record in seeing the wood through the trees is very good." He smiled generously and waved his large hand to shepherd her though the doors that led behind the scenes in the police station.

When they were all four seated around the table Burrows waved a handheld audio recorder towards Alice and smiled. "Let's just get your statement about yesterday evening's events out of the way, Alice. You say you were in town with the youth group when you received the request to deliver Sammy Marshall to us."

"That's right," said Alice. "After I finished with Jordi Campbell here,

I went directly to the EXIT project in a black taxi. We worked all afternoon on a banner and some placards and then joined with other local groups to make our way to the Women's Centre. We walked together in to the City Hall and there were a huge number of people so we stood a little off side. It was the young peoples' first foray into street activism and I suppose we were making sure there was an easy escape route in case things got a little fraught."

"Was it you or your co-worker who chose the place where you would stand?" Burrows asked.

"Well, I think it really came about serendipitously. We just happened to arrive there and the opening of the side street seemed a good place to stop." She was clear that there was some connection between Hugo and the Women's Centre and the planned handover of Marshall but she had no desire to expound that theory. There had been no harm done and what point was there in exploring the connections further? She would have to decide later how much of all this she would share with Caroline and the implications any concealment might have for their relationship.

"Was the envelope with your name on the front handed directly to you?"

"Not exactly." Alice explained that there were vast crowds and there were people handing out political leaflets and various forms of printed material. "I honestly couldn't say who gave it to me. By the time I became aware of it in my hand there was no one about who might have been the source. I opened it immediately and explained to the group that I had been called away and I made my way to the Jurys Hotel where Mr Marshall had been left in the ladies' toilet."

"I assume no one there had seen him deposited there? Of course, we'll follow up on all that."

"To be honest, there was no one to ask other than a very long queue of women waiting to use the toilet and quite unconcerned with an older woman in a wheelchair who looked as if she was dozing. A woman who might have been talking to our subject left as I arrived but there was nothing to differentiate her from thousands of others I saw that evening. I thought it was best just to deliver Marshall to you as quickly as possible. I know that it has been a priority of the inquiry to find him so I thought it best to act quickly." She looked sincerely at the three people hanging on her every word. "Was Marshall able to offer any insights?"

The deflection was effective and Burrows recounted that Sammy Marshall had nothing useful to say about his captors, where he was held or how he was released. He said he had never seen the women who picked him up on the Shankill or the place he had been held. He only saw a bathroom, a bedroom and a kind of sitting room that were very bare and where the windows were blocked out with sticky-back plastic. The men who looked after him were kindly and wore masks all the time. He said they were clearly bodybuilders but he couldn't describe anyone at all and he was very grateful to have been released.

Alice remembered then what Marshall had said to her about Fenians and feminists but thought the better of passing on what might imply too much information about his captors.

"The significant thing he did say," she said, "was that he couldn't actually remember killing Donna. He remembered falling and apparently knocking himself out and when he came around she was dead and he was holding the knife and covered in blood."

McVeigh was nodding in confirmation of what she was saying. "He told us several times that he didn't remember killing Donna but did recall killing his sons because he didn't want them to grow up knowing he had killed their mother."

Pradić said quietly, "I'm not sure if everyone has seen the latest input from Sandra Woods from Family Liaison. She is still spending most of the day with the Nelsons, especially since Bull has been in custody. The mother broke down this morning and talked to Sandra about her concerns about Bull. She worried about the fact that he never bothered with women and was so close to Sammy."

Pradić looked for a signal that she should continue and Burrows nodded and waved his hand to indicate that she should.

"Apparently he spent all his weekends and lots of evenings with him. She was worried that he was coming between Donna and Sammy because Donna told her Sammy was never home and she spent most of her time alone with the kids. After being out with Bull, Sammy would come home very late or even the following morning looking very dishevelled and was often still drunk or high. Donna said to her mother that she didn't think that it was a normal way for a married man to behave. When Mrs Nelson tackled Bull he became angry and stormed out of the house. After that he was cold and distant with Donna and Mrs Nelson said that she thought he was so upset now because he felt guilty for being annoyed with Donna and shunning her."

Alice had been thinking about another perspective on all this. "There is another reading of this but you will know better than I do how the forensics and other evidence support my theory. What if Bull was really very fond of Sammy and angry with Donna for coming between them? He was fine as long as things remained unsaid but she had taken another step and brought unwanted attention onto him. Might he not have killed her and framed Marshall?"

McVeigh looked perplexed. "But why would he frame Marshall if he was the object of his affection?"

"Because it was spoiled now," Alice said calmly. "Donna had named a relationship that he wanted to be secret. While it was nameless, it was his to enjoy but then it became remarked and therefore more visible. His repressed sexuality and his internalised homophobia did not let him openly make relationships with men because he feared the judgement of his macho peers. From my chat with Jordi, it sounds as if this type of self-censoring behaviour was happening back in their schooldays too. It's in character and has a long tail to it. We know he went to Goliath Row around the time Donna was killed. What if he found Marshall knocked out? He saw an opportunity and seized it. He killed Donna and made it seem as if it was Marshall … to the extent that even Marshall believed it. Then he has Marshall lifted by his henchmen next morning and creates a whole distraction that seems to be about an unpaid loan but is really just to give himself distance from the murder and time to figure out his next steps. Then the additional tragedy, Marshall who believes that it's he who has killed Donna, kills his sons."

Burrows is nodding now. "We have no evidence of Bull being upstairs in the house so that fits with your theory, Alice. It also explains why Marshall keeps mulling over his memory blank about murdering Donna."

"Yes," says McVeigh. "Bull arrives after Marshall falls and bangs his head. Donna is very much alive. Bull attacks her and she defends herself. She scratches his face and he cuts his knuckles in the tussle. Then he stabs her and smears her blood onto Marshall and puts the knife in his hand, creating the dreadful circumstances that provoke the murder of the innocents. Then he leaves his sister's house, neglecting to close the door, as observed by Marshall. We might consider that the killing of the boys was not something that Bull wanted and yet his actions led directly to it happening. It explains how difficult it has been to read Bull's moods. That scenario is almost beyond imagining really ..." He stopped there, realising that Alice had, in fact, just imagined that very nightmare situation.

They all sat in silence contemplating, in their own way, how the sequence of events had unfolded in Goliath Row on that fateful evening. Alice thought that both men had lashed out against their wounded masculinity and a woman and two small children had been the innocent victims. It was difficult to see how such cowardice and self-indulgence could ever find a road to redemption but Jordi Campbell's story said otherwise. She would try to keep that thin thread of hope in her grasp.

Burrows pushed ahead with a strategy. "Let's see if we can get this explanation backed up with some more evidence. We have strong forensics and digital phone data. Can we get Bull on CCTV after he's been in Goliath Row? Might he have gone to his gym and showered and changed his clothes? Can we get the bullyboys in Bull's pay to spill the beans about their part in the abduction and release of Marshall? Their car may also provide some corroborating evidence."

Pradić spoke up again. "We also have another possible source of information on Mr Nelson. As I said at the time, I was convinced that there was an insider in the force involved in letting Bull's men know that we were about to find and arrest Marshall. I wanted to get to the bottom of that but other priorities meant I have only now completed that search. I now have everything I need to be able to put the finger on Officer Caldwell. He was the PSNI in Bull's pay who gave the word for Marshall to be released. I'd say he might be happy to tell a few stories in exchange for some leniency. Self-interest will continue to be his primary motivation." She scowled at the thought of a colleague's betrayal.

"That all seems quite doable," said Burrows with satisfaction.

"Before we get back to talking to Marshall and Bull, let's line up the supporting evidence. I'll also let DS McCluskey know we are approaching the denouement of this particularly eventful mystery. He'll be delighted to be able to tell the global press that the Belfast Murder Squad record of resolving cases remains exemplary. Great work, everyone! Another job well done."

CHAPTER 42

On Monday morning Alice and Jordi Campbell took an early flight to Girona. They sat separately and parted at the arrivals gate where a subdued Marcella was there to meet Jordi. Alice knew from Caroline that the Mossos had brought Kyle in for questioning the previous evening and that it was looking as if he might be charged with the murder of Duxo. Alice declined the offer of a lift from Jordi who was clearly not up to date with the latest developments. She said she had already made an arrangement.

Caroline was sitting outside in the rented car, smiling broadly as Alice emerged. The sky was a delightful shade of cornflower blue and the sun was startlingly bright after the insipid Belfast weather.

"I think we should restart our holiday, Alice," Caroline murmured in her ear as they hugged each other tightly in the car. "I've packed a bag and I wondered if you would like to begin with a trip over the border into France. I thought you might enjoy some freshly caught fish and cool white wine for lunch at a little place I know by Collioure harbour? We could stay the night."

"That sounds like a perfect new beginning and there will be absolutely no talk of work," Alice said emphatically.

Caroline winked and said she was in total agreement. As Alice switched off both their phones, Caroline swung the car out of the airport waiting zone and took the direction towards La Jonquera and the border with France.

Endword

Whether you read this as an eBook or in paperback copy and enjoyed the experience, please take the time to post a short review on bookdepository.com or amazon.co.uk or amazon.com. This reader feedback has become one of the main measures of the success of a book … to the extent that it is possible to buy a batch of favourable reviews and thereby boost ratings. I prefer to hope that reader response will be the honest judge of whether *Wrestling with Demons* has merit as a murder mystery. Thank you for supporting me in this.

Acknowledgements

This third Alice Fox murder mystery is located in Catalonia and Ireland. Although it is a work of fiction, it is sadly rooted in a terrible reality. The National Women's Council of Ireland has recently used the term *EMERGENCY* to describe the persistence and escalation of domestic violence and femicide in Irish Society and the evidence sadly tells us that this is a global issue. In the hope of raising awareness of this massive social injustice, this murder mystery aims to generate questions and entertain at the same time. I have allowed myself some imaginary resistance to systemic inaction on violence against women because, despite the statistics, I needed to keep believing that change is possible.

Much of *Wrestling with Demons* was written in Catalonia and good friends, Clara Dato and Joan LLuis, the real life proprietors of Hotel Aiguaclara in Begur, shared invaluable local and cultural knowledge. They introduced me to Paco Coll and Xevi Machado from the Mossos

D'Esquadra who responded to my questions about the Catalan justice system with expertise and great generosity. Vicente Contreras Mancebo was a gentle guide to Spanish political history and everyday life in Catalonia.

Critical readers did much to help me sort out errors of one kind or another and any remaining mistakes are completely my own. Susan Miner, Ursula Barry, Izzy Baker, Niamh Wilson, Trina Barr and Ann Hegarty read drafts of the book with eagle eyes and highlighted inconsistencies. Jackie O'Toole helped resolve some bothersome IT issues and averted a bit of a melt down. Michelle Page answered queries about police procedures and protocols and friends and family encouraged me on a continuous basis: Brian Feeley, Margaret Ward, John and Petrena Baker, Chloe and Jessica Knox, Anais Tapia Knox, Leah, Nessa, and Jerome Finnegan and Bojana and Vesna Jancović all fed me with love and kindness and kept me at my desk.

My thanks to Poolbeg's Paula Campbell and David Prendergast who make publication happen and to Gaye Shortland where the editing buck stops. Her very skilful labours show that when you think a book is all done, really you are nearer the beginning than the end!

My lovely Ann Hegarty makes all things better and keeps me full up – heart, body and spirit. I am most thankful for the abundance of her love.

Printed in Poland
by Amazon Fulfillment
Poland Sp. z o.o., Wrocław